The Counterfeit Matter

Lou Rossi

Printed and published in the United States by Five Count Publishing, LLC.

www.fivecountpub.com.

ISBN (paperback): 978-1-943706-19-8
ISBN (e-book): 978-1-943706-20-4

Cover Design by: Ritchard Bentley

Cover Photo Courtesy of: Daniel J Ruggiero of WNY Hitman Photography

To my great friend, Tom Cavagnaro, who left us was too soon. Rest well, my friend. We miss you.

And to my parents, Pasquale (1932-2009) and Josephine (1936-2010), my biggest supporters.

PROLOGUE

Buffalo, New York. City of good neighbors, located in the rust belt of the Northeast USA. Buffalo is a mostly blue-collar town whose best days are in her rearview mirror, where its people work hard and play just as hard. Businesses left Buffalo because taxes are too high and its politics screw everything and everyone. However, in spite of the incompetents that run our government, Buffalo is making a slow comeback. Maybe things aren't like they were in the fifties, when the city was a major player in America, but a comeback nonetheless.

Once neglected and impoverished, Buffalo is now turning itself around—all this in spite of the city's politics and the fact it's taken twenty years to decide on a new Peace Bridge as a gateway to Canada and the good ole USA. They *still* haven't decided on a design. One design they came up with the nature lovers decided it's a hazard to birds because they might fly into a support span. My god, they're birds, they have the best frigging eye sight in the animal kingdom. Yet that's what these politicians and goody two shoes worry about. So I'm guessing we'll have the same old bridge for another fifty years. Oh well, you can't have everything.

All this being said, it's a great city to live in and raise a family. But like all cities, not all neighbors are good neighbors. And thanks to those special few I am able to make my living.

My name is Lou Romoso. I'm a private detective, or if you prefer you can call me a private eye, shamus, gumshoe, or just plain-old private Dick. My office is located on the corner of Chicago and Carroll Streets in a small office building I own, on the second floor. It's decorated with my collection of authentic autographed NFL, CFL, and Arena Football helmets, a Sirius satellite radio, and pictures of those famous fifties detectives. The likes of Phillip Marlowe, Sam Spade, Richard Diamond, Joe Friday, Pat Novak, the Saint, Johnny Dollar, and Nero Wolfe. I like their wise-cracking dialogue and quick wit. Why Wolfe, you ask? Because he was a big man too, and it just reminds me not all shamuses are Hollywood good-looking.

My view from the second floor of my office is not spectacular by any means. I have the corner office and my desk faces the corner windows. If I look straight ahead I get the silos of the General Mills factory along the Buffalo River. On a good day you can smell cereal all day long. A great smell. Brings you back to when you were a kid and opened a box of cereal and took a big whiff.

To my left I can see the back of Chefs' Italian Restaurant. It caters to people from all walks of life and has been a Buffalo mainstay since 1923. This couldn't be a worse view for a guy that likes food, especially Italian. My friends at Weight Watchers thought it'd be better if I move to an area less tempting, like the thirty-first floor of the HSBC Tower so I only could see the roofs of Chefs' and General Mills. It's nice to have such wonderful friends.

My detective fee is five hundred per day, plus expenses.

High price, for sure, but I only get the best of the best clients because of my talents. To most of my clients, my fee is a mere pittance. They pay because I'm the best and I get results.

I wasn't always a private eye. Used to be a Homicide Detective for Buffalo's finest for twenty years until that fateful day three years ago called upon me to retire. Was it by choice? No! Lead poisoning, unfortunately. Three bullets managed to find me, and since I'm a big guy, six foot two and nearly three hundred pounds, I wasn't too hard to find. Just ask my leg, arm, and chest.

Never did find the shooter, but I have my suspicions of who was at the bottom of it.

***

Goddamn it. I haven't run like this since my football days. Hot on the trail of this dirtbag, though, I couldn't let myself stop. Never have I been able to get so close to wrapping up a case so quickly. And on New Year's Eve, no less.

"Leary!" I panted. "Knock . . . it off! I'm not . . . going to chase . . . you all night!"

He didn't listen. Didn't stop. Just kept running like the asshole he probably was. I'd lost track of where we were by this time. The chase had killed my sense of direction.

How in the hell did I get here? My relaxing New Year's Eve wallowing alone in my office interrupted by this? Some stupid case that looked like a hoax? Running down some punk on the icy streets of Buffalo? Goddamn it, I hate this stupid made-up holiday more every minute.

The man I suspected to be Leary, some no-good, two-bit swindler who took a pal to the cleaners, rounded a corner and was now out of sight. I came barreling around it, not thinking the punk had the balls to turn on me. Not some prick who was a few sandwiches short of being two hundred pounds.

He did.

We had come to a dead end, and he was waiting around the corner with a board and took a swing. Somehow I ducked, and it just caught my right shoulder. He'd pay for that. No more badge to hold me back now from roughing up some asshole who deserved it. Just me and him in a dark alley. Leary bit off more he could chew.

I came out of the duck and threw a vicious uppercut. Didn't quite catch him flush, though, but it was enough to knock him on his ass. He scrambled to his feet while I was doubled over breathing heavy. Gotta get back in shape.

He was rubbing his jaw and looked a little woozy. Like any good Irish gangster, he could take a punch.

"Alright . . . Leary," I managed to say as I straightened up ready to resume the fight if needed. "Enough of . . . this shit. Let's go."

He smiled. "You know, Romoso, what we've got going on is way over your head. Why don't you walk away before you get yourself hurt."

How'd he know my name? I just learned who he was not more than twenty minutes ago. No time to think about that now. Either way: Wrong answer. I made a lunge at him and he feinted left, then went right to get around me and out of the dead end. No way could I last any longer in a foot race. I needed to make a move and finish it.

I planted my left foot and dove, managing to grab onto Leary's leg. My meaty paws were no match for his thrashing. Instead he kicked at my face and connected. Then did it again. But I refused to let go. I'm stubborn that way.

I managed to look up, and Leary had something in his hand. My eye was starting to swell from the boot to my face, and my vision was blurry, so I couldn't quite tell what it was.

Looked like a gun.

"Say goodbye, Romoso," he said, with that same shit-eating grin he gave me before.

His boot came up again, and he kicked one more time. I fell back, my grip loosening. He was managing to wiggle free. The world started to spin, and the ground felt like it was shaking. Some weird voice was talking, maybe Leary's, maybe not, then everything went black.

1954

CHAPTER 1
PAST CONSIDERATIONS

My slumber was interrupted by a pair of giant hands slapping me back to reality. I looked at the culprit. Couldn't be, but it was; Duffy. Duffy, of course, is of Italian descent and wasn't a tall man, probably around five foot seven and about two-hundred pounds. He was barrel chested and had arms like telephone poles. Shaking hands with Duffy was like shaking hands with a cement block. He was wearing a white button-down shirt and brown pants, which were held up by a thin brown leather belt. I got the best look at his shoes because I was on the floor. A nice-looking pair of brown loafers.

I said, "Uncle Duffy, what are you doing here? You're dead."

He looked at me, shook his head, grabbed me by my shirt, and lifted me off the floor. He told me I'd better get looked at; he was tired of coming up here and picking me off the floor. "And I ain't your uncle, dumbass."

"What are you talking about?" I said. I was still shaking out the cobwebs.

I sat down on the wooden chair behind the wooden desk and Duffy gave me a shot of BV whiskey, then told me my name. Why, I don't know. I started to argue, but he told me to shut up and listen. One thing I knew about Duffy is you did what he told you or you'd live to regret it. So I did. Duffy was, well, not quite the law-abiding citizen you'd like your family members to be. He'd been arrested a few times and served time for some minor offenses. Now he ran a bar on the corner of Chicago and Carroll called Marco's with his brother, Marco, plus a little bookmaking on the side.

Marco's was a family run bar, in what used to be an old house built sometime in the early 1900s. It had two stories. Like most homes built in the city, it was long and thin with not much of a yard. The bar was downstairs and a couple of apartments upstairs. The bar itself was long and glowed with a fresh coat of varnish. The wall behind the bar was lined with mirrors with rows of bottled liquor in front.

The rest of the bar was filled with wooden tables, chairs, and a jukebox. The customers were mostly all working-class types. They came from the auto plants, steel plants, wax factory, box factory, and government jobs. They came to drink, eat lunch, talk, cash their paychecks, and place a bet or two. There were women who came, too. They did not work in the steel mill or auto plants—not in manufacturing, anyway. The lights were always low and a thick cloud of smoke from cigarettes and cigars lingered in the air, leaving a hazy halo around the lights. The kitchen was in the back and they served a variety of Italian and American dishes. Beyond the kitchen were the bathrooms and stairs to the apartments.

A short, plump, smiling woman walked up into the room with a wet towel. She was wearing a black dress, almost a mourning dress. Then I remembered: Angeline. She approached me with a cold towel for my head and turned to Duffy and said, "He passed out again? The poor thing."

I grabbed the towel, shook my head and said, "What's going on? You're . . . my grandmother?"

She looked back and then again toward Duffy and told him to set me straight.

When she was gone Duffy lit another cigarette, blew the smoke in my face. He must have thought it was smelling salts. He blew so much smoke in my face I felt like I might die from smoke inhalation.

Me and him were third cousins twice removed, or something ridiculous like that. Bottom line, we were family. After being forced into retirement from the police department, I came to him a couple years ago to open up my private detective agency.

I looked around at my office. I got to my feet and steadied myself and sat down in a wooden bar chair. In the corner was a big old-time Phillips radio on a rickety table. I put my hands to my face to get myself back to reality.

On the wall there was a picture of me in a WWII fighter jacket standing next to a P-51 Mustang with the expression "Death from Above" on the nose. An old football picture of me was on the table next to the radio. I picked it up and looked at it. There I was, plain as day in a 1940s football uniform. My hands began to shake as I looked at the picture. Somehow it slipped from my hand and fell to the floor. The glass shattered and covered the area around the table in broken glass. My knees began to buckle as I looked at a wedding picture of me in a black tux with a beautiful blonde.

Duffy noticed I was about to go down again. He grabbed me and eased me back to a seated position on the ground.

"Duffy, what's wrong with me?" I said.

He took a finger and put it on my forehead, then pushed. "You've taken too many shots to the head, stunad! Here, look at these, maybe they will help."

He tossed a couple newspapers at me. The papers, *The Courier Express* and *Buffalo Evening News*, told my story: A Buffalo Police Detective, former WWII Ace, and College Football All-American and his wife were gunned down by an unknown shooter at midnight on January 1, 1952. The articles said I was shot in the arm, chest, and leg, and that my wife was killed along with my unborn child.

My hands went to my face in disbelief and I felt the places on my arm, chest, and leg where I'd been shot before. No! This can't be! But it was. Sadness for losing the wife I couldn't quite remember hit me hard.

Duffy picked up where the articles left off and told me that I had to retire from my job as a cop because of my injuries, even though I fully recovered, and that I opened a detective agency that catered to the who's who of Buffalo.

"You getting this!" He said.

"Yeah, yeah," I told him.

Duffy went back to the bar after a bit, telling me over his shoulder to stop messing around and get back to normal. Like I had a choice in the matter.

The little hamster in my brain began churning on his wheel, recalling some memories. I went back as far as I could; my high school days at Hutch Tech on Elmwood Avenue. How I got into that school I'll never figure out. You had to be a math wizard and I have trouble with addition. My days of playing football for the Hutch Tech Engineers played in my mind. Then a flashback to college playing for the University at Buffalo Bulls and having a great college career there, then to joining the Army Air Corp and flying a P-51 Mustang. How's that even remotely possible? My shoulders are wider than the plane.

Then I stared at the picture of the woman that was supposedly my wife, Ellen. Beautiful blond hair with blue eyes that made the Caribbean look pale.

My mind skipped a bit to New Year's Eve 1951. I knew it was a Sunday because of the spread; salad, pasta, meatballs, spareribs in the sauce, braciole, Italian bread and my favorite, fried dough with sugar sprinkled on it for dessert. My family, Lou, Elvira, Pasquale, and Frank in his Italian dinner jacket and white t-shirt were there. Elvira was a strong, short, stout Italian woman with broken English who could strike the wrath of God into anyone that made her mad. She's also deadly with a shoe, not to mention her other weapon of choice: the wooden spoon.

Ellen, who was Irish, never got used to eating at 2 p.m. on a Sunday. But that's Italian. It was after dinner that Ellen, who adopted the Romoso clan as her own, broke the news that we were going to have a child. I was in shock and Elvira was ecstatic, like it was her grandchild-to-be, and of course that warranted another meal.

Later that night Ellen wanted to go for a walk at midnight to celebrate the New Year and the news of our child. So I went and froze my ass off with her. The night air was crisp and you could see your breath with every word you spoke. There was a light flurry coming down and the snow crunched beneath our feet as we walked to the corner.

Then all hell broke loose.

A black Ford sedan whipped around the corner, slipping and sliding on the snow-covered street, and the barrel of a gun came out from the back seat. Shots rang out. I grabbed Ellen to shield her from the bullets, but it was too late. I got hot hit three times and she got hit in the chest. I grabbed her as blood flowed from her wound. I did what I had been taught to do in the Army Air Corps: took my hand and put it over the sucking chest wound and applied as much pressure as possible. I was getting light headed as the blood oozed from my own wounds. I told Ellen to hold on and not die on me and screamed for help. The patrons of the bar came streaming out at the commotion.

Ellen was gasping for air and fought as hard as she could, though eventually she lost her battle for life. She closed her eyes for the last time and died in my arms. Her last words were: "I love you."

***

More memories rushed though me as I thought of Ellen. She was that special one. I met her in college during my sophomore year of the spring semester in 1941. We were both in the same history class. I got to class early because I hadn't been to sleep from a party the night before. She sat down next to me. My eyes were red; hers were the deepest blue I ever saw. I just stared at her, or at least I thought I did, but I could have been paralyzed at the time from alcohol consumption. Either way I couldn't stop staring. Ellen looked my way and smiled and started laughing.

"Long night for the All-American?" She said. I just stared and Ellen kept smiling. "Your eyes are a little red, big shot."

"They match the color of my blood," I managed. "I like to be fashionable."

Ellen laughed out loud and the class turned to look and saw me blushing a lovely shade of red, which now matched my eyes *and* blood. I looked up and flashed a little wave. Ellen just kept laughing.

Ever since that day in class Ellen and I were inseparable. She would wait for me after practice at the library and we would study, and then I'd walk her down to her dorm room. Getting into a female dorm back then was like getting into a convent. It rarely happened. I would kiss her good night and start everything over again the next day.

Ellen came to every home game and listened to every away game on the radio. She loved football, especially when I played. That was just one of the million things I loved about her. She was funny, articulate, loved my friends, and she loved me as well.

World War Two raged on as Ellen and I graduated from college and I enlisted in the Army Air Corps. I asked Ellen to marry me, and she accepted. My friend, Father Pat, married us in a small but quick ceremony. I had to head off to basic training, then onto flight school.

I came out as a second lieutenant trained to fly P-51 Mustangs and was assigned to a fighter group in England. I didn't get leave and had to get to my base ASAP. Ellen cried at the news and told me she loved me and I told her the same. We hung up and I left for England. I would write her every day and tell her everything I could and she'd write me back.

I got discharged in the summer of '46. Ellen worked as a hospital administrator and I became a cop. Ellen and I tried to have a kid but it wasn't happening until that fateful New Year's Eve night when she told me she was pregnant. You know the rest.

***

My thoughts returned to that night everything went to hell. My head was spinning as the blood rushed from my body, but I tried to hold onto Ellen as long as I could or until I died. I didn't that night, but now I wish I had.

The ambulance took me to be treated at Columbus

Hospital on Niagara Street where I was in a coma for a month. Ellen was taken to Meyer Memorial where she was pronounced dead and taken to the morgue for an autopsy.

Ellen and our son's funeral was held at St. Lucy's Church located around the corner from my house. Ellen's parents named the baby Louis Jr. St. Lucy's was a beautiful church with a tall spire over the entrance. As you walk in there is a long aisle with pews on the right and left. The aisle led to the altar where Ellen and Lou's coffins were set so they could receive their final sacrament. The church was overflowing with mourners. Father Pat delivered the Mass.

Ellen and Baby Lou were laid to rest in Forest Lawn Cemetery on Delaware Avenue and Delevan. I was still in Columbus Hospital. I never got to attend the funeral or say goodbye. That would haunt me forever.

My family, Ellen's parents, and friends were at my bedside when I woke up. They told me what happened and I began to cry.

I was hooked up to IVs and nurses were dropping in to check my vital signs every hour. Sleep? Forget about it. That's what the coma was for.

My boss on the force walked in as I was crying. He shed some tears as well. His name, dammit . . . Lieutenant Thomas DeRosa, that is his name. A big man, standing six foot two and weighing 220 pounds. Built like a truck. Tom was one of my best friends. He served in the Army as a Captain and was a tank commander in the 3rd Army under General George Patton. He had stories you wouldn't believe. He loved serving under Patton and said he was the finest general in the U.S. Army. He could be a mean son of a bitch but if you did your job he'd back you up.

After the war Tom decided to join the police department and got promoted fast. He was a great guy to work for and a good friend. I missed working for him. Tom retold me the events of that night and said that he suspects it was the Young gang who did the shooting, but had no witnesses.

Why do I know that name? Young, Young . . . Kyle? Kevin? Is that right? Are these memories even right? It feels like I'm experiencing someone else's life. Why is that? But I *am* Louis Romoso. The rest has to be accurate then, too. Right? Maybe my head got hit a lot worse than I thought.

Chapter 2

Damsel in Distress

Ten to five, New Year's Eve, 1954. Dark outside already. Wind howling, snow coming down hard, and it was a balmy fifteen degrees outside in downtown Buffalo. Frost was on the windows, and Duffy downstairs was swearing at the coal furnace.

Absently my hand was rubbing the bullet wound on my arm. Being shot seemed right. That had happened. Wasn't I alone, though? I don't remember anyone else being around, especially my wife. I know I can be an asshole and piss people off, but not to the point of shooting at me. At least I hope that's the case.

I thought more about Ellen, a real catch. I choked up a bit. The best part of me gone, and an unborn son to boot. Anger was back. These emotions inside of me were foreign, yet they were undoubtedly mine. It was confusing the hell out of me.

While I was doing the mental gymnastics a knock came at my door. Who the hell is this now? Then I remembered, I was a private eye. Maybe it was a client? But who would be knocking on New Year's Eve?

I said, "If you're coming here to hire me to keep you alive you better have a check with two zero's preceded by a five. That's five hundred bucks for all you mathematicians out there." That's what I get for listening to Richard Diamond, Private Detective. He'd always start out with a wiseass remark.

The knob turned and in she walked, a blonde about five foot eight with sad, brown eyes, a beautiful white smile. She wore a low-cut blue dress, blue high heels, and a mink fur coat. I looked at her and went pale and my head began to ache. Where do I know her from?

The blonde entered and asked, "Are you Mr. Romoso?"

"Why yes, I am," I replied. I asked her what brought her out on such a nasty New Year's Eve night.

"I need your help. It's a matter of life and death for my mother and I." Then she began to ramble about her suspicions.

I interrupted and said, "Slow down, Doll, I don't even know your name."

"Doll?" She said it with some authority. I put my hands up in surrender and apology. "Sorry, my name is Ingrid Reitman."

What . . . do I know her? I must have fell back in my chair, because she had some concern on her face. "Are you all right, Mr. Romoso?"

"I'm fine." I lied. "Haven't I seen you somewhere before, Miss Reitman?"

"It's *Mrs.* Reitman, Mr. Romoso."

"Oh, I see," with a sad look on my face, like I just lost my best friend. "Please, call me Lou."

She nodded and didn't say anything. I didn't either. Something wasn't sitting quite right. But I needed to figure out what she needed. Time to do what I do best: solve a case.

"My fee is fifty a day plus expenses, and that is nonnegotiable."

Ingrid raised her eyebrows a bit at my bluntness. "I gathered that from the unique way you greeted me. Didn't you say five hundred?"

"Yes, well, I must have misspoke. Mrs. Reitman, or may I call you Ingrid? I like to be creative and give my clients their money's worth. Can I assume that my fee is affordable to you? If not, I can recommend another detective, but you won't get my quality of work or my company to enjoy." I don't know what made me say that, who the hell else did I know? Ten minutes ago I didn't even remember my wife!

She smiled, let out a chuckle, and told me that Ingrid was fine. Then without any explanation she buried her face into her hands and began to sob uncontrollably.

Just great, another "Happy New Year" in the books. I went to the bar and poured her a shot of Canadian Club whiskey.

"Here, drink this, it will calm you down," I said and handed her a tissue or ten to wipe her tears.

She looked up, downed the shot like a professional, and cracked a weak smile.

"Okay, now tell me, how I can help you?" I said.

"Your fee is not a problem and I would not have come to you if you weren't the best. You've done work for a few of my acquaintances, and they highly recommend you. I had my doubts after inquiring after your brash reputation, but a close friend reassured me."

I smiled. Must really be good at what I do if people I can't remember were recommending my services. "Tell them thanks for me next time you see them."

As I stared out the frosted window of my office looking at my 1953 Blue Lincoln Continental—wait that's mine? Damn, that's a nice car—Ingrid began to tell me her predicament.

"The trouble started when my mother, her name is Jessica,

met a man named Heinrich Mueller at the Park Country Club. She fell for his suave demeanor. He's an art collector and dealer from a well-to-do German family."

"However, you didn't buy a word of this story and told your mother that you have, shall I say, *doubts* about the validity of his story. Is that correct?" I asked. Already my mind was grinding its gears. Working a case was exactly what I needed to refocus myself.

"Why yes, it is," Ingrid said. "Heinrich had fled the fighting to Switzerland, where he hid at a family estate in the mountains. He regaled her of his stories of visiting all the famous art galleries in Europe and the homes of the world's most famous artists, rediscovering pieces that were thought lost to the War."

I asked how he did this when the war took most, if not all, German wealth and destroyed most of their homes. She said Heinrich answered this by saying his family lived in a villa in the country that was untouched by the Allies, and that they also invested heavily in gold before the war and put most of it in the Swiss Banks.

"How fortuitous for him," I said sarcastically. I listened intently and asked her if she thought Mueller was after her mother's money.

"Well, Lou, I think he is going to kill my mother, not only for her money, but for something she may have overheard. But mother swears she doesn't know anything."

"Why do you think that?"

"I visited with her on the twenty-third of December to ask if she wanted to do some last-minute shopping, when I heard this yelling and screaming coming from the study. I walked into the study and saw my mother, Heinrich, and Heidi screaming at each other. I heard Heinrich tell my mother, 'if you breathe a word of this, it will be your last!' I also think that

I am now on his list to be killed as well, and I'm scared!"

"Tough guy, threatening a woman," I said. "Who is this Heidi?"

"She's Heinrich's sister. He says they are all alone now. Their family died in the War, when their town was bombed." Ingrid paused for a moment to collect herself. "You know what else is funny? He also said his family's villa was untouched."

"I picked up on that, too," I said. "Did you call the police?"

"No! He would have killed us already if I did. They would have just came by and asked questions, and as soon as they left we would be in trouble. I just can't take that chance and my mother is terrified. She's only at ease when I'm over, which is every day now, or when Livingston her butler and Maggie her maid are in."

"Livingston and Maggie, do they live in the house?" I asked.

"They used to until Heinrich and Heidi moved in, now they're only in the house from nine to five. My Mother felt horribly about this and offered to let them live in the carriage house on the property, rent-free. Heinrich wanted to deduct the rent from their salaries. Mother would have no such thing.

"Things had been frosty between them for the last few weeks before the fight. They sleep in separate rooms and hardly talk. Heinrich is always with his sister and some mysterious man my mother has never talked to or been introduced to. As I told you before, he threatened Mother and I, and now I'm here asking for your assistance. Can you help us?"

I stared at her and said, "I have a question to ask, have you told your husband?"

She looked down at the floor and shook her head no and began to cry again.

"What's wrong?" I got her another drink and a dozen

tissues and waited for her to stop crying.

She wiped her tears away, looked up at me with her sad brown eyes and said, "Do you have a bathroom?"

Yes? Maybe? I didn't know. I thought hard about it. "Down the hall on the right." Hopefully that was right.

She stood and walked out of my office. I scrambled to think. I know I've seen her before, but where? And why does her name seem so important?

As Ingrid closed the door, the name hit me. Reitman. From the war. My head began to throb and I got that funny feeling again as memories flooded in.

***

I saw myself sitting in a briefing room with other fighter escort pilots and the crewmembers of B-17s and their pilots. We got our mission details and got ready for our flight. Take off was in an hour. I saw a B-17 pilot I knew was from Buffalo. Captain Tom Reitman. We had flown fifteen missions together without so much as a scratch. He had painted "Ingrid's Bunker Buster" on his plane's nose, and also had her picture on the dash. That must be why she was familiar.

Both of us for some reason were rather quiet. No small talk about home or personal lives, just "hey" and "good luck."

It was raining in England when we took off and I got my guys in formation around the bombers as we flew towards Germany. It was uneventful until we reached the outskirts of Berlin. Gray, black-crossed Messerschmitts came through the cloud cover. German fighters packed the sky. The flak was so thick you could walk on it amongst the clouds. The Messerschmitts were all over us. They had us out numbered. We tried to hold formation but it was impossible.

They continued coming from the clouds, on us like locusts.

We zigged and zagged, looped and looped again until we could get an advantage on them. The tide turned as we knocked them off one by one.

I was able to loop behind one and held the advantage. He tried to climb for more air space. His plane was no match for the better-built Mustang. I was behind him as he climbed. I fired my .50 caliber gun and hit his right wing and watched him explode as my bullets ripped through his gas tanks. The Germans broke off and I got us back into formation.

To my right one of the B-17s lagged behind and out of formation with smoke coming from his number three engine. The pilot shut down the engine and put out the fire, but the drag slowed the bomber down. Then came another wave of German fighters. They were all over this bomber. I broke off with two other planes in my command and told the rest of my air group to stay in formation. I banked left got behind one Messerschmitt and let a burst of .50 caliber rounds go. He banked left into the clouds and I missed him. I pulled my stick back and shot through the clouds hoping to get above him and praying he didn't get behind me. This guy was good. I got above the cloud cover and saw him below me.

I banked right, pushing the stick forward to dive behind him. The Messerschmitt pilot looked back and I could see the surprise on his face wondering how I managed to pull off the maneuver. I wondered that too and figured the man upstairs was with me that day. He banked right. I followed. He tried to loop in behind me and I stayed right on his tail. He couldn't shake me. I let go another burst and this time his luck ran out. I destroyed his rudder and stabilizers; he had no control. I saw the canopy of his plane slide back and watched him bail out. I could have shot at him while he floated to Earth but thought better of it.

I flew by the cockpit of the B-17 and saw it was Captain

Reitman. I gave him a thumbs up and he returned it. His gunners and my other two fighters were able to knock off three more German planes. We got above the big plane to protect him as long as I could, when three Messerschmitts came up from behind. We saw them and we looped back behind them and were able to knock out one more. The other two got away from us and blasted the big bomber out of the sky. The wing was almost shot off as the crew began to bail out. I counted ten parachutes in the sky. They all got out. Then I saw one of the Messerschmitts go after the downed crew's parachutes.

I banked right got behind the bastard and let him have it. I blew his plane out of the sky. I watched as the crew touched the ground and ordered my other two fighters to join the rest of the formation. I flew over the downed crew as long as I could and then rejoined my fighter group. That was the last I ever saw of Captain Reitman.

And now his widow was in my office. Happy Fucking New Year!

CHAPTER 3
MEET, GREET, AND SHOOT

The door opened and Ingrid walked back in, reclaiming her seat across from me. I shook my head and tried to reassure her.

"Are you sure you are okay?" I asked.

She was done crying, for now, and nodded. Thank God. I'm terrible with women, and never know the right things to say. After a bit, she started back up with her story.

"You see, Lou, the reason I started crying when I came into your office was, I saw your picture next to the plane and thought of my husband. He was a Captain in the Air Corps stationed in England at Thorpe-Abbott Airfield and flew B-17s. He was shot down over Berlin. He and his crew parachuted to safety when, as one witness told it, they were shot by Gestapo troops patrolling the area. They were unarmed, and shot in cold blood for no reason."

She dropped the glass and leaned forward with her hands buried in her face and cried some more. For the third time I offered tissues. Remind me to pick some more up next time I'm at the store. Ingrid got ahold of herself and apologized.

I said, "No need to. Your husband was Captain Thomas Reitman of the eighth bomber group."

Ingrid raised her head and looked at me. "He was, did you know him?"

Did I know him? My memory certainly seemed to think so. I filled my glass and took a drink. I told her my version of the day he died. Saying it out loud, I felt a little guilt for not being better that day.

Ingrid told me it wasn't my fault. We sat there in silence for a while. Ingrid broke the silence and asked me again, "Lou, will you take my case?"

I looked at her, smiled and said, "Yes."

***

After I agreed to take Ingrid's case I offered to buy her a New Year's drink downstairs at Marco's.

Her eyes were still watery and bloodshot from the crying, but she smiled and said, "Why not, I haven't any plans."

The bar was crowded. The wax factory, steel plants, auto plants, and various other industries were closed for the holiday and it seemed like most of those employees had filtered into Marco's. We managed to find a table in the corner of the bar. Cigar and cigarette smoke filled the air. People were standing shoulder to shoulder with a bluish haze hovering over them.

A big band played a rendition of "In the Mood" by Glenn Miller. People were dancing, laughing, and having a ball waiting for the stroke of midnight. Ingrid and I watched them dance and enjoyed the music.

A man, about five foot seven with black curly hair wearing a white bartender's apron covering his white shirt and black pants, stopped over and asked what we were having. I looked at him funny . . . Marco, Duffy's brother. He returned the look, but with a smile. He must have known something I didn't. Make that everything I didn't.

I ordered myself a scotch and water and Ingrid a seven and seven. I asked Ingrid if she would mind if I lit a cigar. She said she didn't, and as a matter of fact took a drag of mine. I looked at her and laughed and she told me her father used to smoke cigars, and she enjoyed the taste.

For dinner I ordered a porterhouse steak with a salad and baked potato. Ingrid ordered the veal parmesan with a salad and spaghetti.

Marco brought them over and said, "Dinner and drinks on me tonight, Lou."

I said, "Thanks, how come?"

"Big occasion tonight, Pasquale and my niece Josephine are engaged."

Pasquale. Josephine. I know those names. "That's great!" I said, realizing I was staring over Marco's shoulder with a faraway look in my eyes. Marco this time looked at me with a bit of concern, like he wanted to ask me something, then shook it off and pointed out the newly engaged couple. They finally reached our table and we gave them our congratulations. Josephine was all decked out for New Year's Eve, wearing a beautiful red and black dress and black high-heeled shoes. She looked beautiful. Pasquale was dressed in a black pinstripe suit, looking very handsome with his hair perfect.

Pasquale said, "I see you that you heard the news."

"Good news travels fast. When is the wedding?" I asked.

"Next February," Josephine replied. "Save the eleventh because you're invited, both of you."

I looked at Ingrid. She looked up at Josephine and said, "We'll be there," and smiled.

They left us and continued making the rounds. I pointed after Josephine. "She your friend?"

"Can't get anything past you, detective," Ingrid answered with a smile. Did she just lighten up and tell a joke? "Yes, she is a dear friend, and it was her who led me to ask for your help."

We ate our dinner, made small talk, and I agreed to meet at her home on the 800 block of Delaware Avenue tomorrow at 6 p.m.

I walked her to her car, and there waiting for her by a beautiful blue 1932 mint condition Cadillac with a V-16 engine was her chauffeur, Russell. He was a big boy, six foot three and all of 275 pounds. Ingrid introduced me after he opened her door.

I said, "Is he part bodyguard, too? Because if he is, I'll take one."

They both laughed as she got in the car. Russell closed the door, got behind the wheel, and began to leave. The car stopped and Ingrid jumped out. She gave me a kiss on the cheek and whispered, "Happy New Year," in my ear. She got back into her car and they left just as quick. I put my hand to my cheek, pinched it and left another mark before heading back to the bar.

It felt strange. As the night went on Ingrid was becoming less square and actually flirting with me, but something was holding me back. My luck with women was nothing to write home about. But this was something different.

You have to let go, Lou, I am fine, and so is your son. I began to tear up but dried my eyes. Ellen, her voice in my head. Sorrow once again overcame me.

Just as I was about to go back inside, in the corner of my eye a black Ford idling on Carroll Street, with two guys in it and smoke coming from the open windows. A funny feeling in the pit of my stomach formed. The engine revved from the black Ford and it came racing down Carroll and around the corner of Chicago Street with its passenger window down. I saw the barrel of a gun come out and dove to the sidewalk. Shots flew over the top of me into the brick wall of Marco's. The black Ford sped away and vanished into the night.

I got up, brushed myself off, shook my head and said to myself, "I hate New Year's Eve."

The bar emptied out and Pasquale ran over to me to see if I was okay. Duffy also came flying out of the bar to see what happened. He asked if I was all right as well. Then he looked at the bullet holes in his bar and told me he'd send me the bill for the repairs. Thanks for the concern, Duffy.

As I dusted myself off I thought about the car. A black Ford. Same model involved when Ellen was gunned down. I was pissed, because now I was a target, and they got away again.

A patrol car pulled up after a couple minutes. They got out of their squad car, Officers Hoffman and Walters, and walked over to me.

"I'm fine, boys, they missed me, and most importantly missed my car."

They laughed and I gave them as many details as I could, but had no idea why they took a shot at me. My mind was still foggy, and details were slowly creeping back into my consciousness. But I'd give them twenty to one it was the same gunmen who tried before.

Walters told me he would have to give this information to Homicide and to DeRosa.

DeRosa? Wait, that's right. My captain when still on the force. I said, "No sweat, have him call me in the morning. I'll be home." Happy New Year to me.

CHAPTER 4

THE HOST

New Year's Day, 1955. After finally getting some rest, I woke up early—around 11 a.m.—because I wanted to get to Marco's and place a few bets with Duffy.

I got dressed, went upstairs to see if Elvira had any breakfast going. I was in luck. After giving her a kiss on the cheek I sat down to some coffee with a little whiskey in it. My father's favorite. I wonder whom he got that from. I had a couple of fried dough cookies with sugar, spoke with Elvira, thanked her for breakfast, and headed to the bar.

I met Pasquale at the foot of the stairs and he asked if he could go with me to Marco's and learn some American football from me. I said sure, as long as I didn't have to watch soccer with him. The deal was sealed with a handshake.

We took my car and parked in front of the place. Duffy was on the phone and writing. I assume he was taking bets on football and not orders for food. He hung up and I gave him my four bets: Georgia Tech over Arkansas in the Cotton Bowl,

Navy over Ole Miss in the Sugar Bowl, Ohio State over USC in the Rose Bowl, and Texas El Paso over Florida State in the Sun Bowl. Something told me I was going to win all four bets, like I already knew the outcome. But then again, I felt that way every time when placing bets. My confidence led me to put a hundred dollars on each game.

Duffy raised his eyebrows at the amount and said, "You'd better be able to pay if you lose."

I took four one-hundred-dollar bills from my pocket and gave them to him and said, "Is this proof enough?"

"Okay, okay!" He threw the money back at me and laughed. "Your bets are in."

Pasquale wanted some action; I informed him it wasn't a good idea to gamble. It could lead you down a bad path. He nodded and had a coffee and whiskey and we watched the game as I explained to him what was going on.

***

Almost 6 p.m. I remembered I told Ingrid I'd meet her at her home. Shit. I may be late. Hopefully she's not big on punctuality.

The 800 block of Delaware Avenue, and for that matter most of the blocks on Delaware, were homes to the wealthiest families in Buffalo. Mansions up and down the street, every one different with all the architectural beauty you would expect from the wealthy.

I arrived at the big stone mansion located on Delaware Avenue and Barker Street around 6:15 p.m. It had a big curved driveway and was kept immaculate. I parked in the driveway, got out and rang the doorbell. Chimes went off and I thought I was in St. Lucy's Church. The door opened slowly and a hulking man answered. It was Russell. I said, "Hello, Russell,

36

Happy New Year."

"Same to you, sir, Mrs. Reitman is expecting you. She is in the study with her mother, Mrs. Mueller."

"Lead the way."

I was admiring the lavish hallway that led to the study as we walked. It was bigger than my entire house. The artwork alone was worth more than my house, probably the entire block I lived on. On one wall was Monet's famous painting, "The Boy with Fife." I thought that was in the Louvre in Paris. Maybe it was a copy, but what the hell do I know about art.

Russell opened the door to the beautifully decorated study and let me in. A roaring fire was in the big fireplace, the wood crackling in the background. Russell introduced me as I walked into the study.

"Mr. Romoso is here, Mrs. Reitman."

"Thank You, Russell," Ingrid said, "could you get Mr. Romoso a drink please?"

"Well, Lou, what are you drinking tonight?"

"I'll just have a ginger ale, thank you," I responded as I looked at the paintings on the wall. One was of a young Air Corps Captain standing by his B-17 with the name "Ingrid's Bunker Busters" over a big bomb painted on the nose. On the other wall hung their wedding picture, and on the desk were several other photos of Tom, Ingrid, her mother and father, and a young boy who had a striking resemblance to Tom.

I said to Ingrid, "Nice pad you have. Rather small, isn't it?"

Ingrid laughed. "Have a seat, Lou."

So I did. It was a big comfortable chair and I felt like I could sleep forever in it, but there was work to be done as Russell came in with my ginger ale.

"The young boy, is he your son?" I asked.

"Yes, Tom Jr.," Ingrid answered. "He never met his father. I got pregnant during the war when my husband was on leave.

Thankfully he is away at boarding school and away from this mess."

Mrs. Mueller entered the room. She was maybe a shade over fifty years old, an attractive blonde with green eyes and an hour glass figure. She could have been Ingrid's twin, other than the eyes. She was wearing a black dress and heels. Around her neck was a diamond necklace that sparkled brightly. However, no wedding ring on her left hand. Her hair was perfect, like she just came from the beauty parlor, but her lovely face told a different story. One of hurt, betrayal, fear.

"Mrs. Mueller, I'm Lou Romoso, and I'm a private detective. I was hired by Ingrid to see if I might be of help to you. So if you will, indulge me. What about your husband has you fearing for your life?"

"I'm not scared, I'm *terrified*," she said. "Mr. Romoso, something is not right."

I interrupted and said, "Call me Lou, Mrs. Mueller."

"I will if you'll call me Jessica or Mrs. Wright, just not Mueller. I was a fool to marry him." A tear came down her cheek.

I took my handkerchief from my suit coat pocket and gave it to Jessica to wipe away her tears and then passed it to Ingrid to do the same. One woman crying is bad. Two, what the Christ. I patted Jessica on the hand and told her she was no fool and that we all make mistakes. I also told her I would help her and Ingrid. She stared at me with her big green eyes as the corner of her mouth started to show a smile.

Ingrid smiled at me but couldn't hide the worry and fear in her eyes. We all sat around the fireplace. The room warm and quite cozy. Ingrid said that she and her mother hadn't eaten all day and were starved. She had her maid prepare us food. Dinner consisted of carved roast beef, mashed potatoes, gravy, salad, and dessert. We adjourned to the dining room and sat at a table designed for sixteen but at the moment sat three. We chatted a few minutes about Ingrid's husband, father, and Ellen. It was sad and happy all at once.

A pretty redhead with steel-gray eyes served dinner; the eyes are what gave her away.

***

The girl triggered another memory, that of one Michael Sullivan. He had been getting ready for a fight that would give him a shot against the lightweight champion at the time, Jimmy Carter, if he won. Sullivan was to fight a boxer from New York City named Johnny "Lead Hands" Carmini in the undercard at The Aud. The fights were sold out, not an empty seat in the house.

Sullivan had sold out, too. He sold out his friends who supported him, his manager, corner man, his fans, and, most important, his best friend, Mary O'Toole.

I happened to be there for the fight. The bell rang and the two fighters went at it. Carmini caught Sullivan with a glancing blow that barely touched his jaw and he buckled his knees. Sullivan made a halfhearted attempt at a left to Carmini's jaw but missed. Carmini kept on connecting with his punches, snapping back Sullivan's noggin like a bobblehead doll. Sullivan was just throwing punches anywhere he could, hoping to make it seem like he was trying. The crowd sensed something was wrong and began to boo and throw anything they could in the ring. A pile of trash was growing on the mat. The ref counted to ten and called the fight with Sullivan lying in a heap of garbage. Boos continued and no one came to get him off the mat. Not his manager, corner man, doctor, nor Mary. Sully was alone in the ring with nothing left.

Sully was later found shot in the head by a .38. Before that, he was shot in the knee two nights after the fight. I got a call over to the ER, where Mary was still wiping the tears from her steel-gray eyes. You could see the hurt and fear in them at the same time.

"Who did this?" I asked, then she broke into more tears. I'm not a saint, so I don't have the patience of one. I grabbed her by the shoulders shook her and said, "If you want me to help both of you, you need to trust me and tell me what happened."

Finally Mary relented and told me what she knew. It wasn't much. I had to wait for Sully to get out of surgery so I could talk to him.

Three days later I got a call and went up to Sully's room. A cop was stationed outside his door. Mary sat in a chair next to his bed holding Sully's hand. No one said a word. I approached the bed and asked Sully how he was doing.

"Fine, gumshoe, now beat it and leave me alone."

My blood boiled and I got pissed, which is the norm for me when someone acts like an asshole. So I got close to Sully's ear and whispered to him, "Look, asshole, I'm here to help you. If you don't like it I could give a shit, but you're going to tell me what happened or the cop on your door goes away and it's just you and Red over there left to deal with Young and his gang."

His eyes grew as big as saucers. "How did you know?"

It was more a shot in the dark than anything. But if something happened in the First Ward, chances were they were involved. "I find out everything. Now talk!"

Sully did. He told me about taking the dive, and how it was Young who came to him and promised him five grand in cash, plus a piece of his now booming business at Mickey Finn's. Since Sully had grown up dirt poor, and was only making a couple hundred for the fight, the decision wasn't tough at the time. Afterwards he felt terrible, and knew he made a big mistake.

The first thing he did was go to Young and confront him. Johnny O'Connell, one of Young's thugs, told him Young wasn't in. O'Connell always wore a neatly groomed beard and was a bruiser of guy. He stood six feet tall and weighed over 250 pounds. Just plain mean. It was said once that when he was in the first grade he pushed his mother in front of a bus for yelling at him for fighting a fifth grader and beating him up. He was one of Young's bodyguards.

With Young not around Sullivan walked out to the bar to get a whiskey and drown his sorrows. He finished his shot, taking the bottle with him and walked towards the back door. Before he left a beautiful black-haired, green-eyed lady walked in. Sully said her green eyes made jade jealous and would give any man cause to freeze. He played up to her and tried to win her affections. No luck. This woman was an ice queen. She rebuffed Sully, telling him, "I don't waste my time with lowlifes."

Drinking whiskey combined with a big mouth and stupidity caused the little Irishman to yell at the green-eyed beauty, "If it wasn't for me and that dive I took, the Irish bug you're looking for would be tending bar in the shithole this place once was!"

She laughed and he slapped her hard across the face. She put her hand to her face, reached in her purse, and pulled out a .38 revolver. Sully's eyes bulged as looked down the barrel of the .38, which looked like a howitzer from his end. He tried to apologize and blame it on the whiskey to no avail. The mysterious green-eyed lady shot Sully in the knee. He went down like the Titanic and screamed.

She turned to walk out and told Sully, "Tell Young I was looking for him and to call me tonight, he has my number, swine," then spit on him and left the bar. Sully never saw her again.

O'Connell saw the whole thing and wouldn't stop laughing about it the whole time he dragged Sully out to a car and dropped him off on the street at his apartment. Mary happened to see it from her window, and that's when she called an ambulance.

When Sully was telling me this I thought we finally had a case to bring down Young. He'd been a pain in the ass to Buffalo PD for years. So we hid them in an apartment above Marco's—my future private-eye office. The apartment was a one bedroom flat with a kitchen and living room. The furniture was old and left there by the previous tenant who met his maker somewhat unexpectedly. Cops hovered all around until we could make an arrest, and then we'd hide them out of town until the trial. We didn't want to lose our star witness.

Several days passed and Sully was getting restless. He wanted to get out into the fresh air. I told him sit tight a little while longer until I was able to get more facts to satisfy the district attorney. Sully nodded yes, but I knew he wouldn't stay put.

I didn't have long to wait before Sully decided it was time to take a walk. Mary begged him not to go but he threw her to the floor and left. The noise caused Duffy and the two cops on lookout to rush upstairs. That's where they found the bedroom window open and Sully shimmying down the drainpipe. They shouted for him to stop and get back in the house to no avail. Sully hit the ground running and took off down Carroll Street.

The rest of the day and most of the evening passed. No word on Sully. I asked Mary where he might go and she had no clue. Time continued to move slowly. I left Mary, continuing to search for Sully before going home. I got home about 3:30 a.m., beat from looking for Sully all day. As I got to my door I heard the phone ring, my wife Ellen answered it.

"I'm sorry, Tom, Lou's not home yet—wait, I think I just heard him come in." Ellen turned around. "It's for you."

"Thanks." I took the phone and listened.

"Lou, its DeRosa, they found Sully."

"Great," I said, "Where is he? I'll be right there."

DeRosa said he was at the General Mills grain elevator but not to rush, a night watchman had come out for a smoke and found him about a half an hour ago floating in the Buffalo River. They beat him bad. No open casket on this one. DeRosa said it's the worst beating he's ever seen someone take.

"Don't know what exactly happened," DeRosa continued, "but when they dragged Sully out of the river he had a bullet hole in his head and quite a few holes in the rest of him. I'm having the coroner pick him up now. I'll see you in fifteen."

I told Ellen what happened and that I had to go. She kissed me goodbye, told me to be careful.

As I drove, I rode past Marco's and shook my head. You stupid bastard, why didn't you listen? You didn't have to die! I thought about Kevin Young and how I'd like to twist his head off and throw it into the lake. Then there was Mary. What would she do now that Sully was gone? How would I tell her? It hurt to think. I drove the rest of the way staring straight ahead and into an abyss called night.

The Buffalo River was like glass when I got to the scene. Sully was gone by the time I'd got there. The evidence team, which basically was a photographer and a couple of Homicide detectives and patrolmen, was walking the area looking for anything that would help us solve this case.

I walked over to DeRosa and asked him if they found anything. They hadn't. The only witness to the whole thing was the watchman.

I took the night watchman aside to talk to him. Asked him what he did that night, why he was out there, did he hear or see anything and did he know the deceased, Michael Sullivan.

He didn't give me much. Just that he walked out of the guard house for a smoke and noticed the body. That's when he called the police. I thanked him for his time and sent him back to his shack to do whatever it was he did and headed back for my car; I was pissed and left in a hurry.

Morning came and we went to see the coroner. The coroner's office was located in the back of Meyer Memorial Hospital. I went over to take a look at Sully. I pulled back the sheet and almost puked. He had black and blue marks all over him. They beat him bad. His face was unrecognizable, his fingers broken, and his ribs destroyed. He had bullet holes in his chest and one in the head. No man deserved to die like this.

The coroner gave us the report, which stated basically what we knew. Sully was beaten with a blunt object about the head, face, arms, legs, knees, and back. He was most likely unconscious or dead when he got shot in the head with a .38 and was shot ten more times in the torso area post mortem with a .45. I shook my head.

Sully's funeral was held on a hot, rainy Monday. Lightning arced through the morning darkness, lighting up the inside of the sparsely filled church. The thunder roared with anger as each crack sounded like artillery fire. I looked up at the dark sky and thought Sully must be pissed; he is causing such a ruckus up there. Or he is fighting the devil? Either way I was glad I wasn't Sully.

The funeral Mass was held at St. Lucy's where I had Father Pat do the Mass for him. It was great as always from Father Pat. His sermon was right on and he made us all feel better.

Pat didn't know Sully, but he spoke as if he knew him for twenty years. He talked about his childhood and how difficult it was for Sully. Spoke of his boxing career and about what-ifs. Father Pat is honest so he also spoke of Sully's bad side. His drinking, gambling, and millions of other bad choices he made, and that God gives us free will to make those choices.

Sully had no family. His mother and father were dead and all he had was Mary. Mary, my wife, and I followed the Hearse to the cemetery, Mount Calvary, in the suburb of Cheektowaga. Father Pat drove with the Hearse and said a few words and prayers. Mary threw some roses on the wooden casket and sobbed as she said her final goodbyes. I just bowed my head and held my wife's hand.

They say you can tell how a man lived by the people who attend his funeral to pay their last respects. If it wasn't for me, my wife, Father Pat, the funereal director, the hearse driver, and Mary, Sully would have been put in a box and buried in a six-foot hole and covered up. The only ones who would have cared would have been the worms.

Rest in peace, Sully, you stupid bastard.

CHAPTER 5

SHOTS, ON THE HOUSE

"**M**ary O'Toole, what are you doing here?" I
said.

She looked over at me and almost
dropped the roast beef. No! Not the roast beef! I asked Mary
how she was and told her that she looked great, which earned
me a kick in the shins from Ingrid. "What!" I Held up my hands
as if to project my innocence to Ingrid.

She asked Mary to sit for a minute so she could catch me
up on her life. "Well," Mary started, "I needed a job after Sully
got killed so my mother Maggie asked Mrs. Wright if she knew
anyone looking to hire a maid. Mrs. Wright had Mrs. Reitman
call me and I've been working here since we buried Sully." A
tear trickled down her face. "He didn't have to die. He just
wouldn't listen to you. He thought he could work it. Now he's
gone. It's funny though . . ." she stopped mid-sentence, shook
her head. "Sully had to die in order for me to move on, and as
much as I loved him, I finally saw in those last few days we

were together that I had no future with him. I still miss him. I want to thank you for being so kind and understanding through that whole mess. I only wish you were able to get that Kevin Young, because all he's done is ruin lives."

Ingrid looked at me as if to say what is she talking about. I looked at her then down at the floor. My wife Ellen and our unborn son crept into my thoughts. As if reading my mind, Mary said she read about me getting shot and my wife getting killed. She blamed herself for it by dragging me into the case.

I said to Mary, "It wasn't your fault. If I can finally prove it was Young, I'll get him for that, and for Sully."

Mary got up and resumed bringing in dinner. Ingrid looked at me, her eyes moistened, and told me that she was sorry about my wife and child and held my hand. It was warm and tender and I could feel how sorry she was for me.

I said thank you and took a sip of my ginger ale as I tried to hold back a tear.

Ingrid asked Mary and Russell to join us for dinner and they reluctantly accepted. It was a great meal. After we ate I asked Jessica to continue filling me in on what was happening with her second husband.

"Well, Lou, as I'm sure my daughter has told you, I met Heinrich at the Buffalo Country Club," she said. "I was lonely and heartbroken over the loss of my husband. Heinrich came over and I guess I was taken by him and his cultured ways."

"Taken is right, Mother. I told you he was no good," Ingrid said, as if to scold her.

"Ingrid, that won't help now," I said. "Please continue, Jessica."

Ingrid gave me another friendly kick in the shins. Jessica said that life with Heinrich was good for a few months. Then his younger sister, Heidi, moved in. Ingrid let out a sarcastic cough. I gave her a friendly kick in the shins and smiled as she said, "ouch."

"Weird things began to happen," Jessica continued. "They were inseparable. We spent less and less time together and they were always at some art show or another. Always with another man whom Heidi said was a friend from the old country. I never could get a good look at him. It's' like they purposely kept him at a distance. However, one afternoon recently, I overheard a conversation between Heinrich and Heidi."

"What were they talking about?" I asked.

"At first they were talking about some art they needed to bring over from Switzerland, and how it was worth a fortune. Then they started discussing a pressroom and a man helping with distribution. I had no idea what they were talking about. I tried to walk quietly away and that's when Heidi opened the door and saw me. She began to yell and swear and accuse me of eavesdropping. I told her she was crazy and I wanted her out of the house by Christmas. I went down to my study and that's when Heinrich confronted me. Ingrid walked in while Heinrich was screaming at me in a mix of German and English. Heinrich began to threaten me and turned to Ingrid and said the same went for her—"

She was interrupted when Mary let out a scream and pointed to the window; a man with a gun. I yelled for everyone to get down as I saw the man bring the Thompson machine gun's eyesight up. They were all frozen. I lifted for all I was worth, but the big dining room table barely moved. Russell jumped in and helped me lift the table upright, blocking the gunman's view of the room. As the table hit the floor the gunman fired. I dove and knocked Jessica and Ingrid to the ground, covering them with my body. Russell did the same with Mary as bullets sprayed around the room.

The shooting stopped and I pulled out my gun and Russell

did the same with his. I looked over at him and smirked as I went for the front door and Russell the back. I got to the front door, opened it slowly, and heard the engine of a car roar to life. I looked in the driveway and saw a black Ford racing away. Just then Russell came running from around the back of the house. He got close to the car and took a few shots, managing to knock out a taillight.

We rushed back into the house to see if the women were okay. They were shaken up but no one got hurt.

What in the hell was that black Ford doing here? Once again it was used to try to kill me, but mine and everyone else's luck held up. Did it follow me? That had to be the case. Unless . . . unless somehow Ingrid's case is related?

The dining room was a mess. Glass was strewn all about the room. There were bullet holes in Ingrid's wedding picture. Ingrid held it together pretty well until she saw the busted glass and frame. She burst into tears. I stood there looking at the damage thankful no one had been hurt. I put my arm around her and hugged her. She buried her head in my shoulder and cried herself dry. She dried her eyes and told me she was sorry. I told her not to worry about it and couldn't blame her for crying for once.

Russell called the police as I checked around the house and by the window. There were footprints by the window and throughout the yard. The ground was muddy and the police might be able to get a print or two.

The police arrived and it was Hoffman and Walters that rang the doorbell. I said, "Hello, boys, Happy New Year."

Walters shook his head and said, "Romoso, this is becoming a New Year's tradition with you!"

I glared at him. I could see the change in his face, as he remembered my wife's shooting. He was about to take the joke back, but I stopped him. "No Shit," I said, and laughed.

Walters and Hoffman eventually joined in. Mine was more of a nervous laugh. The adrenaline right after a shootout can cause weird things to happen to you.

Hoffman asked to use the phone and called Homicide, which always got called in the event of gunfire. Walter walked around the house and began to secure the crime scene. I had another drink and waited.

Hoffman and Walters searched the area and marked where they found the shell casings and footprints. Walters checked the driveway for anything and found bits of the broken red taillight and a snuffed out cigarette.

I asked Mary what she saw.

"I saw a man with a gun," she said.

"Anything else?" I asked. "Could you see what he was wearing, what color his hair was or anything, Mary? Did you recognize him or see him before?"

Mary lifted her eyes as if to look at the top of her head to think, but just shut down and started crying again.

***

Russell walked Lieutenant Tom DeRosa and Detective Sergeant Jim Ruff to the living room where we were all sitting.

Ruff, the department's first black homicide detective, was about six foot one and thin but well-built and could handle himself in any situation. He was well educated, articulate, and was a member of the famed Tuskegee Airmen during WWII. We had a lot in common and spoke of our flying days often when I worked in Homicide. Ruff knew his business and was a great street cop who could defuse the most volatile situations with his calm demeanor. On the streets some punks would often confuse his calmness as a weakness and they soon discovered they made a grave error in judgment and found out that you couldn't push Ruff around. I enjoyed working with him. Ruff had great interview techniques and could get confessions out of some the hardest criminals. He was that good. Same with witnesses. He could get them to remember some minute detail that would help break a case. I was glad he was on tonight.

Ruff took Mary aside to talk through the events again. About thirty minutes later they came into the study where I was with DeRosa talking to Ingrid, Jessica, and Russell. Ruff informed us Mary had seen that man who was in the window before. She'd seen Sully with him at Mickey Finn's, and she may have seen him hanging by Sully's locker room the night he lost his last fight.

"Whats's the name?" I asked, getting impatient with Ruff.

He gave me a look, but let it slide. "One Tom Leary."

"He was also there the night they dropped Sully off after he was shot in the knee, some black car," Mary added.

"Didn't happen to be a '51 Ford?" I asked.

Ruff looked to Mary, who shrugged her shoulders in an "I don't know" motion.

"Wait, did you say black Ford?" Ingrid asked. "Lou, I just remembered something!"

We sat and listened as Ingrid explained. She and a friend had gone out for a drink a couple days before Christmas. Her friend chose Mickey Finn's, despite Ingrid's objections. Heinrich and Heidi walked in, creating slight fear in her. She called Russell to come pick her up to avoid a confrontation.

After Russell pulled away from the curb, a black Ford followed with its lights off. The Ford was swerving back and forth behind them. Eventually it tried to pass them on the left, in the opposite lane of traffic. An oncoming car honked its horn in panic. The black sedan sharply cut its wheel to the right, forcing Russell to pull to the right as well to avoid a collision. The Ford cut left and Ingrid's Blue Studebaker slid on the ice-covered road, narrowly missing a light pole, and slid to a stop in a snow bank.

Within a few minutes a police car showed up on the scene. The cops got out and introduced themselves as officers Christopher and White. They could only tell the officers it was a black sedan. Didn't get a plate number or a look at the driver. The officer's called it in and helped push Ingrid's car from the snow pile.

Before they left, though, Ingrid asked them about a private detective. Both White and Christopher assured her they could help if there was something wrong, but Ingrid played coy with them, saying it wasn't really a police matter.

"They gave me your name, Lou," Ingrid said. "So that is how I came to find you, after speaking with my friend Josephine. They told me you used to be a homicide detective before retiring, and that you're the best in town. They told me you were expensive, but not to tell you they said that or you'd kill them."

I laughed a little, but made a mental note to cuss out Christopher and White next time I saw them. "Russell, you have anything to add?" I asked him.

He shrugged. "No, Lou. Had I thought it was anything different than some drunk asshole leaving Finn's I would have mentioned it sooner."

I agreed with Russell. He had not reason to suspect anything. He didn't know about my previous run-ins with the black Ford, so wouldn't have known the implications.

DeRosa asked us to leave for the night, to allow the crime scene crew some space to see if they could find anything. Also, as small as it was, there was a chance the shooter could come back. He borrowed Ingrid's phone to make a call back to the station to issue a BOLO on Leary and the black Ford.

Ingrid suggested we go to her mother's home, only a block away. I thought that was good. I could continue to ask the questions I needed answers to before the Tommy gun interrupted us.

Jessica hesitated. She didn't want her husband to catch wind of what she was up to. I told her it would be all right. She could tell Heinrich I was a friend of Ingrid and a bit of an art collector. Hopefully he didn't ask any questions, since I know as much about art as I know about women. After a bit she relented, but was still quite nervous about it.

Mary and Russell stayed behind, and would lock everything up after the police were done. As we left they were boarding up the shattered window to keep the winter weather out.

We took my car, even though we were only traveling a block. Too cold out to be walking around. I asked Russell if he could get my car and he told me he had it warmed up and ready to go; that man is better than Kreskin.

CHAPTER 6
DOPPELGÄNGER

J essica and Ingrid got in and off we went to a bigger mansion, if that's possible, on the 700 block of Delaware Avenue. The mansion was all stone. The main entrance had a carport, so guests wouldn't have to get rained or snowed on. After pulling into the carport I opened the door for the ladies and walked them to the front door. As soon as I was about to open the front door it opened. It was their butler.

Jessica introduced him as Livingston. Do you have to be a mind reader to be a butler? These guys were everywhere and anticipated every move.

I walked in and was immediately impressed by the vastness of the front entrance. The floors and walls were marble. The ceiling was twenty feet high and had a solid gold and crystal chandelier hanging from it. The entrance opened into a giant greeting room with Brazilian cherry wood floors. The walls were painted a forest green halfway down and the other half was more Brazilian wood and molding. To the left side of the greeting room was a series of rooms, all with French doors.

Jessica suggested we go into the library. It was unreal. If all public libraries were like this we'd all be geniuses. There was a long oak table in the middle with oak chairs all around. Giant bookshelves lined the walls. Blue leather chairs that were so big they looked like sofas were tastefully about the room. Oak end tables accompanied each chair, each with a cigar humidor and ashtray. The room was painted a country blue with oak molding. On the outside wall was a large stone fireplace with a roaring fire crackling in it. In the middle of the giant oak table was a large wooden replica of Tom Reitman's B-17, the same from the picture at Ingrid's. The plane was stunning and exact to every detail.

Livingston brought us some hot drinks and we all took a seat. Jessica offered me a cigar. I walked over to the solid oak humidor and pulled out a nice Cuban Monte Cristo 2. I lit it and savored the taste. Ingrid came next to me and reminded me how much she enjoyed the smell of cigars. I knew I liked her for a reason.

The quiet was broken as the door opened and a surprised man walked in. "What are you doing here, Jessica?"

I stood up walked over to him and extended my hand to introduce myself. He must be Heinrich. As I walked toward him I saw a gorgeous black-haired female with beautiful green eyes wearing a black dress that clung ever so tight to her body. She had a body that would make the figure eight commit itself to an institution, and her bright green eyes would make emerald envious. Next to her was a man in a black overcoat and fedora tilted toward his eyes, covering them like a total eclipse.

As I got closer to Heinrich I got a glimpse of this mystery

man as he looked up for just a brief moment. He could have passed for Heinrich's twin. Heinrich stepped in front of me, keeping me from getting a better look. The man sauntered back down the hall.

He took my hand and shook it warily. "Mr. Romoso, I presume? I am Heinrich Mueller. This is my sister, Heidi."

"Pleased to meet you both, and, pardon me, but you seem to have the advantage over me. How did you know who I was, have I met you before?"

"Ah, Mr. Romoso, my apologies, Jessica said she was going over to Ingrid's to have dinner and to meet her new friend. I just assumed that was you."

I nodded towards the hall. "And him?"

"Just a friend, my driver. No one of consequence. We escaped the War together and I'm helping him adjust to the U.S."

"I couldn't help notice he looks like you."

Heinrich dismissed me immediately. "Nein, a childhood friend."

Doubtful, but I let it slide. What proof did I have? I just met these two about a minute ago.

"Helping him, huh! More like supporting him with Mother's money," Ingrid said under her breath.

Mueller heard it. He gave Ingrid a death stare and then gave the same look to Jessica. An awkward silence ensued. I stood there not knowing what to do, but finally had to try and keep the conversation from turning volatile.

"So . . . Heinrich, what is it that you do?"

He pulled his eyes from the women, who were still seated behind me. "I am a man of many tastes. Art, mostly."

I nodded, allowing him some room to expand if he wished. I absently moved towards the replica plane on the oak table, and laid my hand on the nose.

"Did you fight in the war?" Heinrich asked.

"Fighter pilot, stationed in England and flew bomber escorts for the Eighth Bomber Squadron."

"Did you know Ingrid's husband?"

"Yes. I flew escort for him on a few missions."

Now a smirk crept up on Heinrich's face. "I guess you could have done a better job protecting that squadron, Mr. Romoso, or Ingrid might not have become a widow."

Jessica stood up now, her face full of fury. "Heinrich, stop. I want you to leave this house right now!"

I curled my hand into a fist and was about to take a swing at Mueller when Ingrid quickly grabbed my arm and said, "Don't, he is not worth it."

Heinrich let out a chuckle. "Enjoy the rest of your evening, Mr. Romoso." Heidi grabbed Heinrich by the arm and they turned to leave. "Try to stay away from the windows. You never know who may be out there."

I followed them to the large foyer and heard them talking. Since I can't speak a word of German, listening to them talk in the hallway was useless. They hopped into a Blue 1954 Cadillac Eldorado and sped out of the driveway and right onto Delaware.

***

Back in the library Jessica was holding a sobbing Ingrid in her arms. They were both crying, actually, and I heard Ingrid tell Jessica, "I hate that man. I wish he were dead. I'd kill him myself if I could get away with it."

"Ingrid, get ahold of yourself," I said upon re-entering the room. "We have to figure out what Herr Mueller is up too. I shouldn't have reacted like that. It's my fault. I apologize, Ingrid, and to you too, Jessica."

"No need to, Lou," Jessica said. "I'm talking to my lawyer in the morning and filing for divorce."

"Jessica, be careful now. This man threatened your life and he is up to something."

Something wasn't right and I just couldn't figure it out. Heinrich and the other man looked almost identical, yet he says he's a friend. That doesn't add up. Another question to add to this riddle. And who was Heidi? She was about as beautiful of a woman I'd ever laid my eyes on. She couldn't be the one who shot Sully, could she? Her green eyes were incredibly cold and beautiful at the same time; hadn't Sully said something about eyes?

As usual, more questions than answers!

Livingston and Maggie walked into the library as I was lost in thought. Livingston brought in another round of tea and cookies, even though neither were touched before. Maggie poured more tea and stood silently looking over the room.

Livingston was a tall, lean, and gangly fellow. His clothes neat and pressed. Not a single gray hair out of place, and he had a touch of nobility about him. His keen sense of awareness was obvious.

I asked Livingston if something was on his mind.

He nodded and said, "I happened to walk by and heard your exchange of words with Mr. Mueller, and I might be able to help shed some light on this matter."

"Please, call me Lou, and your first name is?"

"Livingston, sir. My last name is Cornwall."

"Oh!" was the best I could come up with besides a red face. "Go on, Livingston, I could use some answers instead of questions."

"Well, sir—I mean Lou, I've been with the Wrights for over twenty years, except for the years of the war. I was called back to London for duty with British Intelligence. I was in intelligence during the First World War as well. My job was to interrogate German soldiers and officers that we captured, so obviously I speak fluent German, a skill unknown to Mr. Mueller."

"Okay . . ." I said, liking where this was going. "There has to be a point here somewhere."

"As I said I've interrogated many German prisoners during the war and have picked up little nuances about the German soldier. First, many of the German chaps captured suffered malnutrition and were haggard and demoralized. The German officer, though, always maintained an arrogance about them. Mr. Mueller, for a man who claims to have avoided war, is awfully arrogant, and reminds me of many of the high-ranking men I was tasked with interrogating. He also doesn't treat or talk to his Heidi like a sister. "

I moved to the edge of my seat. "Go on, Livingston, I'm all ears."

"I hear them talk often—not that I eaves drop, mind you."

"Of course not."

"They figure I do not speak German and talk freely when I'm around." Livingston made some sweeping hand gestures, I guess signaling him moving about the house unnoticed by Heinrich or Heidi. "They talk of presses and money, as well as art. Buying and selling, but mostly selling. What this means, Lou, I do not know, but I hope it is of assistance."

This was the first sort-of answer I had gotten to any of my growing list of questions. "It helps, Livingston, more than you know."

Thanks to Livingston this gave me an idea. Thoughts of a case I worked brought me in contact with someone at Immigration and Naturalization. I could call to see what information he could gather on the Mueller family. I'm a betting man, so I'm sure nothing will turn up. But at least there is a chance it may get me some more answers.

Maybe the old codger wanted back in the game of intelligence. "I have no right to ask you this," I started, "But I'd like you to use your skills as an intelligence officer and get me as much dirt on the Muellers and their mysterious friend as possible. If you don't want to it's okay."

Livingston smiled. "I'd thought you'd never ask, ol' chap. I'm very fond of Mrs. Wright and Ingrid, and I want to insure no harm comes to them. So I'm in, Detective, I'm in."

I explained what I needed from him. Immigration would need a photo of each, so I tasked Livingston with searching the home top to bottom. I also told him to keep his ears open, and take notes on anything suspicious he might overhear.

"If you come up with anything, don't call from the house. Take a walk and find a phone booth and call me. If you can't reach me call Lieutenant DeRosa at Buffalo PD, he'll know where to find me."

"I will, Detective. And one more thing," Livingston said, "Heinrich often mentions some pub from down in the First Ward."

"Let me guess, Mickey Finn's?"

Livingston thought hard about it. "Not sure if that's the one. He never mentions it by name."

A final question. Was there a connection between Young and the Muellers? What other place could Heinrich be talking about?

Whatever the answer was, one thing was a fact: Mickey Finn's and Kevin Young were likely at the center of it all.

***

January 2, 1954. Another cold, bitter day in Buffalo. My plan was to sleep as long as I could. But that wasn't meant to be. I hardly slept before Lieutenant Tom DeRosa woke me up at 4 am. I was pissed. It took me a second to remember where I was. At least the phone was right next to the bed.

"Doesn't anyone sleep anymore?" I screamed into it.

"It's me, Tom," DeRosa said.

"What the hell do you want at four in the morning? I don't work for you anymore!"

"Remember the Sully case back in fifty-one?"

"What's a Sully?"

"Really, the last case you were working before you had to retire? You don't remember? We have another body at the same place Sully was found."

I jumped out of bed, dropped the phone and yelled into it, "I'll be right there!"

He started to say something else, but I hung up the phone and started fumbling around in the dark trying to find my clothes. Things must have been so much easier when Ellen was alive. I suck at housework, but I do my best. As I was putting my pants on I tripped and fell. Tried to put two legs into one pant leg. For future reference it doesn't work and you make a lot of noise when you hit the floor.

Damn, I hate DeRosa!

I finally managed to get dressed without killing myself and went to the garage to get my car. Thankfully I had a garage. That way I didn't have to scrape the frost off the windows or brush snow off the car. It was cold but the Lincoln started right up and off I went.

On my way to the General Mills grain elevators I thought about Kevin Young. Those thoughts made me angry. I'd been trying to nab him for years, going back to even before I was at Homicide. Maybe we could finally get him.

I also thought more about Sully, Mary, and everything else that was mounting in this case.

The scene at the grain elevators was dark and cold. A full moon and plenty of stars littered the night sky. I got out of my car and walked about ten yards as my feet crunched in the snow. DeRosa and Ruff were with the watchman. I walked up and asked the watchman, "Aren't you the same guy who found the body three years ago?"

"Yes, sir."

"What's your name?"

"Andre."

"Did you see anything?"

The watchman said he saw nothing strange.

"You didn't hear anything?"

"No, sir, I had the radio on and was eating a sandwich."

You might as well have had Helen Keller watching this place, she'd have done a better job. At least she'd make an effort. I wouldn't pay this guy to watch my TV. Thank God he smoked or you'd have never known he was alive.

We found a few clues this time. Thanks to the snow we had tire prints in the mud by the road, where a car pulled over. Also we had footprints, which were left in the snow and mud. A .38 was found in the dead man's pocket when they fished him out of the drink. He was a small man, standing barely over five and a half feet with red hair and a matching beard.

I gestured to the body, to see if it was alright if I flipped him over. DeRosa nodded, handing me a pair of gloves. Once bent down I grabbed the small man's shoulder and moved to flip him over. As I did, a small device slipped out of his pocket. Quickly I looked around, but DeRosa and the other cops had stepped away. I picked up the device. Like nothing I'd ever seen . . . wait, I have seen this before. But where?

I finally looked at the man's face, and fell back. It was Thomas Leary.

"Lou, Lou! What's the matter with you?"

My eyes fluttered a bit, and I was no longer staring at Leary's blank eyes. Instead, DeRosa's ugly mug was about two inches from mine. I pushed him away and shook my head to clear my mind. "What?"

"You fell backwards, looked like you might pass out," Ruff said. "You okay?"

"Yeah, I'm fine. Need to get some sleep, getting shot at sucks. Have I told you how much I hate New Years?"

DeRosa and Ruff stepped back and laughed, and I was in the clear.

Did we maybe catch a break? After Sully's death, the case against Young died with him. Maybe the lab could compare the slugs found in Sully to Leary's gun, and for the hell of it the slug found in Leary himself. It was just a hunch, but you never know.

If the hunch proved to be right, we would have our first solid clue as to who killed Sully, and in turn who killed Leary. Leary couldn't have shot himself and then put the gun back in his pocket, now could he. Well, could he?

I was suddenly overly tired. I needed some sleep. Then I'd get back to this case. Maybe it was finally time to pay Kevin Young a visit.

INTERLUDE

*T*he tall man was impatient. He had reason to be. He'd been asking questions for almost fifty years. Finally, through an old friend, he'd found the one person who may have answers.

An assistant led the tall man through a maze of corridors until they made it to a small office. The place was a mess. There were books scattered in piles throughout, and papers filled with all kinds of strange drawings and formulas.

Seated behind the desk was a small, shriveled man. The Doc had thick classes, no hair, and small, beady eyes. He couldn't have been more than five feet tall. The tall man took a seat across from him, in a chair much too small for his frame.

"Hello, sir," the Doc said. "From what I understand you have many questions." He spoke with a slight accent. Possibly Austrian, or German. His W's sounded like V's.

"Doc," the tall man said, "Through our mutual friend, I assume you know why I am here."

The Doc nodded, said nothing.

"Okay, then. What can you tell me?"

The Doc smiled, then started his story. "During my youth, I was always fond of science. I—"

"Come on, Doc, you know why I am here. Is your life story necessary?"

"If you wish to know the truth, my friend, yes." He pushed his spectacles back up on the bridge of his nose, and continued. "I was always trying to discover something new. I routinely tested Newton's many theories as a child, which led me to deeper studies in physics. Later I was fascinated by the theories of Albert Einstein, Max Planck, and my countryman, Erwin Schrödinger. I excelled in school, and was soon recruited for my talents. Shortly after Hitler took control of Germany, I was recruited again, but this time by the SS.

"As a youth in my early twenties, I was much more interested in scientific study than politics. Now I am ashamed of my actions. However, at the time, it didn't matter. Hitler enlisted the Hauptamt Wissenschaft to bring in scientists and experts to work on new technology. Weapons, mostly."

"The Hap-what?"

"Hauptamt Wissenschaft, German central office of science."

And you? What were you recruited for?" the tall man asked.

The Doc smiled again. "My task was much more secretive."

2014

CHAPTER 7

OUT WITH A BANG!

ecember 31, New Year's Eve. I am not a fan of any Eve, especially New Year's Eve, for a couple of reasons. One being that nothing ever changes at the stroke of midnight, and two, this is the day that some unknown douchebag decided my time on this Earth was up and it was time for me to retire permanently. Well, he was only half right. I retired, just not from life. As I said before they never found the shooter, but I have a good idea who it is. The evidence I need to put them away has eluded me, but I will find it sooner or later.

It all started a few years ago, back when I was still on the force. I caught the body of a John Doe. It was the last case I worked, and *has* to have something to do with me getting shot up. Me and my partner at the time, Joe Campanelli, initially chalked it up to a drug overdose. The John Doe was found dumped in the old warehouse district on Ganson Street. His teeth were all rotted out from what looked like years of meth addiction. He was in rough shape all together. To make matters easier, he was holding. Both Joe and I considered it open and shut.

I took out his wallet and fanned through it, hoping to find an ID. No such luck. What I did find were a few crisp hundred-dollar bills, though. That was strange to find on a junkie, especially one who looked so strung out. To make matters more confusing, the bills didn't look right.

I must have had a confused look, because Joe came up and grabbed my shoulder. "You okay, Lou?" He asked.

"Yeah, this money seem strange to you?"

I handed Joe the wallet. He took it and with rubber gloves on removed a few of the bills. He held them up to the sky.

"Looks fine to me," he said. After another moment, though, he too looked confused. "That's strange, the date on these say 1951. Never seen a bill look this crisp that's sixty years old."

"Bag it," I said. "We should get someone to look at it."

Joe gave me a worried look, like I was going to go off on one of my witch hunts again. Most of the time my hunches turned out right, but it didn't make it any easier. Pending toxicology, this one was all but solved.

"Come on, Lou, we're backed up as it is on cases," Joe said.

"I'll look into it on my own time, just gotta be sure, you know?" I hauled my frame up from next to the body and made my way over to the crime scene techs. "Any idea on identification?"

One of the techs looked up from his clipboard and said, "After the autopsy. Dental looks bad, so hopefully his prints are on file."

I took one last look at the body then nodded to Joe. He was likely right, but I couldn't leave it alone if I got a hunch. This one felt like more than a hunch.

A few days later I had mostly forgotten about the body until I got the ME report. The deceased was one Benny "Biggs" Remington. I recognized the name. Biggs was more of a joke than a nickname. He stood about five foot eight and weighed maybe 150 pounds, if he was holding a cinder block. He was a small-timer who'd been in and out of jail over the past few years. I'd busted him once myself with possession with intent to sell back when I was still a beat cop. As bad of shape his body was in when discovered, it's no wonder I didn't recognize him.

Toxicology confirmed our original instinct. He had enough meth running through his system to kill himself three times over. An overdose on its own wasn't that unusual, but the fact a user would pump himself full with that much was different. Even so, the case was looking solved.

I pulled up his record for next of kin or someone to notify. There wasn't anyone listed. Remington's family had either disowned him or wasn't around anymore. His known associates were a good lead, though. He had been known to run with the River Rats, a biker gang in Western New York. They were a ruthless group. Extortion, drugs, prostitution, even murder for hire was on their résumé.

Interesting. Probably wouldn't amount to much, but me and Joe were mostly wrapped up on our caseload now. So I had the time to investigate.

I spoke to Vice and they had some more stuff for me. Apparently in the past few months the River Rats had branched out from their normal criminal activity. Now they added in loan sharking. That seemed quite odd, considering their other areas of expertise were likely much more profitable for them. I asked Vice if they had any hard evidence of it, but it was mostly just rumors from the streets. As usual, they couldn't get anyone to talk on the record about it, for fear of repercussions.

I still didn't do too much with it, but I wasn't ready to close the case just yet. Joe was harping on me about it, but I told him tough shit.

Two weeks after the body was found we got a report back on the bills found in Biggs' wallet. They were counterfeits, and, according to the report, damn good ones.

There was definitely something going on here. But still I had nothing concrete. That wouldn't work if I wanted to rule Remington's death a homicide. Campanelli was getting antsy. He wanted the case closed. The year was almost over, and he wanted our clearance rate to be as good as possible. I understood, because he was up for a promotion. Me, I didn't care, I just wanted to make sure there wasn't some bastard out there responsible for Remington's death walking free.

I told Joe to give me two days to see what I could come up with, then we could close the case. He conceded, but said he wasn't going to help me with it.

"Fine, Joe, but when I bust up some huge conspiracy, you don't get any of the credit!" I said to him. I know, sometimes I can be a dick. I was mostly kidding. Mostly.

The two days passed and I couldn't turn up anything. I kicked over all the stones I could think of, and reached out to everyone I knew on the street. Nothing. Maybe I was getting too old and my hunches were just that, hunches. Maybe they could no longer be relied upon to help me solve crimes.

Oh well. Camp was happy with it. He got to close the case, two days before the end of the year. I was still left wondering.

***

I grabbed some ice from the fridge, poured myself a double McClelland's Single Malt scotch, and sat back in my leather chair in my office. Lit a nice Romeo and Julieta 6x60 cigar and watched the cigar smoke drift in the air. And as I always do on New Year's Eve, I pondered my life and thought about what could have been.

For example, like making a relationship work instead of sabotaging them. It's in my DNA to destroy a perfectly good relationship. Me and commitments never got along. I have one question: what the hell does "I love you but I'm not in love with you" mean? If you know, give me a call. I'm in the book under Private Detective.

I could have gone to Williamsville, a lovely suburb of Buffalo, and joined a few friends at the Box, a cigar store.

I was there not too long ago and had a weird experience, so I wasn't too keen on going back just yet. Mike Spoo was holding court, pontificating on the Bills and the Sabres. The Bills, according to him, were a lock for the Super Bowl. The Sabres, with their last-place finish, were going to get a superstar in the draft and a shot at the Stanley Cup. Normally I'd join in to give him shit about how stupid he was but I was too tired.

I was sitting down in the chair next to him and The History Channel was on. I bought my usual, a Ditka Comacho and a scotch and water. The show was ending and I heard Spoo shout, "Romoso, you're on TV!"

I ignored him, then lit up my cigar and casually gazed at the TV to catch the end of *Hitler's Money Men*.

"You're on TV," Spoo repeated, "or you have a twin running around who is about a million years old now." Spoo pointed to the screen. "Look."

On the screen was a guy who looked like me, only thinner, walking out of warehouse with a group of people. The picture was fuzzy so I couldn't make out whom the others were. My head began to spin and sweat poured from my forehead.

"Lou, Lou, are you alright?" Spoo had asked, as his face

grew ashen.

I shook my head clear and said, "Yeah, yeah, I'm fine. Just need a sip of my drink."

I sat in silence the rest of the night, finished my cigar and drink, and headed home. No need for another dizzy spell, so scratch the Box.

So then I thought about going to Virgil's, which was close to my office on Hertel Avenue. A few of my buddies hung out there, too, but they always have Paula's Donuts there. I need a donut like I need a hole in the head. Scratch Virgil's. I just smoked my cigar and pondered the journey known as my life.

***

The night of my shooting was three years ago to the day. I was on call for New Year's Eve, which I didn't mind because I'm not a fan of amateur night. I was over at my brother John's house in Cheektowaga. Our parents had lived there before they passed. It was the house we grew up in that he bought from my youngest brother Mike and me when it came time to settle the estate. We were having our traditional Italian sausage while waiting to ring in the New Year with my nieces and friends. My phone rang; shit. It was my soon-to-be new boss, *Lieutenant Joseph Campanelli of Homicide.*

Camp told me to get to the corner of Spring and Swan Streets where an unknown female caller reported finding a body laying on the sidewalk.

I looked at my watch: 11:30 p.m. The sausage was just coming out of the oven and I was going to light a nice Liga Privada 9 cigar and have a New Year's smoke with my brother. I told Camp I was on the way. Wished my family a Happy New Years, and smiled to myself because I wouldn't have to watch that damn ball drop. Did I mention I'm not a fan of New Year's

Eve?

Once in my unmarked car, a dark, funny feeling that something wasn't right came over me. It stayed with me the whole way to the crime scene, but I kept going anyway.

I got to the scene at about 11:55 p.m. A patrol car was on the corner, its emergency lights flashing a brilliant red and blue against the cold and dark sky. The two officers were out of the car looking around. No body was in sight.

The air was crisp and cold that night; each breath hung in the air like fog. Snow crunched beneath your feet as you walked. Stars twinkled against the blackness of night as they too waited for the New Year to arrive. I looked up and thought to myself, what a beautiful winter's night. That was the last thing I remembered, as three loud shots rang through the night—BANG! BANG! BANG!—followed by a burning sensation in my leg, arm, and chest.

I was down for the count, or as my wiseass friends liked to say, "Down goes Marlowe." Why Marlowe, you ask? I love those fifties detective shows so much and my wonderful friends say I dress just like the old gumshoes. Hence the nickname, Marlowe.

I was unconscious and barely had a pulse. EMTs loaded me into an ambulance and rushed to Erie County Medical Center. The medical staff was waiting, and so was my youngest brother, Mike. He was the trauma surgeon on call. Yeah, I know, doctors don't like to operate on relatives. Well life's a bitch and he had no choice. He operated and managed to save my life.

When I awoke a few weeks later, I looked like the space shuttle readying for takeoff. There were all kinds of tubes coming and going hooking me to machines that did things I knew nothing about. The pain was unreal and I'm not sure if it was from the bullets or the surgeon who operated. The first person I saw was the surgeon. Dr. Romoso was shaking his head telling me how lucky I was to have him on call that night, so that he could save my life. Lucky me. I'll never hear the end of it.

Quite a bit of pain greeted me with consciousness when I heard my brother ask me if I was ever shot before. I looked at him like he was nuts, or maybe I hadn't heard him correctly because of pain meds they gave.

He asked again, and I replied, "Are you on crack?"

He looked at me, shook his head, and grabbed the medical chart. "Wait, this isn't you. This is someone else's chart . . . how did that happen?"

"Mike, what are you talking about? I wasn't ever shot."

"Yeah I know, someone messed up the medical charts."

He told me the chart showed there were three identical bullet holes in the same exact place where the bullets had got me. He also proceeded to tell me I was lucky to be alive and that my police career was probably over. Thanks, Bro!

I thought about who shot me, who would be stupid enough to shoot at a police officer. Campanelli visited me shortly after I woke up and said there was nothing. No leads at all. Nada. In fact, there wasn't even a body. Whoever had called had set us— no, *me*—up. That pissed me off, and I told Camp about it. He said they weren't giving up, but I didn't have much hope. Most of the time, if you don't get something within the first few days of a case, your chances of solving it are kaput.

CHAPTER 8

WE MEET AGAIN?

The time was 5:50 p.m. as I looked up at the clock on the wall. I just wasted fifty minutes of my life reminiscing that I will never get back. Some cases still gnaw at you, and I don't think I'll ever let go of finding out who shot me.

My brooding was interrupted by a knock at my office door.

I shouted, "It's New Year's Eve, so either have a drink in one hand and a check in the other or you'd better leave."

The door opened and in she walked, wearing my favorite color dress. ANY. She was five foot eight, wearing a mink fur coat over the dress. Smooth blond hair reached down to her shoulders. Brown eyes, a very cute face, and a smile that would make angels check their dental plan looked out at me. I froze in my chair and stared. I was speechless.

She asked, "Aren't you going to ask me to sit?"

All I could do was point to a chair. She sat and I stared. She asked if I was Mr. Romoso and I stared. I finally shook my head yes, like a fifteen-year-old schoolboy. Then she asked if I spoke.

"Y-yes," and finally, I was able to straighten out my tongue and introduce myself. "I'm Lou Romoso, and what can I do for you besides take you out to dinner?"

She smiled; I melted as my mind began to wander out of control. Where have I met this woman before? Nothing clicked. But somehow she was familiar.

I said to her, "And you are?"

"Miss Reitman." She had a pained look about her. Even then, it couldn't hide her beauty.

"Drink, Miss Reitman? You look like you could use one right about now."

"I think I will, Mr. Romoso."

"Please, call me Lou."

"Only if you call me Ingrid."

"Deal! Now what can I do for you, Ingrid?"

"You're going to find this extremely confusing, because I really don't know how to explain it."

I chuckled a bit. "Give it a try and we'll work our way through it."

She lowered herself down into one of my leather chairs and ever so slowly crossed her legs. I'm a guy so I stared all the way down until she was comfortable. I swallowed hard, blushed, and asked her to tell her story. It was like watching the PG version of *Basic Instinct*. You won't hear me complaining. Anyway, Ingrid got serious.

"Lou, as you may or may not know, I'm extremely wealthy. Old money, some people call it. Others say born under a lucky star. I don't particularly care for either since I've been able to do well for myself in my own business ventures."

"What might those be?" I asked.

She gave me a bit of a sassy look before continuing. "I don't see how that's of any concern, but if you must know, I'll tell you. I'm an engineer by trade and I have a few patents that made me quite a tidy sum of money in the defense contracting business. I also have a few retail operations around town. I sold my defense company recently and now I'm enjoying the fruits of my labor. I never knew my parents, they passed away when I was young. My grandmother raised me. I was left quite a sum of money by my parents. With the interest over the last thirty something years I've amassed almost four hundred million dollars."

"Okay, so what's the problem?" I asked impatiently. Here I am, a gorgeous woman in front of me, and I'm looking for a way to get rid of her.

She didn't catch my meaning—thank God—and continued on. "Recently my grandmother passed away. I was the only living relative, so everything was passed down to me, including her big house over on Delaware. I never met my grandfather, either. He was killed during the World War Two, just before my father was born."

She paused, and took a sip of her drink, then picked up her bag and pulled out a folder and held it on her lap. "I think this may help explain everything. I certainly don't get it, but hopefully you do."

She passed the folder to me over the desk. I opened it and inside was a letter. It looked to be addressed to yours truly.

Dear Lou,

I don't know where to begin. In my heart I still love you, and forgive you for leaving without any explanation. For a long time I wanted to kill you for making a fool of me, but I talked to Brian about it, and he calmed me down.

This letter is mainly concerning my granddaughter, Ingrid. I believe her to be in danger through no fault of her own. Someone is passing counterfeit bills through her businesses, laundering it without Ingrid's knowledge.

I don't know how else to say this, but I think Kevin Young is somehow involved. I think he has some local gang helping him, but so far I haven't been able to figure out who.

I'm worried for my granddaughter's safety. I need you to look after her. Talk to Brian, he'll know what to do.

Just know that I will always love you.

Love,
Ingrid

Kevin Young? Who's that? Counterfeiting? This crazy old bird still loves *me*? What the hell is going on?

None of this made any sense to me. I began thinking someone may have slipped away from the looney bin and decided to drop by my place. As I set the packet and letter down, ready to show this strikingly beautiful woman, who was probably crazy, on her way, two small envelopes slid out and landed on my desk.

I opened the first and pulled out fifteen crisp one-hundred-dollar bills. They looked immaculate. The feel was just like a real bill. I brought one to my nose, though, and the smell was off. The dates were also wrong. Bills from 1954 shouldn't look this crisp.

The second envelope was labeled 1955. I opened it, and it contained ten more bills, identical to those from the first.

Suddenly it hit me. My mind moved to the bills Camp and I pulled out of Biggs' wallet. Can't say for a fact, but they were the same. Same feel, same smell, sixty years old.

What if this is somehow related to me? Could the gang mentioned in the letter be the River Rats? If so, my investigation into them just became validated. The loan sharking could be all this so-called Kevin Young's doing. I bet he and the Rats are dolling out the fake cash, then when they get repaid it's all pure profit. Quite a scheme.

And now they are laundering it through local businesses? All under the nose of the owner? That takes some balls.

We had sat in silence for what seemed like forever. I had forgot someone was even there with me. I looked up and asked, "When did she pass away?"

"About a month ago," Ingrid answered.

"I'm so sorry for your loss. Do you believe this letter?"

"Yes. Towards the end she was getting frantic. At first I reluctantly chalked it up to the ravings of an old woman. But then I started overhearing some of her conversations, mostly with some man named Brian. I don't know the last name. After she died, the letter was with her final will and testament, along with some other documents that pointed to you. She never got around to mailing it. That's why I'm here today."

I didn't say anything for another few moments. I wasn't terribly interested in having someone to look after, not now, not on New Year's Eve of all days. The last place someone should be on New Year's is under my protection. That's more likely to get them killed than if they were on the corner of the street with a megaphone asking the killers to come get them.

No, I needed more than ever to take down the River Rats and settle the score.

"My fee is five hundred a day, plus expenses." I said.

She looked surprised. "Excuse me?"

"Do you want me to protect you? I can't work for free, Ingrid, take it or leave it."

"No one talks to me that way, *no one*," she said with some fury behind it.

"There's the door, don't let it hit you in the ass on the way out."

She turned and hightailed it out the door and slammed it as she left and called me a jerk. I've heard that before. Thank God I don't need the money.

Perhaps I should be a little more patient with the nuts of the world. Maybe a Dale Carnegie course might help. Nah! Perhaps more sarcasm. I laughed, put my feet up on the desk, and lit a Camacho Mike Ditka Signature cigar to relax. I don't know what it is with women and me, but I seem to have a low tolerance for banter with them. Apparently they do not get my sense of humor. Oh well. I sat at my desk thinking about another early New Year's Eve night. Sure I had parties to go to if I wanted, but I just wasn't in the mood. I'm sure there is a *Three Stooges* marathon to watch, so I decided that's what I'd do.

I sat there and took it all in. A case in the twenty-first century tied to counterfeit bills from the fifties? Interesting, if not ridiculous!

I absently sorted through the rest of the packet. Most of it was old *Courier* articles from 1955. I didn't bother reading them. One sheet did grab my attention. It must have slipped to the ground, as it was under the chair Ingrid had sat in. I walked around my desk and picked it up. Another letter.

Mrs. Reitman,

Your old boyfriend is in danger, and you need to alert him. I cannot say what will happen, but I do know something is going on. Please do what you can, this all needs to stop.

Who wrote this letter? And who's the boyfriend? I know it can't be me. I may be desperate, but not enough to be going out with some ancient broad.

Over at the window I tried to look out at the Buffalo landscape. It was covered with frost so I wiped it away, using the body heat from my hand. Snow began to fall and stick to the street. It wasn't wet snow; just flakes lazily falling to Earth in the background. The lights of the General Mills plant shone in the distance. Down at the street a slow moving, dark-colored vehicle circled my office building. I didn't make too much out of it because the Seneca Indian Casino was nearby and people usually got lost and circled my building. My radio was on and playing a Jack Benny show.

I heard the show but wasn't really listening. Maybe I jumped the gun dismissing Ingrid. Maybe she really is in danger. This letter, if authentic, certainly implicates as much. Maybe the boyfriend is already out of the picture? I shouldn't have dismissed her so soon. Now too many questions were swarming in my head, with no hopes of answers without more information from her.

But one thing is for sure: If the River Rats are involved, they are going down.

CHAPTER 9

FAUX DOUGH

F eds never stop working. At least that's what I thought as I pulled out my phone to dial up an old buddy from the Secret Service. Why Secret Service? No, I don't need the level of protection the president gets for Ingrid. They also handle counterfeiters, and I couldn't think of a better guy to talk to about all this funny money I'm wrapped up in than Agent Paul Wozniak, the guy who helped clean up the counterfeiters in Western New York.

Six rings later Woz picked up, shouting into the phone. There was some noise in the background. Sounded like a crowded bar. Maybe Feds did take a little time off. "Lou, you locked up in a bunker somewhere?" He said. "Don't come out until after the bell tolls midnight. I'd hate to hear about you getting gunned down again on your favorite holiday."

What a prick. "Hello to you too, asshole," I said. "What do you know about counterfeiting in this neck of the woods?"

"More than you."

"Good, then I can just hand this case over to you, and get back to feeling sorry for myself," I said.

He laughed a bit into the phone. "What have you got for me, buddy?"

I delved into what I had, going all the way back to my last case on the force with Biggs Remington and the bills we found on him. He was intrigued.

"You know, Lou, I'd like to get a look at those c-notes you have. There's been bills like that floating around since the fifties. I don't think anyone's ever recovered that many at once, though, not since a big bust back in the day.

"Are you in town? Sounds like you are at a party."

"No, I'm somewhere warm, where you don't have to worry about your balls freezing to the car seat before it warms up. Go talk to Pops. He'll know what you've got yourself into. I'll be in touch."

He hung up before I could ask anything else. My original assessment was correct. Prick. But a good friend and good agent, nonetheless. He covered Western New York as part of his assignments, and had helped me track down one Pops Franchetti.

Pops was a great nephew of a big-time bootlegger in the twenties who made tons of cash. But like most gangsters, greed got the better of him. Franchetti trained to be an engraver when he was young, following in his family's criminal footsteps. He's also quite the artist, so he decided to combine the two and engrave counterfeit plates. This scheme worked well for a bit. Someone always gets caught and talks, though. Pops landed in jail for ten years, and was out in six. When he got out he vowed to go straight, or at least as straight as he could, and wound up working and eventually owning a club. He lives upstairs with his daughter and grandchild. His son-in-law is serving time for burglary. I guess it's nice to carry on a family tradition.

Pops actually owed me a favor when I overlooked his venture into gambling and bookmaking. I kept him out of jail and he helped me with some information that led to a nice arrest of a murder suspect. Quid quo pro, as they say in Latin.

Pops was on the shorter side, about five foot seven, in his fifties, olive skin, slicked-back black hair with sides of gray, and always wore a toothy smile.

After the short drive I parked and walked in and was asked if I wanted some coffee with a shot of whiskey in it. No point in refusing. It was cold out and the coffee was hot.

Pops was behind the bar and waved me over. "Lou, heard you were lookin' for me."

What the hell? Wonder if Woz reached out to him. "Does everyone know what I'm up to?" He laughed and then I got right to business. "Pops, I need some information about counterfeit money and I thought you could help out."

The smile from laughing left his face quickly. "You know I went straight years ago."

"I know, just want to pick your brain," I said. "I think there is phony money being circulated and I need your expertise."

"Okay, Lou, Woz gave me the heads up. What do you need to know?" He still sounded skeptical, but if he was willing to talk, I was willing to listen.

"Everything."

Pops leaned forward on his elbows to get close to me, so no one else could hear us talk. "This much I do know, your suspicions are correct. And before you get the wrong idea, I've got nothing to do with it. Word is the crew responsible is dangerous. But no one knows who they are. They just pop up out of nowhere, do some business, and bail. They are working with a few locals. You have probably busted some of them."

Huh, could be the Rats. I pushed Pops a little, but he

wouldn't give up who the locals were. It ticked me off, but I understood. If it got out Pops could be in trouble.

"Where would they be printing?" I asked. "Are presses available here in Buffalo or would you need to get them from somewhere else? And where would you buy the ink and the paper to print this money?"

Pop took a seat behind the bar and pondered the questions. I sipped my coffee and waited. Pop finally stirred and answered, "If I was to start up again I'd get an old warehouse in a secluded area, fix up the inside and leave the outside alone to keep that abandoned look. I'd say somewhere by the grain elevators, or the old Ford Plant on Furman Boulevard.

"The ink you could buy anywhere, and with all the printing companies around no one would think twice about a big order. You only need green, red, and black, nothing out of the ordinary.

"The paper is the toughest to get and nearly impossible to produce, but I did read that the Germans during World War Two managed to come very, very close to replicating it. A German Colonel named Kryer or Krutz or something like that perfected the best counterfeit money ever made. He disappeared after the war. But he was picked up ten years later, ironically right here in Western New York. Don't know what happened to him after that. The paper is the key. Don't know where they'd get that."

"What about the actual money, you know anything about that?"

"What I hear is that there is a gang in town spreading the money, through a number of operations. Loan sharking, laundering, you know, the works. Each instance may not be a large amount, not enough to warrant detection. However, add it all up, and you are talking millions, easy."

I pulled out a couple of the bills and handed them to Pops. He took a sniff.

"This ink hasn't been used since the war. The Nazis used it to print their currency and other counterfeiting activities. It wasn't quality ink, but it did the job for them.

"And another thing: These bills weren't printed recently. They have been sitting somewhere for a long time. So whoever is passing them through town must have been sitting on them for a while."

"How do you know?"

"This was my business for years, Lou, I'm right. Where did you get those?"

"That's *my* business," I responded. If Pops was going to hold out on some info, so was I.

He held up his hands in an I-give-up way. "Okay, big guy, I understand. Just know, I have nothing to do with this. I've been straight for years."

"Except a little bookmaking now and again."

Pops looked like I just kicked his dog. "We worked that out, you know that. No need for that. You need me for information, remember? Maybe I'll start forgetting things I may or may not know."

I apologized. Why, I don't know. The man was an ass at times. We talked on, but he didn't know much else that could help me. I thanked him, and told him I owed him one. No doubt he would collect on that. Just the way it works sometimes.

CHAPTER 10

FINNEGAN'S PUB

After my row with Ingrid and talking to Pops I decided I didn't want to go home and pout again. No more sitting at my desk as the only guest at the pity party.

I put my car in gear and headed towards the Pub, Finnegan's. I thought about my buddy Brady and what he'd been up too. It's been a long time since we've seen each other. The last time I saw him was when I was in the hospital recovering from my fight with the Grim Reaper. Brady was a good man as well as a big one, too. About six foot five, 320 pounds, dirty blonde hair and beard. Brady always wore a black beret and a long black trench coat with orange sneakers. He is one of the few guys I know who could get away with that look, probably because he'd kick your ass from here to eternity in a blink of an eye. Brady had boxed in Golden Glove matches throughout the city during his younger years. Like his dad Brian before him, it was said getting hit by Brady's fist was like running face-first into a concrete wall.

Brady gave up the fight game and decided to run his father's pub. I met him when he was in the beginning stages of taking it over from his father. We shared the joy of old-time radio. He loved the detective shows. His favorite was Boston Blackie, as well as anything that included Jack Webb: Dragnet, Jeff Regan Private Detective, and Pat Novak. Brady even has a replica of Jack Webb's Dragnet badge, number 714. We would talk for hours about radio, sports, and sports memorabilia over a drink and a cigar.

I glanced into my rearview mirror and caught a glimpse of a car I'd seen before. It was too far back to get a plate or make, but it looked similar to the sedan that was circling around my office. Maybe I was getting paranoid from Ingrid's visit, but I wanted to make sure he wasn't tailing me so I made a couple of left turns, then right turns, and a couple of U-turns. The driver was either good he stayed just far enough away, or wasn't really following me. Tough to tell. I had enough of this cat and mouse game and decided to turn the tables.

I got to Michigan Street by the Buffalo Creek Casino and made a quick U-Turn. The sedan made a turn at South Park, seemingly oblivious to me. He was lucky; I got caught at the light before I could continue following him, but I managed to get a quick peek at the driver and plates. It was a Black Mercedes Benz, a full size one. Maybe a 500 or 700 series. The first three letters of the vanity plate were CAS. I couldn't see the rest as he rounded the curve.

I decided discretion was the better part of valor and stopped chasing him.

***

The sun had gone down hours ago behind Lake Erie's grand sentinels, the grain elevators, and the temperature had already dipped quickly to a frigid negative five. Throw in the wind picking up, and it was cold as hell outside. I pulled my car up in front of an old two-story brick building. In its heyday it was a flophouse for the merchantmen that traveled the lakes, with a bar on the first floor.

The bar had a large glass picture window with a great view of the casino. How lovely! I got to the front door and pulled hard to open it. It was the original door made of steel with a peep door in the middle. I'm guessing this building was a speakeasy during prohibition. It was tough to break a steel door down and this gave the bartenders plenty of time to get rid of the alcohol.

As you walk in, the first thing you notice is the timber frame interior. It was beautiful. All the wood shined and there was a giant circular fireplace in the middle with a sofa surrounding it. Tables, chairs, and booths filled in the rest of the bar. The second floor was turned into a one big loft which housed dart boards, pool tables, and a nice cigar lounge filled with leather chairs and two 60-inch TVs. To the left was layer upon layer of clear lacquer protecting a giant oak bar. Carved out on the panels that formed the skirts of the bar were Irish Symbols; the shamrock, four-leaf clovers, and a shillelagh. It was amazing.

Finnegan's served great bar food. The standard Buffalo fare; wings, burgers, beef on weck, as well as salads, chicken fingers, and as expected corned beef and cabbage on St. Patty's Day. Even for New Year's Eve the place was overly crowded.

I took a seat at the bar. A couple of minutes later Brady made his way down to me. He didn't disappoint; he had on the beret, long black coat and orange sneakers. I smiled and went around to the open side of the bar, shook his hand and gave him a big hug.

"Happy New Year, Lou," Brady said. "Long time no see."

"Good to see you too."

"What are you drinking?"

"Vodka and cranberry."

As he poured my drink, he asked, "Where you been hiding?"

"Been busy pondering life."

"Okay, Lou, fess up. Why have you been such a stranger?" Brady asked. "Everyone here asks about you and they miss watching the ball games with you. What's up with that bullshit, you just exit stage left."

Brady was right. Ever since I got shot and had to retire I've been staying off the radar, just working at my business and occasionally going to The Box for a cigar. I made a grand gesture, crossing my heart: "I promise I won't be a stranger, so what else is shaking? I—"

There was a commotion down the bar. Kong, a longtime friend, was yelling about something. He weighed about 120 pounds soaking wet and the next time he finishes a sandwich will be his first. Starving people give him food. Despite the rumors he does not shop in the children's section of Macy's.

Konger was a successful "businessman" always on the cusp of new technology and enjoyed gambling. He was dressed in a long black trench coat and a blue suit with a white shirt. I thought he was making his first communion with that suit on.

"What's got Konger all hot and bothered?" I asked Brady, changing the subject.

"No idea," he said. "But he came in not too long ago flashing a bunch of cash, buying everyone drinks."

I stood up and walked over to Kong. He looked pale, like he had the flu, but he wasn't acting like it. For some reason him being excited was having a spirit-lifting effect on me too. As the moments ticked by I almost forgot I was supposed to hate New Year's.

"Hey Konger, what the hell you yelling about?"

He turned with a shit-eating grin on his face, fanning the air with a handful of what looked like crisp hundred-dollar bills.

"Can't tell ya, Lou, but just know that I'm buying."

He set a hundred down on the counter, and shouted, "Brady, whatever Lou wants, Lou gets! Happy New Year to all my merry asshole friends!"

I continued to stare at the bill, then nudged Kong. "Mind if I take a look at that?"

He nodded, and was off in some other direction. Don't think he even knew what I asked. The bill had a familiar feel to it, and a distinct scent when I brought it up to my nose. Could it be? I slid one of the hundreds from Ingrid's envelope out of my coat pocket, not really thinking about it at the time, and laid it next to the other. Exactly the same, from 1954. What the hell? Where would Konger get his hands on so many counterfeit bills?

I flagged him down, and he moseyed his way over to me.

"Where'd you get these?" I asked again, motioning to the bill on the table.

Kong knew something was up. I didn't want him going back to the source and saying something. We'd probably find him in a deserted alley. He read the concern on my face, and for a second I felt bad for ruining his high. He didn't say anything, though.

"You know these are counterfeit, right?" I said it quiet, didn't want the rest of the bar to hear. As drunk as everyone was getting, things could have gotten out of hand for my boy Konger, and fast.

"The hell you talkin' about, Lou?" He said.

"They're fake, Konger," and I showed him the bills I had. He pulled out his stack, and each one was exactly the same, from 1954.

Now he was getting pissed. "That slimy two-bit Mick bastard! I knew I shouldn't have trusted him!"

"Whoa, whoa, slow down," I said. "Trusted who?"

"Some asshole named Leary. I did some work for him, and he said he'd pay me in cash, and more than I quoted for." He slammed his drink down, as if the alcohol itself was tainted by the bad deal. "What I did wasn't exactly kosher, Lou, and I think he overpaid to keep me quiet about it."

He told me they put a bag over his head to bring him to the job. They through him in a van. "Must've been a bad road, because I was bouncing around like a rag doll in the back. Then I did some stuff for them in an old warehouse. Looked like it was a hundred years old, the tech was so out of date."

"Where can I find this Leary?" I asked. Maybe this asshole could get me close to whoever was endangering Ingrid. My interest in her case was growing. Maybe it could also lead somewhere in my investigation into who shot me. Thin, I know, but one can only hope.

"I met him over on Ganson, the old warehouse district. Don't know if he's still there."

I nodded my thanks, and gave him a reassuring slap on the back. Don't know why, the man just got cheated out of quite a bit of cash he was likely never going to see again. He went on to tell me he got the feeling Leary was "connected," but didn't know to who or where. He had the look, Kong said, like he wouldn't think twice about putting someone down if they crossed him.

Nothing like tussling with an Irish thug to bring an end to New Year's Eve; that is, if I could find him.

I waved goodbye to Brady, but he flagged me down on my way out.

"Lou, I forgot to tell you, my old man has been saying he

needs to talk to you," Brady said. "Don't know what about, but he said it's really important."

I shrugged. Old Man Finnegan was a hoot. A throwback. To a time when men were men. He fought in the war, played a little college football, and had been running Finnegan's longer than most people I knew had been alive. He had to be pushing ninety by now. Hell, might be approaching a hundred. If the old man needed to talk, I'd certainly listen.

Wait . . . didn't Ingrid's letter mention talking to Brian? Could she have meant Brian Finnegan? How the hell would she know him?

As much as I wanted to find out, I had to go. Couldn't pass up the lead I just got from Konger. "Another time," I said. "I've got to run something down while it's still hot. Maybe I'll stop by this week."

I turned to leave, but then turned and leaned in close. "Between me and you, that money Konger's holding is fake. He knows it, and you can tell by the look on his face over there he doesn't know what to do. I'll cover his tab."

"Okay, Lou, I'll keep an eye on him, so he doesn't do anything stupid. Don't be a stranger."

I gave Brady a hug and went out the door. That tab was going to be expensive. The way I looked at it, though, I was on the clock. This was all related to Ingrid's case, so she'd be footing the bill. What can I say? I've never been accused of being a gentleman.

Once back outside, the freezing air slapped me in the face like a scorned woman; hard and without warning. No matter, the hunch was burning inside me, keeping my mind off the blistering cold.

This Leary, if he was still around, was toast.

*T*he tall man remained quiet. He waited for the Doc to continue. It didn't take long.

"I was brought in and put under the purview of an S.S. Major, Bernhard Kruger."

The tall man frowned at the mention of the name, which the Doc caught.

"Familiar with this man, you are?"

"Let's just say he and I are acquainted, yes." The tall man said while absent-mindedly rubbing his hip.

The Doc paused for a moment before continuing. "Major Kruger was in charge of Operation Bernhard. The original purpose was to perfect counterfeiting the British pound and later the American dollar, with the ultimate goal of submarining the economies of the Allied Powers.

"However, Himmler decided to change directions when Major Kruger took over. Instead, he wanted to launder the counterfeit monies to finance German Intelligence operations."

"Really? That's something I wasn't aware of," the Tall Man said.

"Ja, originally the plan was to air-drop the British notes by plane across England. But as the war continued, the Luftwaffe no longer had the aircraft to spare. More efficient use of the money would be used internally."

"Okay, so where do you fit in?"

The Doc took off his glasses and cleaned them with a handkerchief. He then held them up to the light to make sure they were clear. He made a show of taking his time, which caused the tall man to adjust in is seat to show his irritation.

"Patience, patience. You've waited this long, what is another few moments?" the Doc said, then smiled. "Major Kruger was a very shrewd individual. He saw the ability to use his new position to fund other efforts to further the Nazi cause. He siphoned millions from the laundering in order to fund secretive experiments, many of which he kept from even Himmler and Hitler."

The tall man shifted in his seat again, but this time in anticipation.

"That is where I come in, my friend."

1955

CHAPTER 11

MICKEY FINN'S

Mickey Finn's Bar was located on the corner of Miami and Ohio Streets in the old First Ward of Buffalo. The First Ward is all Irish. Most of the men worked in the auto plants, steel mills, or as grain scoopers. Scoopers worked in the hull of grain ships that come to port from Lake Erie during the good weather months. They shovel grain into a bucket on a conveyor belt and then it's taken to a grain elevator. It was backbreaking work and not very steady. Not to mention low wages. When these men got paid on Fridays, a beer or six was a ritual at one of the dozens of bars located in the First Ward.

Mickey Finn's was one such bar.

Finn's was run by Kevin Young, who made most of his money off the sweat of his blue-collar customers. Young was a big boy, standing six foot four and weighing just short of three hundred pounds with dirty blonde hair and a goatee. And he was strong as an ox. He'd loan money at ten percent interest a week to the First Ward, take their bets, serve them cheap beer and whiskey, and finally after all was said and done take most of their paychecks.

Young was not to be messed with. His brother, Brian, was one of my best friends. Brian was an even bigger man, six foot six and a shade over three hundred, and if you pissed him off he could twist your head off without blinking an eye. Brian was a genius and had a degree in accounting from UB, and just so happened to play football with yours truly. He ran his own accounting shop, me being one of his clients, and had a bunch of other small businesses in the Buffalo area. One being a delivery service that offered same-day delivery for all the warehouses and factories in Western New York. He also ran the finances for Mickey Finn's, and tended the bar from time to time when he was bored.

Kevin, on the other hand, was trouble and was good at causing it. He never got caught at anything. He was that good, or that lucky, depending on your perspective. He was very intelligent, planned everything, and always out for a buck. He bought Mickey Finn's from the widow of the former owner with the money he made hustling on the streets. He and I never really got along. I thought he was an asshole from the day I met him. He put up with me because I was good friends with his brother.

Finn's in the early days was a dive. Then all of sudden things changed. The bar was remodeled. In the basement a casino was built, which only a certain few with money could enter. The bookie room was on the second floor loaded with phones and bookmakers. An extravagant dance hall with its crystal chandelier also resided on the second level. Mickey Finn's became the talk of the First Ward and city of Buffalo seemingly overnight. Where Young got the cash to build an empire was anyone's guess, and when I was a cop I was looking for the answers to what everyone was asking.

***

Now nearing noon, after getting some much needed sleep, I pulled my car up to the front of Mickey Finn's. At the curb a valet came out to greet me. I remembered him right away—my head must finally be screwed back on correctly. Sean Henderson was around twenty years old, five foot eight, red hair, and blue eyes. Hundred percent Irish. Parking cars for Mickey Finn's was good work if you could get it. Twenty dollars a night on the weekend and ten dollars during the week. Christmas time was even better. You could earn as much as a hundred a night in tips.

Sean had a fake smile on his face, until he saw who it was pulled up to the curb. "You're not welcome here, copper, now move that piece of shit, so I can park cars for real customers," Sean shouted.

So I did. How could I know his foot was so close to my front tire that I *mistakenly* ran it over? I heard him scream. He was yelling and started swearing at me. "You motherfucker, you did that on purpose!"

I got out of the car to help him out. "Sean, Sean, Sean, if I did that on purpose my car would still be on your foot. It's not that bad, here take a look."

I grabbed him by the back of his head and slammed his head into the fender of my car. "Listen, you little Irish prick, if you ever open your mouth again and so much as say an impolite word, I'll run you down and back over you again. You got that, asshole?"

Sean just whimpered and shook his head yes.

"I didn't hear you!"

I banged his head off the fender again.

"Yes, sir, Detective Romoso."

"That's better."

"What's all the yelling about, Sean?" Both Sean and I turned to see a mammoth of a man walking towards us. Brian stopped dead in his tracks when he saw me. "What brings you here, Lou?"

"I came to see your brother," I said. "Then little Sean here gets his foot stuck under my front tire and then bangs his head off my fender. You know, Brian, if my fender is dented, Kevin is going to have to pay to get it fixed. Isn't that right, Sean?"

Sean was still wincing in pain. "I need to see a doctor about my frigging foot."

Brian then told Sean, "Just go to the Mercy Hospital Emergency Room. Have McMann drive you. Tell him to take my car."

Sean hopped off to get McMann. I told Brian I had some news on Sully and wanted to have a little chat with his brother Kevin. Brian had a puzzled look on his face. "Sully's been gone for a while."

"Kevin doesn't tell you much, does he, Brian?" I said.

"I don't ask questions. Just help out at the bar from time to time."

"I have a few questions for you then," I said. "Where can we talk?"

McMann, with Sean's arm around his neck, walked by, helping him get to Brian's car. McMann was from Hell's Kitchen in New York City, five foot eleven and about 220 pounds, with receding, graying hair. He met Kevin during the war and they became close friends. McMann saved Kevin's life in the invasion of Italy at Calabria in September of 1943. Young and McMann were with the fifth Army, led by General Mark Clark. Young was a sergeant and on point when they went into Calabria. Young did not see the German sniper on the rooftop;

McMann did. He ran full speed behind Young and tackled him to the ground just as the sniper's bullet whistled by his head. The two were inseparable after that. They survived the invasion of Salerno and the rest of the Italian Campaign. McMann, not having any family worth talking about, came with Kevin to Buffalo to work odd jobs for him. Kevin paid you well if you were loyal and did your job.

When McMann walked by, I remembered him as actually not a bad guy, as far as gangsters go. But he was a living jinx. My god, the man *never* won a bet. He loved sports but managed to curse everything he came across. "Mush," as he was not-so-affectionately called, once jinxed a professional baseball player so bad, the great all-time N.Y. Yankee spoke perfect English until the Mush arrived at Yankee Stadium. He asked the man to sign his ball. That man: Yogi Berra! Mush also ruined DiMaggio's 56-game hitting streak, just by going to the game. Not only did DiMaggio's streak end, but every game after that one he attended the Yank's lost. Management banned him from ever setting foot in the stadium.

He looked at me and said, "Was that really necessary, Romoso?"

I looked at McMann and laughed. "Keep going, lackey, and take your bride with you before your foot gets run over too!"

"Enough, Lou, you can be an asshole at times, you know?" Brian said. He had me there. I gave him my best grin, and shrugged.

McMann stared at me, but just shook his head and continued walking with Sean. Huh, that was strange. It almost looked like he wanted to tell me something. And not an insult, something important. Like I said, he wasn't all that bad for a gangster. Next time I see him, maybe I'll get him to talk. As long as it wasn't about gambling.

Brian and I went into the bar. I sat down and asked Brian

for a ginger ale. Brian got me the drink and leaned over and said, "What do you want to know, Lou?"

"I need to know everything you can tell me about Sully's death, and now Leary's as well."

Brian looked surprised about Leary. "When did Leary get it?"

"He was found at the same spot as Sully was a few years ago," I said.

"Damn. The only thing I know is that Sully came in here the day before you found him and said he was heading out of town for good and wanted to talk to Kevin. That's all I know."

"Brian, don't bullshit me," I said. I was getting angry. "How can you not know what is going on?"

"I swear to you, I have no idea what this is about. I just tend bar every once in a while and run the accounting. You know that."

I paused to take a drink of the ginger ale. For being a genius, sometimes Brian was thick as a brick wall.

"What did he want to talk to Kevin about?" I asked.

"He didn't say and I didn't ask."

I got angrier and explained to Brian what happened to Sully, that you couldn't tell the difference between him and a pound of ground beef. Then if that wasn't bad enough someone shot him in the head and then for the fun of it shot him a few times in the chest. Also told him about Leary's death, and how he was shot with the same caliber gun, and dumped in the Buffalo River at the same exact spot. Brian's disposition didn't change.

"I told you, Lou, that's all I know."

"Are you sure that's all you know?"

"Positive."

I told Brian thanks for the help and asked him one more question. "Why is a smart guy like yourself working in a bar for a crook like your bother? I know you're on the up and up, but Kevin, that's another story. You know I'll figure this out. When the smoke clears, I hope you're clean."

He looked at me, winked, and said, "You know I am, Lou. I got your back, just like the old days at UB."

"Only this isn't football," I said, a bit more serious than him. "It's real life, and I hope you're telling me the truth, big guy."

The door behind the bar opened. Kevin. "He's telling you the truth, Romoso. If you want to talk, come on in and we can talk."

I grabbed my ginger ale and walked into Kevin's office. When we got in there I noticed the faint odor of bleach in the air.

Young must have read my mind. "Cleaning lady was in last night. So what do you want, Romoso?"

"Do you mind if I light up a cigar?" I asked. "This bleach smell is awful. Why did she use so much bleach?"

"How would I know? Maybe the office was dirty."

"I'm sure it was, Young!" And I chuckled.

I pulled out a cigar and handed one to Young. No point in smoking alone.

"Thanks. A Romeo and Juliet, the private eye business must be paying well these days," he said.

We lit up and watched the smoke float aimlessly to the ceiling; nothing was said for a few minutes as we enjoyed a few puffs of our cigars. My eyes searched the office for anything that may lead to solving Leary's death. On the wall, mounted, were a pair of matching Colt .45s, military issue.

"Those from the War?"

Kevin followed my gaze, and nodded. Nothing else needed to be said. He may be an asshole, but he still served his country.

"So, Kevin, what did Sully come to see you about?" I said.

"Really, this again? Haven't we been down this road before? DeRosa and that Ruff were already here this morning asking the same old questions."

I shrugged. "Tell me again, like I'm hearing it for the first time." For all my rattled brain knew I was. But maybe what he said would break loose a memory or two.

"Fine. He came to tell me he was leaving town to open a gym and he wanted to settle our business," He answered. "We settled up and he left. That's all I know."

"And then he died," I continued for him. "Got beat up pretty bad, and then someone shoots him for the hell of it. What do you know about that?"

Kevin looked a little pale and tired, but other than that showed no emotion. "As I said before, he came here to settle up and left for the train station."

"I know, you said that. Tell me about the day Sully got shot in the knee and about the black-haired woman who shot him. Sully told me she came to see you."

"I wasn't here for that, so I couldn't tell you anything," he said shaking his head. "As for the woman, never met her."

"What about Leary?" I asked, changing gears.

"What about him?" Young said.

The way he said it, he sounded angry. Was he pissed about his death, or just pissed at Leary? I couldn't tell.

"He was found dead, same spot as Sully, same gunshot to the head. Only he wasn't beaten to a bloody pulp."

Kevin took another long drag on his cigar before saying anything. "Old Tom hasn't worked here for a while. I fired him a few months back for skimming, so I don't know anything about that."

He was lying, but I couldn't prove it. I was getting frustrated. This visit wasn't paying any dividends, except for the amusement of putting that punk Sean in his place. "I know this comes as no surprise to you, but I know you're lying. I know you know that woman and I know you had Sully and Leary killed, and when I finally put my evidence together you're going to fry. So I'll ask you one more time, what do you know?"

Kevin was calm, but the anger was still behind his eyes. "I'm only going to say it one more time: I don't know anything, but it wasn't any of my employees or me." He paused and put his cigar out in the ashtray on his desk. "It's time for you to leave, I'll have Johnny walk you out."

"If that's the way you want it, so be it. But just know I'm going to get you sooner or later." I turned to walk out, but stopped and said, "And for good measure, I will have cops driving around this shithole twenty-four seven. So you have a good day, Young."

"DeRosa already made that same promise not two hours ago," Young said. "And you're not on the force anymore. If I were you, I'd be careful about where you stick your nose."

Threats don't sit well with me. I took a step back towards him, but he put up his hands. "Just a friendly warning, for my brother's sake. My guess is you are looking for some dangerous people. Keep your eyes open."

He was right, in a way. I couldn't go beating up all the suspects and expect something to get done. As I backed off, Johnny O'Connell came into the office and escorted me out the door.

He leaned in whispered, "Mind your own business, Romoso, or you'll get hurt."

I looked at O'Connell, smiled, and said, "Did you hear about the two Irish guys who left the bar?"

He looked confused. "No."

"It could happen." I thought it was funny and laughed.

O'Connell, not so much.

"Kiss my ass, you wop bastard."

As we got to my car, O'Connell accidently tripped and hit his head on the fender. He fell backwards and into the snowbank.

"Don't ever threaten me again or I rip your heart out," I said to him as I got into my car smiling and drove away.

I was sure Young and his gang had something to do with the murders of Sully and Leary, and I was now sure he knew the woman who shot Sully, too. Not certain yet was if he was somehow connected to Ingrid's and Jessica's dilemma. Now I just had to get solid evidence to prove my case and get to the bottom of everything.

CHAPTER 12

CONTEMPLATION AND MORE CLUES

Nine a.m., January 3, 1955. Another bitterly cold day in Buffalo. I got up, had my usual breakfast with Elvira. We talked for a few minutes before I said I had to go to the office. She gave me a kiss on the cheek. She said "stai attento," which means be careful in Italian.

I responded "I sara" in my best Italian, which means I will.

I went down the stairs, out the door, and to the garage. Started the Lincoln and waited for it to warm up. I turned on the radio and listened to a local sports announcer for the football scores. When you gamble you always want to hear that you won.

The car warmed up and I turned on the heat and backed out of the narrow driveway. Pulled on to Swan Street and headed to my office above Marco's. Duffy was busy. He had plenty of customers from the graveyard shift. I walked in and said hi to the guys and then turned to Duffy. He was not happy to see me. After all he owed me four hundred bucks.

"Duffy, you got a minute?"

He had an annoyed look on his face. "Yeah, what do you want?"

"Guess," I said with a shit-eating grin.

"Wiseass, I'll have your money later today. You're a lucky bastard."

"I'm lucky alright. I'm so lucky that someone's tried to kill three times."

"Too bad they didn't. By the way, rent is due. You owe me fifty."

"Take it out of my winnings," I said, and took my coffee upstairs. I turned on the radio and heard *Richard Diamond, Private Detective.*

"*Diamond Detective Agency, I put the ham in mayham.*"

"*It's may*hem."

I sat there listening to program and tried figure out what clues I had and who the players were in this bizarre dilemma I got myself into. The thought that these two cases—Ingrid's and the deaths of Sully and Leary—were connected kept growing inside me until I was sure they were one in the same. Now I just had to connect the dots.

I took out a pad and wrote PLAYERS on the top, and started drawing connections between everyone involved in this case. Young and Heinrich are connected, I was now sure of it. It would be too much of a coincidence. But how? Why are they afraid of Ingrid and Jessica? What did Sully know? What did Leary do or know to get knocked off? Who killed my wife? What is Heinrich's game? Why does a wealthy man need to sponge off Jessica? What is his relationship to Heidi? What is the mysterious German driver's role?

I thought about all these questions and things were becoming clearer—or so I told myself.

I had a thought, and decided to call up an old friend, Agent William Murphy. I had met him years ago when we had a string of car thefts in the First Ward. They were stealing the cars then fencing them across the border. We finally nailed down who was responsible; it took a lot of work, though. Countless hours on the street, working all our connections, and just when we were out of options we caught a break. One of the suspects was from Mexico, so I went outside the box and brought the feds in. Agent William Murphy. With him on the team we were able to make the case federal. We extradited the suspect back to Mexico after he served his time.

Murphy answered on the third ring. "Hello, Lou. To what do I owe the pleasure?"

"Hey, Murph, I might have something for you." And then I dug into the issue, and where he could be of help.

He took it all in. "That sounds like a mess of a case, but I'll help you any way I can. Just give me their names and a little time. I'll see what I can come up with."

"You're the best. Their names are Heinrich Mueller and Heidi Mueller. There is a third man, but he's somewhat of a mystery. I don't know his name, but he looks an awful lot like Heinrich. They are all Germans, but could have traveled through Argentina or Switzerland to get here."

"I'm on it," Murph said.

I hung up and took another sheet of paper and wrote CLUES, then started making those connections. The device found on Leary was an enigma. I had never seen anything like it. It was a small boxlike thing, with what looked like a mini TV screen on it. The screen was cracked. No matter what I did, it wouldn't do anything.

I put my pencil down and rubbed my face with my hands. Other than the mystery device I was dependent on BPD for everything else. Not a position I liked to be in, relying on others. I needed DeRosa to come through with something on the Sully and Leary killings or that black Ford. Then we may find the killers.

As I was considering my options, there was a knock on my door.

"Door's open, and you'd better have a clue because I don't. And have a check ready."

Ingrid opened the door and walked in. "Didn't I already give you a check?"

"Oh! Ingrid, come on in. I was just working on the case, trying to make sense of everything."

"Any luck?" She asked. She sat down in one of the visitor chairs.

"If you call clouding my head with all the information 'luck,' well, then yes," I said.

"How about I take you to lunch to clear some of those cobwebs out?" She said.

I rubbed my temples, thinking it couldn't be time for lunch so soon. "Is it noon already?"

"Noon! It's one in the afternoon."

"My how time flies when one is having fun." Sarcastic, I know. Sometimes I'm a real nice guy.

Ingrid told me Russell had the car running, waiting for us. As I passed the bar, I asked Duffy for the money he owed me and he reluctantly gave me the 350 dollars with a grimace on his face. Ingrid asked what that was all about and I told her Duffy owed me some money and wasn't too happy he had to pay. I laughed, and as we hit the front door there waiting for us was the 1932 blue Cadillac.

Russell got out to open the door and said hello, then asked Ingrid where they were going.

"Buffalo Country Club," Ingrid said.

"Pretty exclusive club!" I chimed in.

"Well yes it is, Lou, but my father left my mother and I his business after he passed away. With it came membership to the club. Anyway, my mother met Heinrich at the club and he swept her off her feet with tales of world travel, passion, and art. My mother, lonely for companionship, bought the story hook, line, and sinker." Ingrid paused for a moment and looked out the window as if all of life's answers were out there. "Russell, make that the Park Country Club. I feel like going for a ride with Lou today."

She smiled, grabbed my hand, and off we went to Williamsville. Russell took the long way to the club as he wheeled the car towards Delaware Avenue. We traveled north then made a right turn and headed east on Sheridan Drive. The Park Country Club is a huge building built almost like a Tudor castle. We entered through two solid arched-shaped doors into the bar area.

The bar was not crowded so we sat there. The bar itself was a solid oak span enclosed by a half-glass wall separating it from the dining room. A big fire burned in the fireplace giving the club a toasty atmosphere.

The bartender approached us and greeted Ingrid. "Good afternoon, Mrs. Reitman, What will you have today?"

"Hi, Jerry, this is my friend, Detective Romoso. I'll have a vodka martini."

"Same for me," I said.

We got our drinks and were making small talk when I spotted Heinrich and Heidi at a table having dinner with a short, bald-headed man. I turned to Ingrid and she started to shake a little bit. She must have seen them too.

"Ingrid, relax. They can't hurt you. I'm here. So let's have a little fun with them. Follow my lead."

She was tentative. "This is not a good idea."

"Sure it is. Call it part of the investigation." I smiled and pushed back from the bar. We went into the dining room and over to their table. "Mr. Mueller, Heidi. So good to see you. How are you?"

Heinrich looked up surprised. "Detective Romoso . . . what brings you to this part of town?"

"I wanted to see how the other half lives, and asked Ingrid to show me," I said.

Ingrid gave my arm a gentle squeeze for that remark. "Who is your friend, Heinrich?" I asked.

"This is Tom Gavigan, my stock broker. We are conducting business, so if you'll excuse us, we have more to discuss."

"Sorry to intrude. Heidi, charmed as usual." That remark earned me a harder squeeze, but I had to laugh. "Enjoy your lunch."

I'm such a wiseass sometimes. Not really; it's most of the time.

"Why did you have to go to that table, Lou?" Ingrid asked when we made it back to our spot at the bar.

"I wanted them to know that I saw them and maybe make them squirm a bit. Funny, isn't it? That this guy is investing money and your mother has no idea this is going on. What's this guy's game?"

"I don't know and I don't care. They scare me."

"Don't worry, Ingrid, you have me to protect you."

"Oh brother!"

She was quiet for a while. We both looked at our menus and ordered lunch when Jerry the bartender came back.

After he took our orders I asked Ingrid if Heinrich was rich enough to be a member at the Park Club, let alone to be talking business with a stock broker. Ingrid didn't know where Heinrich got his money from or how he got it, but her mother wasn't giving any to him for investing purposes. I picked at my salad and began thinking about what I knew of Heinrich and company. He said he was wealthy and that his money was old family money. I had a hard time with that one.

Why would a wealthy man leave his homeland, wealth, and possessions to come to the U.S.? It didn't make sense. And the talk about presses. . . .

I smiled. "Ingrid, we have to go to your mother's house, I need to talk to her. I have an idea about where Heinrich is getting most of his money. We have to act fast."

"What? Lou, tell me!"

"Let's finish lunch," I said calmly. "I need more time to think and I'll fill you in on the way to your mother's."

"This is not fair, tell me now. It's my moth—"

"Not yet, I need to think. Finish your lunch."

That little sentence earned me a black and blue shin. I have no idea what set her off but it seems to be a talent I possess. The kick reminded me of how I frustrated Ellen like that constantly, except she would give me a *gentle* whack in the head. I think I now have post-concussion syndrome thanks to my lovely late wife.

As I realized what I was thinking, my heart became saddened as I thought of my wife. Then I heard her beautiful voice in my head. *Louis, why must you always be stubborn.* Ellen used to call me "Louis" when she was getting mad. *You have to let go and live your life. As long as we are in your heart we are with you. Now, Louis, you listen and listen good. There is a beautiful and charming woman eating lunch with you and has given you enough clues that she likes you. God only knows how you became a detective.*

I loved my wife more than anything. Still do. Which was a really strange feeling since three days ago I couldn't even remember she existed. But I needed her voice in my head, as crazy as that sounds. It helped keep me from going insane.

Ingrid finished her salad ahead of me since I'm such a

deep thinker. I finally finished mine and ordered another round. As our drinks came Heinrich and Heidi passed us on the way towards the exit. So me being me, couldn't resist. "Auf wiedershen. I'll be seeing you."

They stopped dead in their tracks and turned at the same time, giving me a menacing look. I laughed and waved good-bye to them. He was about as intimidating as a two-week-old puppy.

They turned and stormed out of the club. I didn't see who picked them up but I'm sure it was the mystery man from Germany. Ingrid was shaking her head.

"I hope you know what the hell you are doing. I don't want to see another person I care about . . . I mean, someone get hurt because of me. You know what I mean, don't you?"

"Sure, Ingrid."

"How the hell could you?" She said. "*I* don't even know what I mean! Men!"

"What did I do?"

"You know what you did!"

She stormed out the door without touching her new drink. More like ran, like I was contagious. Chalk another one up for me on the board. I'm so good at sabotaging relationships I don't even know when I'm doing it.

Russell had the car out front and Ingrid had already gotten in the back. As I approached Russell had a wide grin forming on his face. I told him to shove it and he started a deep belly laugh. It's bad enough when you know you screwed up without having someone else rub it in.

To be safe, I figured I should sit up front. I did apologize to Ingrid, though, and she forgave me. For what, I still have no clue. Maybe someday.

Chapter 13

Lou Romoso, Cultured Patron of the Arts

Russell drove us over to Ingrid's mother's house. I had to talk to Jessica about her finances. It's always difficult to talk to people about their money, especially the rich, but it had to be done.

Livingston greeted us at the door. What's with these butlers? Is that all they do, wait by the door so they can open it, or do they just hate doorbells?

We walked in and Livingston asked if he could speak to me. I nodded my head and told Ingrid to get her mother and I'd meet them in the library.

"What's going on, Livingston?" I said.

Livingston didn't look scared, but he also didn't seem completely at ease. "Mr. Mueller and Heidi came home very upset. I heard them discussing some plan to get rid of all the baggage. And then they mentioned your name, Detective. I don't think they were planning a party for you. Just be careful,

Sir."

"Thanks." Looks like my plan to rile them up worked a little too well.

He saluted me and led the way to the library. As I said before, I loved that room. The leather chairs were so comfortable you could sleep for days in them. The crackling wood and warmth of the fireplace added to the ambience and made it my own personal heaven.

"Okay, Jessica," I started. "I have a few questions I have to ask you and I need some honest answers if I'm going to get to the bottom of this case. They are going to be personal questions about your finances. Are you okay with this?"

"Yes, Lou, I'm fine with it," Jessica said. "Ingrid knows everything about my finances since it will be hers someday. My husband and I started out very poor and we worked hard to build our business into what it is. Then the war came and turned our lives into a nightmare. Tom and my James both died, leaving Ingrid and I to run the company and look after Tom Junior. We've done a great job in a man's world, Lou, so ask away."

Jessica was getting her confidence back and you could tell by the way she was carrying herself she was done taking shit from Heinrich. She looked years younger than she did when I saw her the day before. I'll take credit for that. With me on the job, how could she be worried? I know, I know, conceit is a dangerous thing, but I was cookin' with gas.

"Let's get started, then. How much are you worth? Just yourself, leaving the business finances out of it."

Jessica paused a moment and turned to ask Ingrid a question.

"I want to know from you, not Ingrid." I said. "If I want her to answer I'll ask her. This is important."

"You are direct, aren't you? I was just going to ask Ingrid

if you finding out how much I'm worth was going to be a problem for her."

They both laughed, and of course me being a guy, I didn't get it. So Ingrid had to explain to me that her mother was worried that I might be in it for the money.

"Of course I'm in it for the money, fifty bucks a day plus expenses. I have bills to pay, you know," I said.

They laughed even harder. It was no use. I wasn't going to win so I just raised my hands and surrendered. They laughed some more. I'm glad I could bring them some amusement.

Jessica wiped the smile from her face but it just kept coming back as she gave a poor excuse for an apology. "We're sorry, Lou, just having a little fun at your expense."

"I'll add that expense to your bill!"

Now I laughed and Jessica continued. "To answer your first question, I'm worth over fifty million dollars, not counting the business."

I was taking a sip of my drink when she said that and spit it out all over Ingrid's dress. She gave me a whack in the back of my head. I sheepishly smiled, and a bit of red must have crept up my neck to my face. "You're worth fifty million bucks? Business must be good."

"My late husband and I invested well and spent wisely. We only splurged on this house and a few cars, which he always wanted. I swear he loved those cars more than me the way he washed and waxed them every week until he died."

I knew the feeling, had a great love of cars myself. Must be a guy thing. "Where is that fifty million? A bank, multiple banks?" I asked.

"Let's see. I have one account with five hundred thousand in it for emergencies, and I keep another account with five hundred thousand to run the household. Those accounts are with Maritime Central. That includes the salaries for

Livingston and Maggie, food, utilities, and taxes. I pay Livingston and Maggie very well because they are good. Twenty thousand, respectively. My friends think I'm nuts for paying them that kind of money, but I trust them, so it's worth it to me."

I do quite well on my own, thank you, but damn, twenty grand for answering a door and serving drinks? Once again I choose the wrong profession. "Do you need any more help, Jessica?"

I laughed and so did Jessica and Ingrid.

"Please continue, Mother, Lou and I are going to Shea's tonight to see a play," Ingrid said.

"We are?"

"Yes, we are. Should be an exciting show, one I think you will enjoy."

Great, just what I need. Some new way for me to make an ass out of myself. "Do we have to? I really should be working on this case."

"You're impossible." But she smiled anyway.

"Continue, Jessica, please, before we are interrupted again by your daughter," I said.

This time Jessica and I laughed and Ingrid slouched and pretended to pout in her chair.

"Where was I, oh yes, that's the household expenses. I keep another million in an account for living expenses. Forty million is tied up in stock, as well as municipal bonds and treasury notes. So I do quite well. The rest I keep in a bank investment, which is still in James' and my name at Maritime Central."

"Who is your broker?"

"He is the best in Buffalo, Tom Gavigan."

That's interesting! What is going on here? "Ingrid and I saw him talking to Heinrich and Heidi at the Park Country

Club and they were quite surprised to see us there. Ingrid, why didn't you tell me you knew Gavigan?"

"I was so scared when I saw Heinrich and Heidi at the club it slipped my mind until Mother said something about her investments. Do you think Tom is up to something?" Ingrid asked.

"I hope not," I said. That would throw a whole new angle into this case. "But I'm going to have a chat with him anyway. Jessica, if you wouldn't mind when we are done here, could you set up a meeting when you get a chance?"

She nodded.

"Thank you. And when the bank opens tomorrow, I want you to go there and get copies of every transaction to your accounts since the day you married Heinrich. Every transaction. Also, do not let anyone know where you are going. Have Ingrid take you as soon as the bank opens and bring the paperwork to my office. I'll be waiting."

"Yes, Lou. We'll be at your office by ten thirty," said a now worried Jessica.

I looked at my watch, 6:13 p.m. The day just shot by and I wanted to talk to DeRosa about the case. Ingrid insisted I stay for dinner before going to Shea's Theatre, so I did. I also wanted to call Murphy at immigration to try to get a line on the Muellers. That would have to wait until tomorrow.

***

We sat down in the dining room as Livingston and Maggie served us dinner. I always felt uncomfortable having people serve me dinners unless they were waitresses or waiters. Of course, I've never had a butler or a maid before either. We made small talk and enjoyed the dinner Maggie cooked up. We had steak, baked potato, salad, and cheesecake for dessert.

Afterwards I thanked everyone for their hospitality and moved towards the door.

Ingrid shook her head and stood in my way. "It's time to go to Shea's and you have to shower and change."

"I have to go home, change my suit. We will never make it." Maybe I could get out of this yet.

"Yes we will, Lou. Stop being such a wet blanket." She had a devilish grin on her face. I didn't like where this was going. "I called Elvira and she put Pasquale on the phone. I had him pick out a suit, shirt, and tie and give it to Russell, whom I had go over to pick it up. It should be here any minute, so why don't you go up to the guest bedroom to the right at the top of the stairs to shower and shave. I had Livingston put out everything you'll need."

"Thanks." Damn, she was good.

As I said thanks, Russell just happened to walk in and Livingston told me everything I need is in the bathroom. These guys are magicians. I shook my head and laughed and went up to use the shower. As I got to the top of the stairs I smelled a faint odor of printer's ink. What is that all about? Where is that coming from?

"Anything wrong, Lou?" Ingrid asked from the bottom of the steps.

"No Ingrid, I was just thinking if I have everything. Whose room is that at the top of the stairs?"

"It's just a storage room, I think Heinrich or Heidi uses it for their art business. Now hurry up, you're going to make us late!"

***

Russell was waiting by the car with that cocky I-don't-know-what-took-you-so-long smile. I hate it when everyone knows what's going on and I'm the last to figure it out. Ingrid turned and said goodnight to her mother. We got into the back of the car and Russell made the right onto Delaware and headed toward Shea's.

"So what do I have to suffer through tonight?" I was not looking forward to this. I'm all for people enjoying the arts, but that stuff usually flew right over my head.

"Oh, you'll like this. It's a Broadway reproduction of Sherlock Holmes. Since you're this big tough guy private eye and former cop I thought this would be something you'd enjoy. I know the stage manager and he will let us go in through the back so we do not have to wait in line."

"Sounds swell." Maybe this won't be too bad after all.

Shea's was a magnificent theatre, modeled after a European opera house and originally opened as a movie house. Many big stars graced the stage of Shea's; Frank Sinatra, Bing Crosby, the Marx Brothers, George Burns, and many others. The stage manager met us in the hallway and apologized for keeping us waiting. Not a problem, Ingrid told him, and thanked him for taking the time from his hectic schedule to show us to the lobby.

As we walked down the hallway we passed a dressing room with the door ajar. So me, being the detective I am and just a little bit curious, thought I'd look in and maybe catch a glimpse of a real Broadway actor. I peeked in and could not believe what I saw. It couldn't be, no way, no how, but it was true. How many coincidences can happen to a guy in one day? I caught up to Ingrid and told her I had to use the restroom and would catch up in the lobby.

I walked into the restroom—so at least part of my story would be true—and waited a minute or so before heading back to the dressing room. The door was still ajar. Heidi Mueller was talking to a woman with a toolbox of some sort, Heinrich nowhere to be seen. Heidi was telling this woman something about meeting at her husband's storefront. It was hard to hear, and I didn't want to move in fear of them noticing me. I then saw Heidi reach in her purse, get her wallet out, and hand the woman five one-hundred-dollar bills.

Heidi turned and started for the door and I took my cue—get it, *cue*, Shea's theatre, play—ah, never mind!

My mind started working over this new information as I walked away. Who was her husband? What was that talk all about? I desperately wanted to follow her, but knew my bathroom excuse was already running thin. If I didn't make it back, Ingrid might kill me, so I headed down the hallway to the lobby.

The lobby was stunning with its marble pillars, crystal chandeliers, red carpet, and my favorite, a bar. The two-minute warning bell went off, as I call it, to signify it was time to get into your seats. As we entered the theatre there were rows of red velour seats facing the giant stage. The carved woodwork and molding was spectacular. All the colors blended together wonderfully. As you looked to the ceiling you saw a large dome with carved wood molding, which again was amazing. I took it all in and began to ponder what the hell Heidi was doing with that make-up artist. There was only one way to find out. Unfortunately, it would have to wait.

Surprisingly I enjoyed the show. Who knew going to the theatre could be so much fun and enlightening, both personally and professionally. Not only was it a great night out with a beautiful woman, I added another clue to what was turning into a complex case. If only Sherlock Holmes himself was here to help me put everything together.

CHAPTER 14

FOLLOW THE MONEY

Seven a.m., January 4. Elvira was pounding her foot on the floor over my bedroom every ten minutes until I got up. I screamed I'm up and the pounding stopped. I then showered, got dressed, and went upstairs for breakfast.

I got my coat and gloves and headed down the stairs after eating. I had to run back up and kiss Elvira on the cheek and thank her for breakfast. In the garage I lifted the door and got into the Lincoln. Started it and my other car, let them both warm up. While waiting I shoveled the small driveway and the stairs to the house. I shut off my antique Lincoln and got into my newer one. The car was nice and warm as I backed out of the driveway.

When in doubt, follow the money!

Is it possible the money to remodel Mickey Finn's had come from Mueller and his old money from Germany? No way had the Mafia backed an Irishman. Young ran a dive before

Mueller got into town then all of a sudden he builds himself a casino. Mueller claims he has old money then latches on to Jessica with some bullshit story.

Follow the money.

My first stop was the Guarantee Building, a beautifully designed piece of architecture that graced the Buffalo skyline. I parked in front of the building and entered through the North Division Street entrance. I looked at the sign that listed the businesses in the building. Found what I was looking for, Tom Gavigan Investments, 701. Jessica had been quick in getting me the meeting. I took the elevator to the seventh floor and headed to Gavigan's office.

I walked in and said to the shapely brunette secretary, "I need to speak to Mr. Gavigan."

"Do you have an appointment, Mr. . . . . ?"

"Romoso."

"Do you have an appointment, Mr. Romoso?"

I took out my badge. "A client called ahead. Mr. Gavigan will see me."

She looked at the badge and got the message. "Yes, Detective, I'm sure he will."

Even though it wasn't a real police badge, just my private investigator's one, it still got the job done.

She went into his office and out he came. Gavigan was a short man in his sixties, bald, and in fairly good shape for a man his age.

"Detective Romoso, How can I help you?"

I barged into his office and the little man followed me in. "We met the other day at the Park Club," I said.

"Yes, I remember you were with Ingrid Reitman. I handle her mother's accounts. What can I do for you?"

"I have a couple questions to ask you about Jessica's husband, Mr. Mueller."

Gavigan swallowed loudly and started to look worried. "Y-yes, Detective?"

"Let me be straight with you, Mr. Gavigan. Ingrid is worried about her mother and doesn't trust Mueller. She thinks he is taking advantage of her and wants me to make sure that doesn't happen. Have you noticed anything strange with his transactions, or has he asked about Mrs. Wright's investments?"

"I don't see how any of this is your business. I am under no obligation to tell you anything."

I like it when people try to get tough. They just never learn. "Okay, I will be sure to let Ingrid and Mrs. Wright know how uncooperative you've been. We'll see how many clients you lose after that."

That must have shaken the little bastard up because he sang like a choirboy. He told me Heinrich was inquiring about opening an investment account. He had millions to invest and wanted to know what kind of return he could get.

"He also asked, and I thought this kind of strange," Gavigan said, "if he'd be able to withdraw money if he were in Europe. Very odd, because Jessica never mentioned going to Europe."

I took it all in and figured that whatever Mueller was up to it was going to happen real soon. I thanked Mr. Gavigan for his time and asked him to call me if Mueller called him again.

It seemed Heinrich was nearing the end of his time in Buffalo and was preparing to move on. Hopefully Livingston is keeping a close eye on him and gets me something I can use.

***

I called Ingrid from Gavigan's phone and told her that I wouldn't be able to meet them today but make sure that her mother had what I needed, and we would get together at my office tomorrow. I apologized but I had to get some answers to other questions first. She was not happy but understood and told me I owed her a dinner and that I was buying, not her. Damn, I hope she likes the Elbow Room in Cheektowaga.

My watch read noon, and my stomach was growling. That needed to be remedied, and fast. I decided to head over to the Big Timer's Club, where hopefully I could find another piece of the puzzle.

Just after my promotion to detective, I was given a case involving somebody suspected of laundering money through the First Ward. That suspect was Freddy the Rat.

He's a small guy, about five foot six, thin and gangly, slicked-back black hair, and about forty years old. He's well-known and well-liked in the First Ward. By the time he got done shaking hands and kissing cheeks crossing a room he could run for president. Freddy got the nickname "Rat" from being a tough, wiry guy who'd gnaw your eyes out in a fight, not because he was a snitch. Freddy never talked and kept his mouth shut. He'd answer a question without really answering the question, just talk circles around you until you either got it or were more confused. It was an art and he perfected it.

I finally busted him doing some small-time money laundering after someone ratted him out. How ironic. The Rat getting ratted on. Ha. The source got out of town, and fast. No sense in hanging around after Freddy got out of jail. Freddy was cool with me. He understood the game, but he was pissed about being turned in by someone else. I couldn't reveal who it was, and he knew that. We had a good respect for each other. If I needed something he's a guy I can go to. Though I know I'll have to work for my answer. That's just the way Freddy operated.

I got in my car and headed to the east side of Buffalo. I got to the Club and the lot was filled with cars of all makes and models. Lincolns, Caddys, Packards, and Oldsmobiles.

The Big Timers Club is an Italian-American club located on East Lovejoy Street on the east side of Buffalo. The Club was started in 1919 by a group of Italian Americans to help preserve their heritage and celebrate being American citizens. There were cheap drinks, good food, great guys, and twelve bocce courts, all in an old turn-of-the-century two-story family home.

You had to be sponsored to get in the Big Timers Club. Ninety-nine percent of the guys were hardworking and successful men in business. I walked in and was greeted with handshakes, hugs, and kisses on the cheek. I ordered a drink and had a seat at the bar. The bartender was named Tommy. He was, if you can believe it, German. He grew up in the neighborhood and worked for the city, but earned a little extra money tending the bar. Since Big Timers was a club it couldn't pay Tommy a wage, but he did earn money from tips. The drinks were fifty cents and I tipped Tommy another fifty and then ordered a sandwich.

"What brings you in today, Lou?" Tommy asked as he gave me another gin and tonic with my sandwich.

"I'm looking for Freddy the Rat," I said.

"He should be here any minute. He's still a little gun shy from that beating he took a while back, but he still makes book and won't let those Irish pieces of shit get to him. He's just more careful now."

Beating, huh? Wonder what Freddy got himself into. "Good, I need to talk to him and pick his brain on something."

"Working on a case?"

"Yeah, Tommy, I am," I said. "It's getting really big and I need Freddy's help."

I sat at the bar and sipped at my drink listening to the

radio. They had the *Jack Benny Show* on. I was deep in thought so I really didn't pay attention; it was more like background noise that was helping me focus. Every time the door opened I'd snap out of it and look to see if it was Freddy. Pretty soon it was almost 2 p.m. Where had the last two hours gone?

I was just getting ready to leave when in walked Freddy. He was like a celebrity; always had a joke to tell and knew everybody. He was sporting a black eye.

"Freddy, how you doing?"

"Like gangbusters, Lou. What can I do for you? Heard you wanted to talk to me."

"How the hell did you know that?"

"I've got my ways," Freddy said with a smile.

"Well, Freddy, since I'm not on the force I have a little more leeway to, let's say . . . make it worth your while to chat with me."

"That's great, Lou, but my throat is a little parched." He made a gesture with his hand, scratching at his throat. This was like a game to Freddy, he was a master at it.

"Okay, Freddy. Tommy, get Freddy whatever he wants."

"I'll have a Simon Pure," Freddy said.

"So what happened? That's a nice shiner you got there."

He didn't look too happy. "Some guys snuck up on me last week. I thought I was about to get whacked, but they just told me to move my business elsewhere, that this was the first and last warning."

"What did the guys look like that slapped you around? Was it the mob?" I asked.

Freddy gave me a look. "I know all those guys, and they leave me alone. I keep my business to the neighborhood, so I'm good with them."

"What can you remember from that night?"

"The only thing I remember was the car they came in. It was a black 1951 Ford."

There it was. That damn Ford showing up again. It was too much of a coincidence not to be tied into my case somehow. "Freddy, how can you be sure?"

"Besides women, my family, and making money, my only other passion is cars. I know cars like the back of my hand, and that was a 1951 Ford."

"Okay, I believe you. What can you tell me about Young's business?" I asked Freddy after Tommy gave him another beer.

"What, you think he had something to do with it?"

"No, no . . . well, he could have. But he's the real reason I'm here."

"Unbelievable story. How did this mick go from a bar that barely makes it serving scoopers to a casino that rivals Las Vegas? I'll tell you. Money! Someone gave Young enough seed money to get this started. The construction cost alone was almost a half million. He paid in cash, I'm told. I know for a fact his bookmaking operation was penny ante. I did more business in a day than he did in a week. Christ, Duffy did more, and he does it for shits and giggles.

"Then overnight there is a Casino in the First Ward pulling in huge money each week when it opens, like one-hundred-grand huge. Movie stars start showing up. You got Sinatra, Crosby, Ball, Elvis, and guys like Berle, Youngman, Benny . . ."

As Freddy rambled on I thought there was truth in much of what he was saying. Could Heinrich be supplying the money behind Young's rapid expansion? Why hadn't anyone caught on to this before?

Freddy eventually quieted down, so I had Tommy get him another drink, to re-grease the machine, if you will. We sat quietly for a little while, but then I got back to my questions. "I know you're no rat, Freddy, but I need an answer or a place to look. My client is in big trouble. What have you heard about this new money coming into town?"

"Not sure I feel like talking anymore. I got a reputation to protect, you know?"

More of the game. I smirked and put a twenty-dollar bill down on the table. Freddy picked up and brought it to his nose. "Ah yes, Lou, my mind is clearing up."

Huh, why'd he do that? "Why'd you smell that bill, Freddy?"

"Can never be too cautious. And, like I said, money is one of my passions. Nothing like the smell of freshly earned bread, is there?

"Well, word going around is that some out-of-towners are behind it. One of them is this bigshot art dealer with a gallery on Main Street. I hear the paintings are originals, and big dollars. He may be the guy reinvesting it in the streets."

"You think this guy is backing Finn's?" I asked.

Freddy smirked again and took a long pull on his third Simon Pure. "You tell me, Lou, you tell me."

That was Freddy's way of giving me the answer without actually telling me the damn answer. It worked, so I didn't care. It also kept his reputation as a guy who never snitched. And it was all I was getting out of Freddy.

***

Freddy was leading me in the right direction, but I needed proof. It was time to pay another visit to Brian Young, and pick his brain. After all, shouldn't the financial guy know where the money was coming from?

I made my way to Brian's operation. He had an office just a couple blocks down the road from Mickey Finn's. It took me a little bit to get there, and luckily Brian was in when I arrived.

"Sweet Lou, how's it going?" He stood up and wrapped me in a bear hug. I'm no small guy, but Brian made me look like a ten-year-old boy by comparison.

"Good, Brian, but I got some questions for you."

He motioned to his visitor's chair, and I took a seat. How should I approach this? If I come right out and accuse Kevin of some wrongdoing, Brian will likely clam up and not give me anything. His love for his brother would get in the way of rationality. Better to play it safe and be real vague.

"I'm investigating some bad investments that have been happening in the First Ward. Supposedly there is someone coming in and working deals with local business owners that they'll float a bunch of cash to them real cheap for pieces of the business."

"So what do you want from me?" Brian asked.

"Well, you being a money guy, I wondered if anyone came to you. These guys are new to town, probably foreigners. You see anyone around, maybe at Mickey Finn's?"

Brian leaned back in his chair and thought about it. "You know, I can't think of anyone. There's so many people coming through there, hell, almost a third of them I bet aren't from around here, coming in on the grain ships."

"You handle the money at Finn's, how'd Kevin swing it to build that place up?"

"Are you accusing my brother of something?" Brian's voice had a little bit of an edge to it.

I backpedaled, didn't want to lose him. "Of course not, Brian. I'm just looking out for you, and by extension him. If someone came in and was trying to swindle the two of you, wouldn't you want me on your side?"

He thought about for a while. I was worried the conversation was over before I could get any real information.

"Yeah, I guess you're right," he finally said.

Brian got up and went around to a file cabinet. I pulled out a cigar and lit up. It'd been too long since I last had a smoke. He came back and laid a file on his desk and started flipping through it. Then he stopped and tapped the page.

"HK Arts. They are the main financier for Mickey Finn's. But everything is legitimate. Believe me. I know my brother's had somewhat of a checkered past, and the casino and betting aren't exactly legal, but I told him I wanted nothing to do with any shady deals going on when I agreed to work with him."

HK Arts? That name meant nothing to me. "You know where they are based out of?"

"They are international. Headquartered in Switzerland, but the office Kevin worked with is on Main. I worked with their bank to secure the financing. Trust me, Lou, I know the deal is clean."

"I heard the deal was paid for all in cash."

"Well, yes, but again, it all went through the bank, Maritime Central."

That's Jessica's bank. Coincidence? Maybe, but I doubt it. He went on to say HK Arts specialized in brokering deals for some of the finest art in the world. They wanted to use the deal with Kevin to broaden their business. I didn't really pay much attention, just eyeballed Brian. He stared right back. Brian was smart, loyal, and if you got into anything physical, there wasn't anyone in Buffalo you'd rather have in your corner.

"I believe you," I said after a little while. I put out my cigar in his ashtray and stood to leave. "I appreciate your time, Brian. Just keep an eye out for me, would you? I don't want to see anyone else from the neighborhood be taken by these assholes."

Brian smiled a big smile. "You got it, Lou. I always got your back."

I walked out of the office feeling a little less confident than I did going in. There was no reason not to trust Brian. He was my oldest friend. And him being a genius made it unlikely for him to be fooled. Possible, but unlikely. I needed to do some more digging on this HK Arts outfit. Maybe they have some answers I haven't been able to uncover yet, or maybe they know about the art dealer the Rat mentioned.

**

The night was lit up by the reflection of my headlights off the falling snow. It was snowing heavy now and it was piling up on the streets. My windshield wipers could barely keep up. The heater worked great; at least I'd be warm. The snowplows were nowhere to be seen. The best I could manage was ten miles per hour without sliding.

When I finally got home I walked up the stairs. It was warm and I realized I was hungry and tired. Driving in a snowstorm was stressful enough. Doing it when you're tired, forget about it. I collapsed on my couch and stretched out and rested my head on the pillow. Too tired to crawl into bed. I started to fall asleep on the couch when there was a knock at the door. I was pissed and yelled, "Who the hell is it! It better be goddamn important to get me up in this weather!"

I flung open the door and what I saw surprised the hell out of me. It was Ingrid holding a tray with dinner on it.

"What are you doing here? And where is your trained bodyguard?" I said.

"Well hello to you, too," she said.

"Sorry, I just wasn't expecting anyone, especially you."

"Why, you have someone in there you don't want me to see?"

I laughed and motioned my arm for her to enter. Ingrid

came in and placed the tray of food on the table. She gave me a kiss on the cheek and told me to sit and enjoy Elvira's cooking. She is the greatest. Italian sausage mixed with fried eggs and potatoes, peppers, and onions stared back at me. The dish is called jambot. Delicious.

"When did you get here, Ingrid?" I asked between bites.

"I had Russell drop me off about eight thirty and I spent the time with Elvira learning to cook Italian. So I hope you like it."

Being me, I couldn't resist, so I made a choking motion. I might have to go see the doctor if my shins get anymore abuse from kicks under the table. "I'm kidding, it's great! Thank you, I was starving."

Ingrid looked around the apartment and stared at the pictures of Ellen and me. There was the wedding picture and various other pictures of us. There were football and Army Air Corps pictures throughout the house. She stared at every one of them without saying a word.

"Your wife was a beautiful woman."

"Thanks, but it doesn't really matter now, does it?"

"What do you mean?" She asked.

"All I have left are those pictures and memories."

I was sad all of the sudden, maybe overwhelmed by all-consuming loss and guilt. I heard a voice in my head, and this time she was sarcastic right out of the gate. *You are so smooth, Louis. You just don't get it. She came all this way to be with you in this horrible weather and all you can do is feel sorry for yourself. Now how are you going to fix this, genius?*

Ellen certainly had a way with words.

"Ingrid, what I meant was that's all *we* have left. You and I only have pictures and memories. I guess I was feeling sorry for both of us."

Ingrid gave me a knowing look. "I know what you mean,

but as long as they are in our hearts they will always be with us. We need those pictures to remind us of a better time."

I smiled, then leaned over and gave Ingrid a kiss.

"What time is Russell picking you up? I asked. "I could take you home so he wouldn't have to drive in this weather."

"Who said I'm going home?"

Ingrid stalked over to the lights with a coy smile. She hit the switch and whispered in my ear that Elvira will have breakfast at 9 a.m. You figure out the rest.

Chapter 15

Two Blondes

Eight a.m. January 5. Didn't even have to use Elvira the human snooze alarm. Ingrid was still asleep so I hopped into the shower and got dressed. At 8:30 Ingrid finally awoke. I smiled at her and she smiled back.

I asked her, "Did you get enough sleep?"

"Yes I did, and you?"

"Slept like a baby. Thank you for coming over, you made my night."

Ingrid smiled back at me shyly and went to shower and get dressed. I looked at Ellen's picture on the mantle, smiled, and looked up, whispering thank you.

There was a knock at the door; who the hell could it be this early? After opening it all I saw were shoulders, torso, and legs.

A smiling Russell looked down at me. "Good morning, Lou, I trust you slept well?"

"You know, Russell, you are a smartass, but I like you anyway."

Ingrid came out of the bathroom dressed and ready for breakfast. She yelled at Russell and me to grow up and pushed us aside and walked upstairs.

Russell and I looked at each other, shrugged our shoulders, and climbed the stairs. We could smell the eggs and bacon cooking and the fresh aroma of coffee. We all ate breakfast with my family and had a genuine good time. After a while I told them we needed to get back to work.

We made our way to Marco's to meet up with Jessica. Maybe her banking records could continue connecting the dots. The plows were out but so much snow had fallen that the main streets were plowed first and often. Swan wasn't a main street so making my way took time.

Jessica and Livingston were sitting at the corner table drinking tea. Livingston was looking bored and was thrilled to see me coming.

We walked upstairs to my office and I turned up the heat, got chairs for the ladies, Livingston, and Russell, who finally made it inside. Jessica was staring at the pictures on the wall. She stared at the wedding picture the longest, then the Army Air Corps picture, and then the college football photos. She smiled and put the wedding picture back down on my desk.

Before she could say anything I said, "Now let's get down to business, shall we?"

Jessica nodded and retrieved her bank transactions from her bag. I opened the file and her passbooks and started looking during the time period when Jessica married Heinrich until now. Something was strange. The balances matched, but not the number of transactions. Jessica's personal passbook for the large account showed she hadn't made a deposit or withdrawal for a few months, but her statements from the bank showed several withdrawals and deposits. Same thing with her household account.

The household account had the earliest transactions on it. Jessica explained she normally used that account to pay her bills once a month. There should have been a handful of transactions. Instead there were over a hundred.

The bank statement showed once a week a withdrawal was made for five grand, and then a few days later a matching deposit was made. The withdrawal always on a Monday and the deposit on a Saturday Morning. Every week, like clockwork.

Jessica also had another account for emergencies with a beginning balance of five hundred thousand dollars. Jessica told me she rarely, if ever, used that account and she hasn't touched it since she married Heinrich. There should have been zero transactions on the account, which the passbook did confirm, but the statements were another story. Again they showed fifty-two deposits and withdrawals, each Monday and Saturday. Five grand, each time.

The third passbook Jessica brought was the big one, which contained nine million. She used the interest earned in this account to replenish the household account each year. Her passbook showed no deposits or withdrawals, as she hadn't transferred the money to the household account yet for the previous year. Like clockwork, the statement had fifty-two matching withdrawals and deposits, except these were for just shy of ten thousand dollars.

Jessica was stunned and visibly shaken. "Who could have done this?"

I didn't answer her because I was doing the math. It wasn't pretty. The household account: $260,000 withdrawn and put back. Emergency fund account: $260,000 withdrawn and deposited. The savings account: nearly $520,000. All told the amount was over a million dollars withdrawn and deposited just in the past year. If I looked back further it was probably more. To the casual observer this looked like a simple deposit and withdrawal of the same funds every week.

"Lou, I feel like a fool," Jessica said. "What does this mean?"

"I know what it means, Mother, you married a crook!" Ingrid shouted.

Ingrid was probably right, but I didn't need the allies fighting amongst themselves. "Ingrid, we don't know that for sure, Heinrich's name isn't even on these accounts," I said, even though I didn't believe it myself.

"Bullshit!" She stood up from her chair. "You know it, Mother married a crook. I always knew that Heinrich was no good."

No one else said anything for a minute or two. Ingrid paced back and forth, eventually sliding back into her chair. We all sat in silence. Jessica had tears in her eyes. Russell and Livingston stared at the wall like it was the most interesting thing they'd ever seen.

Me, I think I had something. Enough was enough, I had to get us back on track. "I know this is emotional, but we have to keep ourselves in check. Jessica, you, Ingrid, and I are going to the bank. Livingston, I need you to go to Mrs. Wright's home to watch, listen, and learn what you can. Please be careful."

"Yes, Detective," Livingston said. "Haven't had this much fun since the war."

"We have to get you out more," I said.

Livingston laughed and said his goodbyes.

***

Russell pulled up to the curb in Ingrid's Cadillac in front of Maritime Central Bank. The ride was quiet; no one said a word. Ingrid looked at her mother, shook her head, and held her mother's hand until we arrived at the bank.

When we got to the bank Jessica asked for Mr. Simon, the bank manager. The receptionist was a middle-aged brunette wearing a blue dress. She hurried to Mr. Simon's door. A minute later, Mr. Simon, a portly bald man in his early sixties wearing a charcoal gray three-piece suit, entered the waiting room.

He went right over to Jessica and said, "Mrs. Mueller—"

"Mrs. Wright," Jessica interrupted.

Simon stammered for a second. "Sorry . . . Mrs. Wright, so good to see you again. It seems like you were here last week, wasn't it?"

Jessica had a surprised look on her face. "Mr. Simon, I was not here last week. I hadn't been here in almost a year prior yesterday to pick up my passbooks."

Now it was Mr. Simon's turn to look confused. "I'm sorry, I swore I spoke to you last—"

"I don't see how that is possible," Jessica snapped.

"Well, maybe I'm mistaken—"

"No you're not, Mr. Simon," I cut in. Everyone turned to look at me. "You did see Mrs. Wright, but it wasn't her."

Now everyone was confused. This was actually fun, usually I'm the one who has no idea what's going on.

Jessica finally recovered enough to introduce me. "Mr. Simon, this is Detective Romoso. He works for Ingrid and I. So if you will, please answer any questions he has for you as there seems to be a big problem with your bank."

"What could that possibly be, Mrs. Wright?" Simon had regained his composure, and seemed a little offended by the insinuation that his bank was at fault for something.

"I'll have Detective Romoso explain it. It could take a while. May we use your office, Mr. Simon?"

"Yes, yes but of course."

Simon's office was in the corner of the bank. It was a large room with a plush rug with the Maritime Central logo sewn into the middle. A big oak desk and leather chair were towards the back where Simon sat. Pictures of his family decorated the desk and a painting of a sailing schooner hung on the wall behind his desk. There were three leather chairs for his customers. We sat down and I told him we needed to talk to him and the tellers who usually handled Jessica's transactions. I showed him the stack of transactions that took place in his branch. It happened to be the same teller every time. That caught my eye, but I didn't suspect the teller was part of any scheme against Jessica. Just an unknowing accomplice. Mr. Simon informed us the teller was working today, a Miss Sandra Jacobs, and he would get her for us when she finished with her last customer.

Jacobs was a woman in her early thirties with blond hair down to her shoulders. Couldn't help but notice her hour-glass figure. She wore an outfit that would make any guy deposit every dime in his pocket just to have an excuse to talk to her. Since I'm a guy and am no different from any other guy on the planet, I just looked and stared and wondered how many dimes I had in my pockets. Ingrid caught me staring. I was so obvious a blind man could have caught me. She gave me a gentle squeeze on the arm—if you call a black-and-blue mark a gentle squeeze. The message was received loud and clear, but it was worth the bruise. I'm a guy, what can I say?

Simon introduced Miss Jacobs to us. When she saw Jessica she smiled and said, "Mrs. Wright, it's good to see you again. I hope all is well."

Jessica didn't know how to respond since she'd never seen Jacobs. She finally acknowledged her after a short, awkward pause.

The pleasantries were now over; it was time to get down

to business. I had Miss Jacobs sit down next to me, a move I'm sure would get me making funeral arrangements later, but it was necessary to go over the paperwork. Her perfume floated through the air and could dull one's senses if you allowed it to. I didn't have to worry about that since my sense of feel was being tested by the constant squeezing of Ingrid's grip on my forearm.

"Miss Jacobs, I'd like you to look over a few transactions if you don't mind," I said.

"Certainly, Detective, and please, call me Sandy." She smiled at me and I was about to propose and ask her to run away with me when Ingrid spoke up.

"He'll call you *Miss Jacobs* since this is business."

"Of course, *Mrs.* Reitman." Sandy smiled again, but this one was a little more devious.

The battle was on. Sandy was not going to be intimidated by Ingrid, and Ingrid was not about to back down from Sandy. I sat back and enjoyed the show since I might be asked by Ingrid later what I would like for my last meal.

Jacobs took the stack of transactions from me and gently brushed her hand against mine and smiled at me. Ingrid caught this and squeezed harder still. How strong is this woman? Jacobs took a few minutes to look over the transactions. She explained what I already knew. Mrs. Wright came in twice a week, once to withdraw money, then to deposit the same amount.

"Do you find anything out of the ordinary about this, Miss. Jacobs?" I asked.

"At first I did, but Mrs. Wright explained to me she used the money to replenish her household funds and would replace it from another account. It was none of my business, so I didn't think much about it."

"Why did she always come to your line?"

"I don't know why. We always strike up conversations about fashion and other things women talk about, like who I was dating, just everyday things. Are you seeing anyone, Lou?"

I knew I was a dead man when I heard Ingrid say, "You're out of luck, the Detective here has someone, and she isn't quite as understanding as I am of another woman flirting with her boyfriend."

"Oh, brother," I muttered under my breath.

"Of course, Mrs. Reitman. I wouldn't want the detective getting the wrong idea."

"I'm sure you wouldn't!"

I was in the middle of a catfight and needed help. I looked to Mr. Simon. I might as well have tried to float with a cement block tied to my foot. He was sweating behind his desk wondering what to do. No help there.

"Ladies, lets calm down and get back to business," I said. "Ingrid, why don't you go check on Russell?"

If looks could kill, I would have died a thousand deaths as Ingrid got up to leave. She'd forgive me later. I hope. But the thing is we weren't going to get anything done with her and Miss Jacobs going at it.

"Okay, Miss Jacobs, so someone came in and withdrew money one day and deposited the same amount few days later, is that correct?"

"Yes, it is."

"What did this woman look like?" I asked

"Now you are joking with me," she said. "It was Mrs. Wright, and she is sitting right next to you."

"I'm telling you, Lou, it wasn't me!" Jessica said.

"Can you tell if there is anything different about Mrs. Wright here and the one you've been dealing with, Miss Jacobs?" I said.

Sandy looked at Jessica and thought for a moment, then

said, "The only difference is the voice. Mrs. Wright's voice is not as deep or hoarse as normal. I was going to ask if she had a cold."

"No accent of any kind?" I asked.

"There may have been, but it was tough to tell," Sandy said.

"How about the way Mrs. Wright was dressed?"

"Very fashionable, just like she is dressed today," she said, and gave Jessica a smile.

I thanked Miss Jacobs for her time, and excused her. If I was going to defraud the bank, I'd have picked her as well. She wasn't putting rockets in the sky anytime soon. Then I turned to Mr. Simon. "Sir, I think we have a major problem here."

He was mumbling to himself, and didn't offer anything intelligible.

"Look, on behalf of Mrs. Wright, I want you to put a freeze on all of her accounts," I said. "We can't . . . actually, don't do anything."

Mrs. Wright looked at me, and started to complain, but I held up a hand to stop her. "We can't let them know we are on to the scheme. If they catch wind of it, bad things may happen and we'll never catch them." Then to Simon, "If Jessica, or the woman posing as her, tries to come in and do anything with the accounts, let it happen, but call me immediately after. I want to know everything going on."

He nodded.

"And also, I need to know everything you know about HK Arts."

"Who?" He tried to remain calm, but I saw it.

"If something is up, and I find out later you were involved, you're going down."

He babbled a little more, but I stopped him and told him to keep his mouth shut for now, and I would do the same.

Ingrid was cooling down with Russell in the lobby. I asked him and Jessica to go on ahead and grab the car so I could talk to Ingrid.

"Look, Ingrid, I don't want to fight. As a matter of fact I don't even know what you were mad about." That was a little white lie, but why add fuel to the inferno I had going? "First, I only want to be with you. I haven't dated anyone since Ellen, so this is all new to me again. That Jacobs woman was just a witness. She means nothing. I'm sorry if I angered you. I don't want to mess this up."

Ingrid was crying. Why, I have no clue. She always seemed to cry and I can't afford to keep buying handkerchiefs. But I gave Ingrid mine anyways and she wiped away her tears. "I'm sorry too, Lou, I don't want to lose you either."

"Well, you are stuck with me, so stop crying, okay?"

She looked up and nodded. I smiled, gave her a kiss and headed towards the car. Russell had the door open and was waiting next to it. I didn't say anything, and Russell stifled a laugh. What a wise ass.

CHAPTER 16
COCKTAILS, ANYONE?

My next stop was the immigration office in Buffalo at 133 Delaware Avenue. Maybe Agent Murphy could help. Immigration should be able to find something on the Muellers, if that really was their last name.

When I got there he had someone with him. He saw me through the glass and held up his index finger to let me know he'd be a minute or so. After another fifteen minutes his door opened and he came out with a tall, lanky gentleman dressed in a blue suit, white shirt, and blue tie, wearing a fedora. I knew him from somewhere, but couldn't get a good look with the hat pulled tight over his eyes.

"Who was that?" I asked Murph when I walked into his office.

"That, my friend, was an old OSS agent named Kolbe," Murph answered. "He now works for the CIA and is still hunting Nazis. Currently he's tracking a group who were high up in Hitler's Reich. They are supposedly selling some of the art stolen from Jewish families during the war. He tells me that the artwork seems to be coming from Buffalo, and he was hoping I had some information on any illegal German immigrants in the area."

Art? Hmmm . . . could HK Arts, the financier behind Mickey Finn's, be involved? I decided to remain quiet for the time being.

Murph further explained who Kolbe was, in case I didn't quite grasp it. Kolbe worked as a low-level employee for the German Foreign Ministry. He knew all the players in Hitler's government and close associates. He developed anti-Nazi sentiment in the early stages of the War and in 1943 decided to contact Allen Dulles, who was working in Switzerland at the time. Dulles then recruited him and Kolbe passed untold numbers of valuable documents about the German war efforts.

Murph continued. "He knows his business, Lou, and probably knows everything you're up to."

"You didn't tell him about me, did you?"

Murph nodded, but before I could yell at him he held up his hand. "I told him you were working a case, but no details."

"Okay," I said. "I just have hunches, but right now they seem to paying off. Did you find out anything on the lovely Mueller clan?"

"They came in legitimately with Swiss passports."

"Any dirt?"

Murph suddenly looked disappointed. "Nothing. Searched high and low. Could hardly trace them back to Switzerland. Can't haul them in here without any proof. A hunch just isn't good enough."

"I understand. Just give me a little more time and I think I will have this all wrapped up in a nice little package for you."

"Okay, Lou. Keep me posted."

I left Murph's office and hopped in the elevator, and lo and behold there was Kolbe.

"Good afternoon, Detective Romoso," Kolbe said. He held the door for me and pushed the lobby button. "How are you?"

"Afternoon, Agent Kolbe. I'm well, and you?"

He smiled. "Your reputation precedes you. How about we go for lunch and put our cards on the table?"

"I don't gamble." I know, I know, I'm a degenerate. But Kolbe doesn't know that.

He chuckled. "Come on now. One doesn't win all four bets on bowl games and not gamble, does one, Detective?"

Damn! Kolbe had me on that one. How he knew I'll never figure it out. But I'd try. "Call me lucky," I said with a wry smile.

The elevator came to the lobby entrance and we got out. "I'll drive, if you don't mind," I said.

We walked to my car and headed downtown and made the left onto West Tupper towards Michigan Street. Neither one of us spoke a word as we made our way to Seneca Street. I made another left onto Seneca and thought about going to Chefs. I decided to keep driving and still he said nothing. I pulled in front of DiTondo's Restaurant and parked.

DiTondo's is an Italian Restaurant and does a thriving lunch business. If you don't get there early you may have to wait. The building is like almost everything else in the neighborhood, a former turn-of-the-century two-story home, now repurposed as a restaurant. Traditional red-checkered tablecloths made it a quaint little spot. Their specialty was the spaghetti and meatballs, and it's good.

The hostess sat us down in a secluded corner of the restaurant without being asked, almost like this was planned ahead of time. I must be getting paranoid. Hanging out with a CIA spook certainly doesn't help. I sat down and caught a glimpse of Fritz winking at our waitress. I wasn't paranoid, I was just right.

"How did you know I'd come to DiTondo's?" I asked.

"I took an educated guess it would either be here or Chefs," he answered.

This guy was good. Very good. We sat down and ordered a drink. I had a beer and so did Fritz.

"Okay, Fritz, what's all this about?" I asked.

"The people I am after have in their possession valuable artwork, taken from Jews across Europe during the War. They are selling them throughout the world as of late for good money. Most, if not all, of these Jewish people paid with their lives. I believe the gang is led by a former SS Major named Bernhard Kruger."

That name didn't ring a bell. "That's all fine and dandy, but what's that have to do with my case?"

Before he could answer, the waitress came over and we both ordered the spaghetti and meatballs. I had a feeling this was going to be a long lunch.

"Did you ever hear of Operation Bernhard?" Fritz asked.

I shook my head no.

"Good. Operation Bernhard was the codename of a secret Nazi plan devised during the Second World War by the RSHA and the SS to destabilize the British economy by flooding the country with forged money. It was the largest counterfeiting operation in history."

"RSHA, really?"

"Yes, Reich Security Main Office. Created by Heinrich Himmler. The organization's main purpose was to fight all enemies of the Third Reich inside and outside Germany. The plan was named after Kruger, who set up a team of counterfeiters formed from prisoners in the Auschwitz concentration camp.

"Starting in 1942, work began on the complicated process of engraving plates, developing the rag-based paper and correct watermarks, and breaking the code so the proper serial numbers could be used. By the time Auschwitz was liberated in April of '45, the printing press had produced over 130 million in British pounds. The notes are considered among the most perfect counterfeits ever produced, being almost impossible to distinguish from the real currency.

"Kruger disappeared without a trace. We believe he married a girl much younger than him and hid in Switzerland."

I wasn't looking for a history lesson, but it was fascinating. Maybe Kolbe was right after all, and we were hunting the same people. Even though Heinrich never mentioned anything about the war, there were some unavoidable parallels to the two stories. "Keep talking, Fritz, you've sparked my interest."

"The bank notes were so perfect that Hitler and Himmler rewarded Kruger with gold and valuable paintings taken from Jews. I believe those paintings are somewhere in Switzerland. The paintings are sold from the United States and Canada, and an employee in Europe ships the artwork to the buyer.

"We got a tip from Simon Wiesenthal, writer and feared Jewish Nazi hunter, who was also a concentration camp prisoner. He was able to get this information from art buyers who were caught with the stolen paintings and artwork. These people only cooperated because they didn't want to be associated with the concentration camps. They told Simon that they wired money to a Swiss bank and the art was shipped to them from Europe. That's all they knew."

Kolbe paused for a bit and had a few bites of his spaghetti. My mind was turning, and I hadn't touched my plate—which is surprising, I know. He wiped his face and continued.

"Bernhard's brother, Erik, was a tank commander in the Kampfgruppe Peiper, led by Colonel Joachim Peiper, which was part of the 1st Panzer Division at the Battle of the Bulge. On December 17, 1944, the Kamfgruppe Pieper overran a small platoon of Americans near Malmedy, Belgium. Pieper took over ninety prisoners that day and decided they would not stop to tend to American POWs. Pieper wanted to keep moving and ordered his tank group to kill them. He gave the order to one SS Major Erik Kruger. Kruger not only arranged the massacre, he took part in it.

"After the war we were able to round up most of this Panzer Division and his officers. All except for one."

"Let me guess, Kruger."

"Correct, Lou. We have reason to believe that his brother was able to smuggle him out of Germany and get him to Argentina. Like Bernhard, he became a ghost."

"So what does this have to do with me?" I asked.

"My information leads me to believe that Bernhard and Erik may be connected to the people you are tracking."

Great. Not only was I tracking master counterfeiters, but possibly evil war criminals? I needed to be sharp in order to take these assholes out.

"I want these people alive," Kolbe said. It was like he could read my mind.

"I'll do my best, Fritz, but I can't promise a thing."

We finished our food quietly and made our way back out to my car. Before I got in, he said, "Keep an eye out for a Ford sedan. It followed us here, but I don't see it now."

"What?"

"A black Ford, from the time we left Agent Murphy's."

"Why didn't you say anything?" I shouted. "I've been trying to track that car down. It's a suspected vehicle in a string of murders, not to mention a few attempts on me. Fritz, I thought you were a spy. Son of a bitch!"

"And I thought you were a detective."

Touché! He had me there; I wasn't paying attention. I guess this was Fritz's way of letting me know I wasn't careful enough and could probably get myself killed.

Fritz had an agency car pick him up, leaving me to get on with my day.

***

Buffalo Police Headquarters is a four story building which houses Homicide, Robbery, Vice, Fraud, and many other divisions of the department. Headquarters also has holding cells for prisoners until they're arraigned and brought to the county lockup.

Once there I took the rickety elevator to the third floor and went into Homicide. I asked a detective, who was sitting at his desk doing nothing, if DeRosa was in without looking at him.

"No, Shamus, he isn't in yet." He said it like my presence was a huge inconvenience to him. Something tickled the back of my mind.

"Don't you have a client to rip off?" He said as I stared at him.

Stanley Kovak, a twenty-year veteran of the Buffalo Police Department and all-around fuck-up. He and I never saw eye to eye on the force. He resented the fact that I got promoted faster than he did. He would always try to undermine my investigations by telling anyone who'd listen, which wasn't many, that I didn't know what I was doing and he would have had the case solved already. I could have taken the high road, but as usual I didn't.

Once I got hold of a pack of his cigarettes and put an exploding load in one and waited for the show to start. I didn't have to wait long. Kovak was pontificating on what a genius he was when he took a puff of his cigarette and it exploded. There was tobacco everywhere. The place erupted with hysteria and laughter. I spit out my coffee I was laughing so hard. Kovak was pissed and screamed an artful string of obscenities my way.

So that's how our relationship went. He'd bust my balls and I'd crush his.

It really came to a head during a big case we solved—the same case I had to call the Hail Mary and bring in Agent Murphy. Kovak, the dumbass he is, made a mess with the paperwork and we couldn't get the warrant. With Murphy brought in we were able to make the case federal and bypass Kovak's mistake.

He should have been busted down to traffic at the very least, but I think DeRosa must have a soft spot for him. I guess when you've gone twenty years as a bad egg it's hard to get rid of you.

After shaking my head I feigned offense by placing a hand on my chest, gasping. "I am highly offended. If you could find your ass with both your hands you might be able to solve a case or two, but since you're sitting on both of them I don't see that happening."

Kovak stood up and was about to say something else when a voice stopped him.

"Ice it, guys!" It was DeRosa. He was standing by the entrance door shaking his head. "Kovak, go back to work—better yet, get me all the files involving the Leary case, and the shooting at the Reitman estate."

Kovak mumbled something under his breath and sulked away.

"What do you have, Tom?" I asked.

"Come into my office, and be quiet." I followed him in and closed the door behind me. After I sat DeRosa said, "Can't you and Kovak get along?"

"He's a waste of space, Tom. He almost blew the Gonzalez case for us with his stupidity. I still can't understand how he has a job."

"It was an honest mistake," DeRosa said. "We were able to convict thanks to you."

No big deal to me now since I was no longer on the force, so after a moment of silence I said, "If he apologizes I'll play nice. Until then all bets are off."

"Okay, Lou, I'll talk to him, just keep the peace."

Kovak came in with a stack of reports and dropped them on Tom's desk. I thought he was going to lay into Kovak but he didn't. Just told him to close the door behind him as he left.

"This is what we have," DeRosa said. "It's not much, but it's better than nothing."

I grabbed the files. First was on the shooting from Ingrid's. The bullets were from a Thompson sub machine gun—better yet, the same gun that hit Ellen and I. The footprints outside the window were from a size ten shoe.

The tire prints had come back from the FBI and match that of a late forties or early fifties sedan. The broken bits of taillight from the Reitman's driveway came back to a 1951 Ford, confirming what Freddy the Rat already gave me.

The second file was on Leary. Leary and Sullivan were both shot with the same gun, a .38, as we suspected. The shot Sully took in the head did not kill him. He had died from the beating he took. The torso wounds were also post mortem, from a .45.

"Well, Tom, it's a start. How can we narrow the scope of this investigation to Young's gang?"

"Here is the problem," DeRosa started. "How many guys wear size ten in the Buffalo area? Thousands? Probably more. And Young doesn't have any Fords registered to him. I do think we are dealing with the same gang responsible for this whole thing, and also agree with you that it is probably the Young gang, but try to prove it."

"I have a source that tells me some of Young's gang may have been driving a Black fifty-one Ford."

"That's great," DeRosa said, "but if there isn't one registered to him or any of his associates, it doesn't do us any good. We are at a dead end unless we can find the car or the guns."

DeRosa was right, at least from the police aspect of the case. "Okay, I'll let you know if I find out anything more." I got up and walked to the door. "And I'll let stupid in."

Before DeRosa could ask what I was talking about I quickly opened the door and Kovak almost fell flat on his face. I laughed and he called me an asshole. I then slammed the door behind him. It hit his ass and Kovak fell into DeRosa's desk. He screamed my name. I was laughing and the entire squad room followed suit. DeRosa's door opened and he stared everyone down. As he did the squad tried to suppress their smiles but couldn't. They all burst out again and even DeRosa joined in.

Kovak turned a lovely shade of red and screamed, "I'll get even, Romoso!"

I hustled out of the squad room and headed back to the elevator before I took it any further.

***

I headed for Shea's to the make-up artist. She was the last piece of confirmation I needed before setting my plan in motion. I got there about 4 p.m. and knocked on the door. The stage manager who worked the night of the Sherlock Holmes play opened the door and stared at me like he knew me but couldn't place me.

"Yes, can I help you, Sir?" He said.

"I was here a couple of nights ago with Ingrid Reitman."

His eyes clicked. "I remember now. I don't see Mrs. Reitman, how can I help you?"

"I need to speak to your make-up girl. Is she in?"

"Alice? She should be here any minute. She usually rides the bus."

No sooner had he gotten that out when an NFT bus came and dropped off its passengers. Out they came: a man in a brown suit, a woman carrying groceries, and finally Alice. As she walked out in front of the bus, I heard a car's engine racing and I screamed to Alice to get back. The black Ford raced down Pearl, aiming right for her. There was nothing I could do. The Ford clipped her and sent her flying into the bus. She let go of her make-up kit and it scattered through the air. The Ford sped away from the scene and I was able this time to get a quick glimpse of the driver, but not much more. The license plate was blacked out.

I rushed over to Alice but she was mercifully unconscious. The stage manager called the police and I waited. This was my fault. They must have followed me and I wasn't paying any attention again. Maybe Fritz was right, this was too big for me to handle by myself.

The cops got to the scene quickly and the ambulance rushed poor Alice to Buffalo General Hospital. How she was still alive was anyone's guess. It had to be a miracle. The two cops on the scene were Walters and Hoffman. They secured the crime scene and I advised them to call Homicide, not the accident investigation unit.

Day was quickly turning into night. The temperature dropped twenty degrees from the time Alice was run down until Homicide got to the scene. By then the entire length of Pearl Street was shut down for a few hours. This did not make the stage manager happy because he was worried his theatregoers would be late.

"How long are you going to block the street, Detective? I've got a show to put on." He stated angrily

"Look, asshole, one of your employees was run down and you're worried about a play?"

"I have a backup artist on hand. The show must go on!"

I had enough of the windbag and hit him with a right to the jaw. Down he went in the middle of the parking lot. Just as he hit the ground Ruff showed up. He came running over to see what happened.

"Lou, why did you hit him?"

"Hit who?"

"Him, that's who."

"Oh! Why didn't you say so?"

"I just did."

"Did what?"

This could have been a great Abbott and Costello routine, but I figured it went on long enough. Ruff was getting pissed and I was getting cold.

"I hit him because he is an asshole and doesn't give a shit about the poor girl who got run down," I said. "All he cares about is that damn play and whether or not theatregoers get to their seats on time. That's bullshit so I smacked him."

"You can't just go around hitting people, Lou!" We walked away from the downed stage manager as a medic still at the scene looked him over. When we were out of hearing range, Ruff said, "Good, I would have hit him myself if I was there."

I laughed and filled him in on what happened. The stage manager finally got up and screamed at me that he would call Ingrid and tell her about my rude behavior. As politely as I could I told him to go fuck himself.

I followed Ruff to the ER to see if we could question Alice. A nurse informed us she would be in surgery for quite a while and she'd need a miracle to survive. He left and I hung out for a bit longer before deciding it was time to leave.

It had been a long day but I wasn't tired and didn't feel like going home. I decided to head back to the office and figure out my next move. My car was parked on North Street, close to the ER. I decided to look my car over. Why, I don't know. Just that old funny feeling I get when something isn't right.

I checked the back of the car. Nothing. Checked the trunk. Again, nothing. The rear doors were fine and nothing was out of place in the back seat, so far so good. I bent down in the freshly fallen snow and looked underneath my car. Couldn't see much. It was a moonless night and the darkness gave way to an eerie feeling. I got up, opened the passenger door and got my flashlight, bent down and looked under the car again. Nothing.

I got up and brushed myself off and checked the engine hood. It was ajar. I ran my fingers along the open crack between the hood and the body and felt nothing. My fingers found the hood latch and I slowly opened it. No wires or anything else wrong until I got the hood open.

"Dammit!"

What an ending to a perfect day. Someone had stolen the coil wire to my car and left me stranded. At least it wasn't a bomb. I swore a bit more, got pissed, and in the end I was still stranded. I slammed the hood and was about to take a step into the street when I heard an all too familiar sound. Squealing tires and two headlights came racing towards me. This time something was different. There was another pair of headlights behind this car.

I froze for a quick second and thought *not again* as the two cars closed the gap. I saw an arm come out the open window and in its hand was a container with a blazing flame on top flickering in the cold wind.

"Oh shit!"

I dove on the hood of my car and slid off to other side and took cover. The container hit my car windshield, shattered, and spread flames all over the front of my beautiful Lincoln. It was awash in flames as it burned brightly and lit up the evening sky. I guess one Molotov cocktail wasn't enough, because the second car also launched one and lit the back windshield. I had no choice but to get up and get the hell out of there. Unfortunately, they were waiting for that. They had turned around at the intersection of North and Ellicott and were heading back towards me.

This time the cocktail bar was closed and happy hour started. Free shots. They had their guns out, spraying the street with round after round of gunfire. I hit the deck behind the snowbank and prayed they would miss. I wasn't that lucky. A few ricochets off the curb grazed my arm, causing a burning, stinging sensation.

I couldn't fire back for fear of hitting an innocent bystander leaving the hospital, so I just laid there and did nothing. The whole thing was over in less than a minute.

Thankfully no one walked out into the shower of bullets. I knew I wasn't hit badly, but that didn't stop it from hurting. Slowly I got up and looked at the burning funeral pyre formerly known as my car. A hospital security guard came running out to see what happened and just stood next to me with his mouth open not saying a word.

Finally he snapped out of it and asked if I was hurt. I showed him my bloody arm. He walked me back into the hospital. A nurse rushed me into the ER and got a doctor. I asked the guard to call DeRosa. Then I also had him call Ingrid.

Why I asked him to call her, I wasn't sure. Maybe I was feeling sorry for myself, or maybe I just wanted someone *else* to feel sorry for me for a change.

CHAPTER 17

NOW WHAT?

I was sitting on the end of the hospital bed when Ingrid and DeRosa came in. Ingrid rushed over and gave me a hug and Tom just stood there with a disbelieving look on his face.

No one said a word for a few minutes so I thought I'd break the ice. "Anyone bring the marshmallows? I have a nice fire going on North Street."

"Do you ever take anything serious, Lou?" Tom said.

"Why, I didn't know you cared," I said sarcastically.

"I don't. I was worried about Ingrid."

"Thank you, Tom," Ingrid said. "My brilliant detective thinks he is indestructible. Jerk!"

"Look, you two, of course I'm worried," I said. "But there is nothing I can do right now. Plus, I'm quite mad that my car is ruined. I loved that car."

Tom shook his head again. "Did you get a look who did this?"

"When I tell you, you won't believe it."

"Let me guess, a black Ford sedan."

"Give the man a cigar!" I shouted. "And here's the kicker, they had a second car behind them to make sure the job got done right."

"What model?"

"Don't know, it happened so fast. I couldn't even get a shot off, that's how fast it happened."

Ingrid was shaking with fear. I don't know if it was the fear of losing me, or what she might have gotten herself into. I wasn't going to ask because I'd get in trouble again for not getting it. Round two goes to me. I always win when I keep score. She hugged me again.

Tom shook his head for the third time. "Lou, we can't mess around anymore, it's time to call in some help and take these guys down. If we spook them, so be it. Too many bodies and no answers. Even if we get them off the street temporarily, it's something."

"No! I asked for some time, and I want it. Besides, chances are Kolbe already knows about this anyway."

"Kolbe?" DeRosa asked.

"CIA," I said.

"What! You've gotten the CIA involved!" Ingrid yelled, and for good measure hit me on my bullet-ridden arm. "Listen to Tom. He is right, you know, but you are too stubborn to admit it. If you don't listen I . . . never want to see you again!"

The tears flowed steadily now but I wasn't going to give in.

"Ingrid, I can't, not now, I'm close to solving this case and I'm going to see it through."

With that last statement Ingrid looked at me and said, "Find your own way home, hardhead. Elvira was right, you don't listen. Goodbye!"

Tom and I watched her go and sat in silence for a few

moments.

"She's is right, you know," he finally said.

"I know she is, but I've got to even things up, and I will. Come hell or high water. You think she's mad at me for not listening, or that I woke her up?"

"You're an ass!" He said and then left.

The doctor came in and checked out my wounds. They turned out to be deep scratches, nothing life threatening. He cleaned me up, put on some fresh bandages, and released me. Tom left, Ingrid was gone, and me in my infinite wisdom forgot my car was molten steel. Hence I had no ride. Shit! Now What? If the black Ford drives by again I might ask them for a ride.

But outside the hospital my lifeline was standing there. Russell.

"Ride, Detective?" He had his trademark grin plastered on his face, ready to break out into laughter at any time.

"Thanks, Russell, but won't you get in trouble for giving me a ride? Your boss is pretty tough. She canned me, and she just might can you too!"

"I'm not too worried about it, considering it was her idea."

"Women, who can figure them out? They leave you one minute and then give you a ride the next. At least with guys when they say I'm out of here, they mean it and leave you stranded. That I understand. This, no way."

Russell's shit-eating grin widened as he opened the car door. I wasn't paying attention because I was pissed about everything that had happened. I hopped in the front seat and asked Russell to take me to my office. I still had to put all the pieces of the case together.

"I'm sorry. I have strict orders to take you home."

"Well, Russell, since I was a Captain and you were a Lieutenant, and I out rank you, take me to my damn office!"

"You fly boys, your cushy living quarters affected your

brains. While you slept in a bed I slept in the mud, sand, rain, high humidity, with bugs and no hot meals. So I'm telling you, I'm taking you home, and that my orders come from above *your* paygrade. So sit back and relax. You'll be home in a few minutes."

"Bullshit, Russell! I'm done with this nonsense where I'm always wrong! Bullshit! I'm doing this for her and her mother to keep them safe. I can't help it's turned into a cluster fuck. If she wants to give orders, get her ass here and let her bark them out!"

Russell burst out laughing. As I said, I wasn't paying attention and didn't know anyone else was in the damn car. A hand reached out and touched my bandaged arm, and a familiar voice boomed. "Well I'm here, Mr. Big Shot Detective, so why don't you tell me to my face."

I gulped hard and looked at Russell. "Please tell me, Russ, old pal, that it's not Ingrid's hand touching me. Please tell me it's a ghost or a reaction from my pain medicine."

"I wish I could, *Capitan*, but you're on your own," Russell said. "Say hello to General Reitman."

Russell laughed even harder as the big Cadillac headed towards my house. I really couldn't argue, so I didn't, but I was still pissed.

The Caddy pulled up and I got out. Ingrid moved towards the door and I closed it before she could get to it. High school antics, you bet, but what did you expect?

Russell opened the door for her and Ingrid got out and followed me to the stairs. Russell's smile still hadn't left his face when he jumped back in the Caddy and pulled away. He was an ass, but I liked him anyway.

"Where do you think you're going?" I said to Ingrid. She was making her way towards my house.

"Inside. Elvira made dinner. So why don't you act your age

and open the door for me? We'll eat, and then you can apologize."

I guess round two didn't go to me.

We went upstairs and waiting for us was Louis, Elvira, Pasquale, Frank, and Mario. They ate earlier but stayed up to hear the details of the night. I spoke while I ate and told them the story. They sat there in silence and were amazed I wasn't killed. Now that I think about it, I was too. No wonder Ingrid was upset.

We finished dinner and thanked Elvira. Ingrid and I each gave her a kiss on the cheek and headed to my apartment. I hopped into the shower and then into bed. Ingrid was waiting. She patted my side of the bed and I slid under the covers. As soon as my head hit the pillows I was out. Ingrid called me a jerk and then kissed my cheek. I just love her terms of endearment.

***

Six days into the New Year. The alarm went off at 8 a.m. Ingrid was already up and dressed. I showered and got dressed myself. There was no time to grab a bite to eat because I had a busy day ahead of me. Just one problem: no car. That's another thing I had to do, call my insurance company to file a claim. How do you explain your car is a pile of molten lava because of careless thugs playing with Molotov cocktails? I don't think that will fly, and that's a shame because my deductible is only fifty dollars. Maybe I can slip it by as an expense and bill Ingrid. Oh, I'm sure she'd love the extra few grand on the bill. Is it any wonder why I'm no good at relationships?

I needed to get to my office and there was no way in hell I was going to drive my 1932 Lincoln in the winter, so I got dressed for the long, cold walk. Told Ingrid I was leaving and heard her say wait. So I waited.

Ingrid was on the phone and just hung up as I walked into the room looking like Nanook of the North. She burst out laughing at the winter outfit I was wearing: Long trench coat with a thick wool sweater underneath, big black rubber boots with snaps, thick wool gloves, and a hat with flappy ear covers.

"Where are you going dressed like that?" She asked after she finally gathered herself.

"What? I'm going to my office. It's cold and I have to walk. In case you didn't remember, my car is still smoldering next to Buffalo General."

"You can relax and dress like a normal person, not like an Eskimo. I have Russell and Mary coming. You can use my Hudson until you get a new car. By the way, the loss of your car is a business expense, and I expect to be charged for it."

I was going to say forget about it but it would be another argument I'd lose so I kept my mouth shut. See, I'm getting better at this relationship crap! Round three to me. It's nice to have a client who's your new girlfriend. They don't argue about cost and even let you pad the expense account.

I thanked Ingrid and promised I wouldn't turn the Hudson into a fireball like I did my Lincoln. Outside the Hudson pulled up with Ingrid's Caddy right behind. I kissed Ingrid goodbye and went out to greet Russell and Mary.

"Thanks for bringing the car down."

"You're welcome," they answered in unison.

Mary stepped in front of Russell and looked me straight in the eye and said, "Detective, these bastards took everything I had away from me and I lost years of my life feeling sorry for myself and treated a lot of people badly because I was angry. Now is my chance for redemption, and if I can help put these murdering bastards away I'm going to do it, whether you let me or not!"

It was too early in the morning to argue with another woman and lose, so I acquiesced. "Okay, Mary, you win."

I got into the warm Hudson and waved goodbye to Mary and the ever-smiling butler. I laughed and drove towards the office. It would have been a brutal walk. The cold winter wind blew through Swan Street like a tornado and penetrated the warmest winter coat. The snow froze and cracked like ice with each step as the temperature dipped to a balmy three degrees. Thank God for the Hudson.

I decided I'd stop at Police Headquarters and speak with DeRosa to see if anything came up on the black Ford or if he turned up any witnesses before heading back to my office. I took the elevator to the third floor, walked in, and saw a pair of size eleven shoes looking at me. Wearing those highly polished shoes was one Stanley Kovak, sleeping with his head resting on the back of his chair and a burned-out cigarette still between his unsuspecting fingers. I just couldn't let sleeping dogs lie so I walked by him ever so quietly and lit the end of his cigarette. It started up again and I walked away.

Tom was looking at a folder intently; in fact he never even bothered to look up. "Hello, Lou, feeling better today?"

"Not bad considering I got shot and my car was turned into a flaming ball of steel. Any luck with finding witnesses from last night?"

He shook his head "Nothing of any use. Everyone pretty much saw what you saw."

"I was afraid of that. What about Alice?"

He shook his head no again.

"Thanks, I'll be in tou—"

All of a sudden a blood-curdling scream echoed through Homicide. Tom jumped to his feet and ran towards the door to see what happened. I burst out laughing. I peeked out and saw Kovak slowly lifting himself off the floor. He kept staring at his fingers as I walked past him.

"Sleeping and smoking are a bad combination, Kovak, you could get burned, or worse, laughed at by your co-workers." I kept laughing as I walked by him and Kovak told me to in no uncertain terms to screw myself. Tom shook his head at me. He knew I was behind it but didn't say a word. He was laughing too hard.

***

I got to Marco's and made my way up to the office. I was exhausted. This had been a long couple of days. The case was also at a roadblock. There were no more clues, no more leads. The person I needed to tie it all up in a nice bow was laid up in a hospital bed because of my stupidity.

One thing was clear to me at that point: I had moved into uncharted territory on this case. I knew in my heart what was happening but needed to align all the facts with bullet-proof evidence to put the final nail in the coffin of Young and the Muellers.

Before I got back to work I needed to relax, and decided to lounge for a bit and listen to the radio with a nice cigar. I turned it on and caught part four of a five-part weekly series of "Yours Truly, Johnny Dollar."

I just sat back and listened to the radio. John Lund played Johnny Dollar, Insurance Investigator in the weekly radio serial. I loved it. I closed my eyes and listened for a while as my mind raced through the evidence and what my next move would be. I needed to find a new way to string everything together, especially if Alice never woke up.

Something beeped, and I opened my eyes. The device from Leary's body was sitting on my desk, and was lit up. Curious, I picked it up. Since it was cracked, I couldn't make out what it said. It started buzzing to the point it was almost shocking my skin. I set it down on the desk and it kept rumbling. Then my radio started to go crazy, getting static and the volume jumping all over the place. My head began to ache and the office began to shake. I stood to try and turn off the radio, but found myself on the floor, not able to gain any footing. The office continued to shake and everything started to go black. . . .

INTERLUDE

"*M*ajor Kruger was also a very cautious man, in addition to his sadistic nature," the Doc continued. "Most of the scientific work he commissioned was related to ways for him to stay ahead of the Allies and avoid capture, should the war turn against the Germans."

This is the information the tall man had been waiting for. He couldn't resist any longer. "So were you directly involved in the time-travel work?" He asked.

"So impatient, that is the trouble with you Americans," the Doc said. "I was moved off the team working on the project, so I did not see it finished. Though some of my formulas and experiments were used by the team."

"How does it work?"

The Doc, who had been sitting back in his chair, leaned forward and placed both of his hands, clasped together, on his desk. His smile was growing larger and larger as he continued to dive further into his story.

"Well, I'm not sure entirely. At the time it was all

theoretical, mind you. The team responsible, using all the data compiled from the leading physicists of the time, combined with their own research, thought they could open up a time portal to the future."

"How?" the tall man asked again.

The Doc pushed himself up from his chair, and walked over to an old chalk board in the corner of his office. He cleared off a small section, and proceeded to draw a diagram to explain the theory.

"Okay, consider time this straight line, here," he said, pointing. "Now, this shows time as linear." He then drew an arcing line from one spot on the line to another. "This line represents the portal. In theory it would allow someone to jump forward in time. Now, our science at the time only found this one portal, which leapt sixty years in the future. We theorized you could only move sixty years, never more, never less."

"So, if I were to use this now, I could jump forward in time sixty years. Could I come back to this time right now?"

The Doc shook his head. "Unfortunately it doesn't work that way. You cannot select a specific time. As I said, it is only a sixty-year window from which you can move back and forth in time."

"Okay, so obviously Kruger figured it out."

The Doc looked mildly surprised. "Why would you say that?"

Now it was the tall man's chance to smile. "Because I've personally seen it work."

2015

CHAPTER 18

BROTHERLY LOVE

"Y ou . . . lucky bastard . . . you don't . . . many . . . left."

I woke up, not knowing who was talking to me. I kept my eyes closed, until I felt a jab to my ribs. The pain was pretty severe.

"What the hell was that for!" I yelled out in pain. When I did finally open my eyes, I was greeted by Mike, my younger brother. He was smiling. I wasn't.

"Happy New Year's to you too," he said. "As I was saying, you are one lucky bastard. You don't have too many chances of escaping alive left."

When he said that, my memory, hazy as it was, started to come back. I was chasing some dirtbag down an alley, and he got the drop on me, kept kicking me and I refused to let go. Then the lights went out.

"How long have I been out?" I asked.

"A few hours. Brady brought you in, said he followed you

from his bar, worried about you. Found you face down in the snow, gripping this." He handed me an iPod. But as I grabbed it, it wasn't an iPod. Where have I seen this thing before?

"Damn thing won't turn on," Mike said. "I monkeyed around with it for a while, got nothing. Looks like the asshole broke it, along with your face and ribs."

My hand instinctively went to my face, and touched the cold aluminum of a nose splint. Every slight jostling caused the pain in my ribs to spike worse and worse.

"Good thing I was here to save your life again. You got one bruised rib, and it will be tender for a while. Nose was a clean break, should heal up fine, if not a bit crooked." Mike started laughing again. If he wasn't my brother, I'd probably kick his ass. Still might do it anyways.

He left, telling me he gave Joe Campanelli a call, and he should be there soon. I had just dozed off again when Camp showed up.

"What the hell, Lou, can't you get through a New Year's in one piece anymore?" Camp said.

"Fuck you, too," I said. God, I really hate this damn holiday.

Camp laughed. I'm glad I'm so amusing to all my friends and family. Maybe I should have been a comedian. At least then everyone wouldn't keep trying to kill me.

When he finally stopped laughing at my expense, Camp asked me what the hell happened. I tried to remember, and my concussed brain was struggling.

"I'm not quite sure, Camp," I said. "I was sitting in my office ... wait, a woman came in, and—"

"Liar."

"Dammit, Camp, let me think this through." He laughed again, the prick. "A woman came in, and needed help with something . . . and she was a beauty, but she looked familiar for some reason, even though I'd never seen her before. A case, she said, that involved me somehow. She had some letter from a crazy grandmother, then I told her to get lost."

"Now that sounds like the Lou I know. Only you would tell a beautiful woman to get lost when she is asking for your services."

"Whatever. I finally said to hell with feeling sorry for myself, so I went over to Finnegan's for a drink." As my brain recalled the previous night, I relayed what I could remember to Camp. From my conversation with Brady, to his old man needing to talk to me, to remembering the name of the woman—Ingrid—to Konger and his counterfeit bills he got from somebody called Leary, and talking to Woz from Secret Service.

He took a few notes, but said chances were the guy supposedly named Leary was long gone. He had already talked to Brady and Konger, and they couldn't provide any helpful information. He was interested in the connection of a biker gang to this new case I stumbled into, and his gut liked the River Rats as well.

Camp left after he had mined my memory for all its worth—not much, these days—and went home. I spent the rest of New Year's Day and the second at the hospital. Not like I had anywhere to go, so why not? It would give me more time to annoy my little brother and make him take care of me too.

As much as I hated New Year's Eve and the bad memories it brought, New Year's Day was just the opposite. Bowl games all day. What more could you ask for? Sitting back and relaxing while watching the best of the best was tradition. My favorite college football team, Boise State, was playing. I love watching them play because you never get the same-old same-old with them. So I had that going for me, despite what else was going on.

But I needed to make things right. No way could I leave Ingrid hanging like that, nor leave a case unsolved.

***

January 3rd. Eight a.m. I took a long, hot shower and tried to put together what facts I had. My ribs were still tender, but I had shed the nose splint. Thankfully the break hadn't caused raccoon-like black eyes.

The steam condensed on the shower door and using my finger as a pen I wrote on the glass. The steam stays on for about thirty minutes and I have two fifty-gallon hot water tanks, so I had a lot of time to think about what I had. Not to mention the hot shower and steam felt good.

As the scalding water cascaded over me, I stared at the shower door and tried to organize my thoughts. Though the fog created by the steam wasn't the only thing clouding my vision. I think I knew who was gunning for me now. The rest I was still having trouble figuring out. Maybe understand—or believe—is a better way to describe it. How do past and present connect? Where was this counterfeit money coming from?

I dried off, threw on a pair of sweats, and sat on the couch by the fire. My fireplace was a nice wood-burning stove with a big mantle, brick chimney, and an all-brick hearth. The fireplace threw off a ton of heat and on occasion heated my entire home when the power failed. And besides, it provided great atmosphere on a date.

My mind was still trying to focus on what was happening. I was chasing down some potential counterfeit bills while still on the force, but that was years ago. The funny money hadn't even crossed my mind until Ingrid showed up in my office with the fake bills. When running down the Leary character, I thought I knew him from somewhere else. . . .

My cell phone started buzzing on the table. Camp. I answered after a couple rings.

"What do you want?" I greeted.

"Nice, that's how you answer your phone? No wonder you're alone." Camp then proceeded to give me some details. He said Konger finally broke down, and told him what he was doing for the man called Leary. He had an old warehouse he was working out of down on Ganson Street, and needed someone to rewire the electric and outfit it with cable wiring for internet. It was all some big secret, to the point they even made Konger wear a blindfold when they brought him in there, so he never knew exactly where on Ganson the place was.

"And Lou, I also looked into this Leary character."

"Yeah, what'd you find."

"You're not going to like it."

"The suspense is killing me. Spill it already."

He paused for a minute before talking. "The only criminal I could find that fit the description from Konger and you, was one Thomas Leary."

"Great, go pick him up."

"Well . . . he's dead."

That couldn't be right. "What! Where was he found?"

"No, Lou, you're not getting it. He was murdered back in 1955, shot to the head, and left on the bank of the river in the shadow of the General Mills grain elevators."

I took it all in. "Come on, Camp, that can't be. It obviously can't be the same guy, then."

"I emailed you one of his old mug shots. You tell me."

I opened up my laptop, and opened up the email from Camp. The picture took a second to download, and I couldn't believe it. The mugshot was in black and white, but there was no doubt. That was the man who kicked me in the face.

"That's impossible. Maybe he's a kid . . . or a grand kid of this Leary in the photo?" I said, grasping at straws.

"Looked into that too," Camp said. "No known relatives. That's not definitive, but very hard to track down, unless we somehow find this guy."

We talked a bit more, but after a while I told Joe I had to go. All of this was making my head hurt. I decided to try and pack each of these confusing memories away in the back of my mind and focus on what was in front of me: protecting Ingrid. First I needed to apologize and make sure she still wanted me on the case. Not that it would stop me from finding out who put me in the hospital.

My gray suit accented with a deep-blue shirt and tie would do for this mea culpa. After putting it on and grabbing my overcoat I got in my car and headed downtown to Ingrid's place.

CHAPTER 19

RECOGNITION

O nce on route 5 I headed for the Skyway, which goes over part of the lake, and I decided to exit at Ohio Street. The General Mills plant was drawing me in. I pulled over and tried to picture in my head the scene of police cars and men all standing by the river at the discovery of Leary. I was at the side of the road for no more than a minute then continued down by the river to Ganson. Nothing clear came to me. With no real idea which warehouse Konger was in, there wasn't any way to know where the mystery man may be, short of staking it out.

I kept driving and finally got to Ingrid's home on the 800 block of Delaware Avenue. I pulled in the long driveway and parked by the massive oak front door. A huge man opened the door and I got déjà vu, like I knew him from somewhere . . .

"Do I know you?" I asked.

"Not sure, I'm George," the man said. "Can I help you?"

"Yeah, I'm here to see Miss Reitman, she hired me a few

nights back." Nothing wrong with a little white lie. I need to apologize, anyway, and let her know I'd do anything I could to keep her safe.

George led me to the library. He opened the beautiful stained-glass French doors . . . Have I been here before? It felt familiar, but it was different, more modern. As the door opened you could see the large fireplace glowing from the flames of the fire. Two of the walls were lined with bookshelves. One wall had a sixty-inch TV on it. By the last wall was a wet bar complete with a sink. It was like dying and going to heaven. The blue leather chairs were big enough to seat an army and between them was a beautiful antique oak table.

"Please, make yourself comfortable," George said. "Miss Reitman will be right in. Would you like a drink?"

"Thanks . . . George, I'll have a Diet Pepsi."

He left and I sat there alone watching the fire roar and thought of how the past and present were connected. I didn't notice that Ingrid had entered the library. She was in a tight-fitting blue dress that showed off every curve in her body. Man she was a knockout.

"What's this all about, Mr. Romoso?" She still had some anger from New Year's Eve.

"Well, Ingrid," I started. "I wanted to apologize. Things are just getting too weird for me, but I still shouldn't have treated you like that."

Ingrid didn't say anything, just continued to scowl.

"You are probably going to think I'm nuts, but I think your grandmother may have been part-way right. And because of that you are likely in danger. I may be a stubborn ass—"

"May?" She interrupted.

"Okay, I *am* a stubborn ass. She was digging into something that connects to our . . . her past. Something I didn't realize until yesterday."

She didn't say anything, but her body language had loosened some. That was a good sign. George came back in with my drink and took a seat. I started to explain about my investigation into the River Rats, and how it turned up empty, but I was still shot up and had to leave the force. Then I went into what had happened after she left me New Year's Eve. How the investigation grabbed hold of me when all I wanted was for it to go away. Ingrid loosened up more, and I could see some sympathy and regret in her body language. I told her it wasn't her fault. Even though it technically was, I didn't need to hurt my position anymore.

After getting through those details, I filled them in on Konger and Brady, then Thomas Leary, and how even though Leary was the man two eye-witnesses identified, he was found dead sixty years ago. Ingrid and George both looked skeptical now as well. Who could blame them? I still didn't quite grasp it myself.

It was making my head hurt, and sweat was forming on my brow. I was getting hot, maybe from the fire crackling in the hearth. Standing up, I walked over to the big window facing Delaware. I don't know why but I opened the window.

Ingrid yelled, "Are you nuts? Its three degrees outside, close that window!"

I heard her but ignored it. Recounting all the details in my head was one thing. Sharing them out loud, even *I* was ready to commit myself and throw away the key. Some cold air on my face would hopefully calm me down.

I stood by the side of the window and looked down. I couldn't believe what I was seeing. The barrel of a gun touched the ledge and then I screamed for everyone to hit the deck. George grabbed Ingrid and brought her to the ground. I jumped back, keeping my eyes on the window.

A bright orange and yellow flash leapt from the gun as the

shooter pulled the trigger. A split second later my gun was out. I fired and saw the gunman fall to the ground, followed by a scream. The shooting stopped. I must have hit him. I scrambled back to the window and saw him opening the door to a dark-colored vehicle. It looked eerily similar to the one circling my office the night before. If only I would have gotten the plates last night. Instead I wrote it off as some lost tourist trying to gamble. The car screamed out of the driveway and onto Delaware before I could catch the plates again. Damn.

I turned back to the room. "It okay, he's gone."

George helped Ingrid to her feet, no worse for wear. I checked the grounds and found nothing but one piece of evidence that was like striking gold in an abandoned mine. It was a Colt .45, lying on the snow-covered grass by the library window. I knew this gun. Not just the make, *this* exact gun. They were issued to officers in WWII. Where did I see one, though? It was recently . . . my head started to hurt again.

***

Lieutenant Joe Campanelli showed up with a couple of patrol officers. Camp said he would call the hospitals to be on the lookout for a white male with a possible bullet wound. If he came in for treatment he was to be called right away. No one was holding their breath on it working, but you got to cover all the bases.

A couple hours passed before the Homicide squad wrapped up its work and left, as did the patrol cars. There wasn't much in the way of evidence. Hopefully the CSU crew could pull some prints off of the Colt. Maybe we'll get lucky. There were three rounds fired from the .45 dug out of the wall. This was too strange. Two men, one who was supposedly sighted just the other day, murdered sixty years ago, and now possibly the same gun was used in an attempt on my life? I ran out to flag Camp down before he pulled out of the driveway. He rolled his window down.

"Lou, what the hell you doing? It's freezing out here."

"I kn-know," I managed, trying to catch my breath. "I j-just thought of something. Run the gun against all solved and unsolved murd—"

"You think I'm a rookie, Lou?" Camp interrupted.

"Of course I do, I did all the work when I was your partner." He smirked, I continued. "Widen your search. Bring it back to at least the fifties. That's an old gun, probably pre-World War Two."

He looked skeptical, but caught the look in my eye. It told him my gut was speaking. He learned during our time together as detectives to listen when it was talking.

"Leary?" I nodded yes. "Will do. And for the love of Christ, try to go at least the rest of the day without getting yourself killed, would you?"

I flipped him the bird, and Camp rolled his window up and backed out of the driveway. An uneasy feeling hit me. It didn't involve the case. I'd seen some pretty serious stuff in my years. No, it involved something a little more disturbing. What was happening to me?

***

January 4, 9:30 a.m. I woke up not sure where I was. I rubbed my eyes and looked around. The library. The fire was still burning. Man, it felt good. I sat up on the couch and noticed that my suit was washed, neatly pressed, and hung up. There was a note attached to the clothing so I got up and read it. George had taken care of my clothes and set some stuff out for me. I need to get myself a butler. And fast.

I walked to the bathroom and stood in the doorway totally in awe. The thing was huge. There was a sauna, a large steam shower, Jacuzzi—no, more like an Olympic-sized hot tub—two sinks, and enough cabinets for ten people. A shaving kit was laid out along with toothpaste and brush. I stepped into the shower which dwarfed mine, turned on the steam and hot water, and began to plan out my day.

After dressing I headed for the kitchen. The aroma of fresh-brewed coffee led the way. It reminded me when I was a kid and I walked down the coffee aisle of the old A&P. Fresh ground coffee beans. Can't beat it.

As we sat eating my phone rang. Campanelli. He had a ballistics report for me, and a possible lead on who did the shooting. I listened as he told me that the bullets fired were from a .45 and the gun we found was the gun they came from. Duh, I figured that already. What I wasn't ready for was the report on the prints of that gun.

"Lou you are not going to believe this. In fact, I don't believe it myself."

"What, Joe?"

"You just won't believe it."

"I will if you ever decide to tell me."

He sighed and finally said it. "The prints on that gun belong to an Irish gunsel from the mid-fifties. It's unreal, Lou. Unreal. Does the name Kevin Young mean anything to you?"

I got a fiery pain in the front of my head as Camp said the name. My cell phone slipped from my hand and my face must have flushed because Ingrid grabbed my arm and asked me if I was okay. What was that all about? Joe was yelling through the phone still. I bent down and picked it up.

"Joe, let me know if you get an address, or any address on this guy, anything at all."

"I don't know what you've got going on but keep me in the

loop."

I paused before asking, "What about the River Rats? Any progress with them?"

"Huh?" Joe was confused. "You think they are involved?"

My investigative mind was running wild. These goons trying to kill me were probably involved with the Rats. The Rats were branching into laundering and loan sharking, and doing it with counterfeit bills. Konger was paid for services rendered with the same bills. I don't believe in coincidences.

Unless . . . could the Rats have stolen the identities of old criminals, to help mask some of their operations? They were getting more sophisticated with their schemes. It was possible. Maybe they got hooked up with some hacker who would have no problem setting something like that up for them.

As I thought through it, this seemed much more likely, but also felt wrong.

"Hello, you there, Lou?"

I wasn't ready to drop my cards on the table just yet. Though maybe Camp could find a link and help me connect the dots. "They might be, what have you got?"

"Let me talk to Vice. I'll get back to you."

I hung up the phone, then told Ingrid and George to stay alert. Things were starting to happen fast and we had to be ready for whatever came at us next.

CHAPTER 20

EUREKA!

The temperature had taken a quick nosedive to about zero and the snow crackled beneath my feet. Froze my ass off walking out to the car. When I got there it was warm and toasty, though. That George. Seriously, where can I get myself a butler?

Before I left I made sure George knew not to let Ingrid out of his sight until I returned. He agreed. Mentioned he was a Marine MP, so there was no issue with Ingrid's safety.

Once inside I grabbed a Ditka from my car humidor, lit it and sat wondering what my next move would be. Snow began to gently fall as I pulled away from the curb. I had time to kill until Joe got back to me so I headed towards home. Instead of hitting the Skyway I was drawn to the empty lot that was once Mickey Finn's, an old bar that ran an illegal gambling and sports book operation back in the day. It was no secret, but for some reason everyone looked the other way on the gambling. Eventually it shut down after its owner, Kevin Young—the man whose prints just showed up on the gun used to shoot at me—disappeared following a riot at the bar.

It was quiet inside the car except for the crunching of the snow beneath my tires as I pulled to a stop. Nothing was left of Finn's. My parents and family would talk about the place often, and how immaculate the place was. Now it was reduced to a empty block, with wispy weeds browned from winter spiking up through piles of broken concrete. If Young is still around, where is he? Or if it's someone posing as him, would they still be using his old haunts as a continued cover of the persona?

Another thought hit me, though unrelated to Young. The History Channel's *Hitler's Money Men*. I had just seen someone who looked like myself in it a few days ago at the Box. At the time I got a bad headache and was sweating. Could it be related? I think it focused on bringing down a counterfeiting operation; I should have been paying better attention before I brushed it off. The man walking the bad guy out of the warehouse was eerily similar to me. Did I have an old relative who worked with the Feds? It was essential that I got a better look at that program.

A knock on my car window pulled me back. It was an old beat cop I'd known for twenty years. The knock grew louder as I shook the cobwebs from my head. Between knocks I heard, "Lou, Lou, you okay?"

I swung my head around, then rolled down the window. "Hey, Teddy, long time no see. How've you been?"

Ted Catalano was an old-time beat cop, about five foot nine, 225 pounds, and tough as nails. He'd been on the force almost forty years. His face showed the wear and tear the job had taken on him. Ted took things that happened on his beat very personal. He was my training officer when I got on the force after getting through the academy.

He was old school. He'd walk his beat and knew the

neighborhood like the back of his hand. The good, the bad, and the ugly. Deputy Commissioner could have been in his future, but he never took the tests. Loved being a beat cop too much.

"I'm good, Lou," Teddy said. "What brings you down here? I've been knocking on your window for a minute to get your attention. You okay?"

"Yeah, just trying to work a case and needed some alone time. Jump in, it's warm in here and a hell of a lot more comfortable than standing in the cold wind."

Teddy moved around the hood and slid into the passenger seat.

"Thanks. Can't sit long, just for a bit. You got an extra cigar?"

I smiled, opening my car humidor to let him pick one. Ted has great taste in cigars and took my last Liga Privada Churchill. He lit up and savored the taste and aroma. He seemed lost in thought and almost drifted asleep.

"What brings you down to this part of your beat?" I asked. "There is nothing but grass and snow here."

"The neighborhood's been complaining to me about strange noises and comings and goings here. The community here is tight and they talk. So they asked me to attend a meeting they had at the Irish Community Center to tell me what's been going on. So I went."

"What'd they tell you?"

"Lou, it's crazy, and you probably won't believe that I even entertained this. Hell, I am having trouble with it myself. There's some new activity that has been going on in the old Ganson warehouses."

I grimaced, my ribs giving me a quick jolt of pain at the mention of Ganson. "Yeah, I found that out the hard way."

"Heard about that," Teddy said. "Never thought one of my trainees would ever let some punk get the drop on him." He laughed a bit, then got back to his story. "Anyways, the older residents, they think they've even seen some of the old guys from the Ward."

"From the old casino? Their rascals got snow tires on them?" Now I let out a chuckle.

"No, no, they ain't old, they look just like they did in the old days, from Mickey Finn's in the fifties. But different, you know? Like they are pale, almost ghost-like."

I paused for a moment before talking. Then got an idea. "Do the names Thomas Leary or Kevin Young mean anything to you?"

Teddy about dropped his cigar. He's lucky he didn't; he'd be on the hook for repairing my leather seats. "Yes! Those are a couple of the old gunsels from back in the day. The old people mentioned those two specifically. I was getting to the point of writing them all off and calling the psych ward, since I myself thought I caught a glimpse of Leary a week ago. And I know he's been dead forever. They found him out by the grain elevators."

"Believe it or not, they aren't crazy," I said. "Same thing happened to me. So you're not a customer for the looney bin. I'm working a case, and both of those names have popped up."

"Lou, if you are involved it has to be crazy. All you *do* is crazy." Ted let out a laugh and took a hit of his cigar.

"You were around in the fifties, Ted, do you remember the casino at all?"

"I was only five or so when it opened. Best thing to hit the Ward since that first grain ship pulled up to the docks. See that back there?" He pointed to the back of the lot. "Used to be a hidden driveway leading around the back and underneath Finn's. An old basement garage. Not many knew about it. Me and some of the other youngsters in the area would ride our bikes all around the place, since they wouldn't let us in. That prick, Steve . . . Sam . . . no, Sean, that's it. He was head of valet, and he would always kick us off the property."

Ted took a puff of his cigar and thought some more. He had nothing else to add about the casino. We had a few laughs and I told him not to be a stranger, gave him my cell number and that I'd meet him at Finnegan's next week for a drink.

I knew I'd never have that drink with him. That was Teddy. He stayed pretty much to himself, and now so more than ever since his wife died a few years ago of cancer. His kids were grown and out of town and all Ted had was his work.

He rolled down the window threw out the butt of his cigar, got out, and zipped up his jacket. Said goodbye and headed for his patrol car. His breath lingered as its warmth and the chilly air collided. I could hear the snow give way underneath his boots as he walked away. He stopped to turn around and wave goodbye. Later, my old friend.

***

I looked at my watch wondering when Joe would come up with something. Might as well try to find a spot to watch that History Channel special. I put the car in drive and headed back to the office, only about five minutes away. I hoped I could get it on Hulu, Netflix, or some other streamer. I slowly pulled around the building, looking in my rearview mirror to see if I had been followed. No one was going to catch me with my pants down again. This case had made me extra cautious. So far so good.

I pressed my garage remote and the big door slowly rolled up like a medieval gate opening to let in the castle guards. My eyes darted back and forth looking for anything unusual or out of place. The garage held fifteen cars and mine took five spots. Since I owned the building no one was bitching. I had a spot for my 1968 Mustang Shelby, Lincoln MKS, 1932 Lincoln, Cobra A/C, and my Bentley. No, the Bentley wasn't new, but it was nice. I always wanted one, and since business has been good I rewarded myself.

The garage was empty except for my cars. I parked near the doorway and got out, hand on my gun just in case. I hopped on the elevator and headed upstairs. Everything was in its place in my office. It felt good to be back in there. I sat back in my nice leather chair, grabbed the remote and scanned the TV for the documentary. Luckily the History Channel had it on demand.

Sitting back I relaxed and started the show. It was about Hitler's finance minister, Johann Ludwig von Krosigk, and his quest to make Germany a world economic power. The Third Reich was failing and they had to do something drastic. That's when they came up with the idea to take down the monetary systems of the United States and Great Britain by counterfeiting their currencies, rendering their economies useless. Krosigk appointed Bernhard Kruger to head up this operation. The money was virtually flawless, except for the paper. If Germany had not collapsed, the plan could have taken down the two super powers of that time.

The documentary was good and informative and got very interesting when pictures of Kruger popped up on the screen. I almost fell out of my chair. I'd seen that man before . . . but that wasn't Kruger . . . why did I know him? My headache started to return.

I stood up and splashed some cool water on my face from the sink, determined to not allow my brain to continue hurting. The pain that gripped me was subsiding, and I hit play on my remote.

The documentary continued to explain what was happening to Kruger and the others involved in Operation

Bernhard. Supposedly he, his wife, and his brother had seen the writing on the wall at the end of the war and split without a trace. That is until the mid-1950s. However, just as the narrator was going to lay out how the man was finally caught, the picture and sound became grainy and garbled. I smacked my cable box to stop it from being fuzzy. That did nothing, just hurt my hand and made it worse.

All I could make out were two people walking towards a camera from an old warehouse. One was a guy who looked exactly like Kruger, but I wasn't sure. There was no doubt about the second. Save a few pounds—okay, maybe more than a few—missing from action, I was staring right into my own face.

All at once the ache returned to my noggin like water bursting from a damn. The sweat dripped from my brow. The room started to spin, and I fell to the floor in what felt like slow motion. I don't remember smacking the ground—I was out before it even came to that.

CHAPTER 21

SHOOT-OUT AT THE L.R. CORRAL

My eyes opened, slowly, and I was staring at the ceiling. I blinked a few times. Gradually everything was coming back. My head was still hurting, but it was more of a dull ache now. My concussion must be worse than originally thought. Was that really me on the screen walking the bad guys out? I don't believe it. There's no way that's possible. Must be someone who happened to look like me—*exactly* like me.

After another minute or two I eased up to a sitting position, then hauled myself up using my desk as a handhold. The TV screen was back to the on demand home screen, so I turned it off and plopped back down in my leather chair to think.

I poured and finished a drink, then refilled the glass and sat back. An unlit cigar lay on my desk astray, so I picked it up and started to chew on it. I tend to do that when I'm deep in thought.

The money . . . the counterfeit bills were tied to this Kruger fellow. I opened up my laptop and did a search on him. There wasn't much. He was operating in Western New York at the time of his bust, where he was brought down by a couple Feds working in a task force of sorts with BPD. Maybe if I see Teddy again I can ask him if he remembers anything about it, or possibly Camp can pull some old files. According to reports, they don't think they ever recovered all of the cash Kruger and his cronies had managed to print before getting taken down. Is it possible the Rats or their new partners stumbled across the secret stash of cash somewhere?

The only way to solve this thing was to take down the River Rats. There was no other way, unless these supposed 1950s thugs came into my office and confessed. That was about as likely as winning the lottery; I couldn't bank on it, even as a gambling man. Instead, if we were able to get to the Rats, somehow drive a wedge between them and their new partners, it could work. Or, if it was the Rats themselves posing as these old-timers, even better. Then we only had to bring down one crew.

Something in my gut told me it was all going to come to a head soon.

I called Joe and he said he had something for me on the River Rats, that he'd stop by with it. Good, maybe we could get to them with this new information. I also told Ingrid to have George bring her. Everyone was to meet at my office at 5 p.m.

***

The big grandfather clock in my office began to ring as the chimes struck the appointed witching hour. They rang out five times as I sat at my desk waiting for the office door to open.

Apparently promptness was not a strong suit for these people. Fashionably late must be their mantra. Ten after five and the door came ajar as the first guest showed up.

It was Campanelli, and he wanted answers. "Tell me, how did you know to look at the Rats?"

"Don't get your panties in a bunch," I said. "Before we start, let's wait on George and Ingrid. Don't feel like explaining everything twice. You want a drink?"

"Yeah. Vodka and cranberry, splash of soda."

I pointed to the side wall. "The bar is right over there, help yourself."

"Some fucking host you are!"

Camp relented and made himself a drink.

"While we wait," Camp said, "take a look at this. It's Kevin Young's jacket, from back in the fifties. Had to do some serious digging to find this in the archives."

I looked through it, and he had a bunch of minor run-ins with the law. He was still wanted for a connection to some counterfeiting ring, but had been MIA for the past sixty years, and was assumed dead. The photo showed a rough customer: blond, thick shouldered, and a mean disposition. He looked like someone I know. . . .

Camp's pacing about the room distracted me. He was getting impatient and wanted to know what was going on and where the hell was the rest of this impromptu party.

I couldn't blame him as I was getting pissed off myself. I reached for my phone on the desk and began to dial Ingrid's cell phone when my office door opened. She and George finally made it. I stood up from behind my desk and walked toward Ingrid, pissed they were half an hour late. Apparently they failed to realize my time is just as valuable as anyone else's on this frigging planet.

Ingrid was about to say something, but I was in no mood

to listen to her or anyone else.

"Glad you could make it. Right on time, I see," I said.

Ingrid could see that I was pissed. Well, it didn't really take a genius to see that, but she continued on anyway.

"Well, hotshot, if you'd just calm down I'll tell you why were late!"

That didn't sound good. Maybe they had a valid reason to be late. Oh well, I was going to get an excuse anyway so I might as well listen.

"I'm all ears."

"So is an elephant!" Ingrid let out.

I had to admit, it was a good shot, so I kept my mouth shut for a second. "Well go ahead regale us with your story, Miss Queen of Ice."

As I said I kept my mouth shut for a second, then promptly got myself in deeper shit with her. Ingrid shot me a dirty look.

Before she could start in on me George spoke up. "Well, Detective, as we were coming down Delaware, I made the left onto North. A black Mercedes was following me some ways back. So I decided to see if he was truly following me or if I was paranoid. Miss Reitman told me to hurry because she knew you'd bitch up a storm—her words, not mine. I just laughed. So I told her that we might be getting followed. Miss Reitman said to be sure, and we were. The last I saw of the Mercedes was when I made the turn onto Carroll from Swan Street."

Damn, if this guy is as good as he seems, we may be in trouble. I decided to look at my security cameras around the building and dammit if he wasn't right. Four men were walking slowly around the building. The entrance would be open since I changed the time on the door lock to 6 p.m. from 5 p.m., to make sure everyone could get in without me having to go downstairs and play doorman.

Shit.

I turned the monitor around so everyone could see. Camp and I were on the same page. He made a call to get the cavalry moving, but they would be at least a few minutes out. Ingrid got in the walk-in gun safe for protection in case shots were fired. George refused. Instead he grabbed one of the shotguns. This was not going to be pretty. Ingrid, for once, didn't give me an argument over my plan.

Plan? What plan, you ask? Exactly. Other than protecting Ingrid, I had none. We had the slight edge on them because we knew they were coming, when they looked to be banking on the element of surprise. Other than the fire escape, though, we had no other way out. Custer had a better shot at Little Big Horn. I heard the elevator doors open—don't ask me how because I can't hear women talking to me half the time. Shit, you're right, that's selective hearing, not deafness.

We flipped my big roll-top desk over for cover. It was over two inches thick, and would provide pretty good protection. Joe and I were behind the desk; George went behind the bar. I told him to stay down and not lift his head until the shooting stopped. When it did, come up ready to shoot.

Their footsteps grew louder and louder as they closed in on my office. The building was usually empty at this hour and the sound carried quite well. My office, as I said, was the corner office on the second floor. There are eleven other offices, mine being the biggest. Why not, it's my building. They are all located on the outside wall with the middle being open so you can look down at the giant fountain on the first floor. There is a walkway around the entire second floor, forming a big square.

My office has a glass lobby, where my secretary, if I had one, would sit. There is a desk out there just in case. It also serves as a waiting room complete with TV and a stocked fridge for my clients' comfort. The furniture is blue leather and large enough for men to sit in, not like most furniture today designed for the weight challenged. I like my clients comfortable and happy. When they're happy they spend money, and when they spend their money on my agency I'm happy.

The footsteps grew louder and stopped all of a sudden. I looked at Joe and nodded. The action would start any second. The sensor sounded on the outside door, a chime to let me know I have a client. In walked our unsuspecting would-be ambushers. As they neared the door to my office they let go a volley of artillery fire that would have made Patton proud. They sprayed my office with enough lead to make any lawyer happy to accept my case for lead poisoning. The thick, oak desk provided enough cover to keep us safe from the onslaught, though. They kicked in what was left of my office door and entered.

As we hid behind the desk I motioned one, two, three with my fingers to Joe. As soon as the third finger showed itself we rose and fired everything we had. The merry band of assassins were caught by surprise. Bullets peppered the four men dressed in biker gear. Their bodies contorted every which way with each bullet that found its mark. They managed to get a couple shots off, but they were nowhere near the mark. Joe and I dipped back behind the desk and George dealt the final blows. He emptied the shotgun into what was left of the four bikers. One by one they dropped to the floor with the look of horror and pain etched on their faces forever. Blood and wood splinters and broken glass were everywhere.

We checked ourselves for gunshot wounds but we were lucky. Except for cuts and scratches from the flying splinters we were untouched. Time had slowed down during the shooting. In reality, the whole thing took maybe five seconds from when they kicked in the door.

Ingrid stepped out of the safe a minute or so after the last shot, working up the nerve to see who won. She was in shock at the carnage. I went over to her with a reassuring hug. She started to cry. I'm pretty sure it wasn't for the dead assholes on the floor.

Campanelli was back on his phone with dispatch. The place was a mess. I examined the dead men and recognized the insignia on their bullet-riddled leather.

The River Rats.

Half of their main crew was on the floor of my office. Mark "Mad Man" Walsh, age thirty-eight, six foot five, 375 pounds, black hair and beard. His eyes stared up at us with a cold, eerie glaze. Nobody home there. Thomas "Rat" Mann, the smallest and oldest of the four, forty-six years old, six foot two and 225 pounds, white handle bar mustache and blue eyes like an Alaskan huskie. "Diamond" Lou O'Shea, six foot four, 295 pounds, a former bodybuilder who got busted dealing steroids and served a few years at Wendy Correctional Facility. He was thirty-seven, clean shaven, and nuttier than a fruitcake. All those years on the juice ruined his brain. Last was Francis "Fat Boy" McDuggle, forty-three, six foot three, four hundred pounds, shaved head and a long, black beard ala ZZ Top. A big man. Several who thought he was fat and slow were shocked to learn that a man this size had the reflexes of a cat. They all misjudged him and paid the ultimate price. That is until now.

These men were mean and tough and did nothing for free. Thankfully they decided to use guns and not their fists. Guns gave us the edge, no doubt about it. They didn't just murder people for the hell of it. It was a business to them, and who ever paid them, paid plenty. Joe rummaged through the pockets and pulled out wads of money.

A voice in the back of my head told me to ask Joe if I could look at the money. He shrugged his shoulders and handed me a stack of bills. I looked at the money, rubbed it between my fingers, and then put the cash up to my nose and took a giant whiff. A smiled crossed my face, as I smelled that all too familiar odor. The dates were right, too: 1954. I took a bill from my wallet, rubbed it, and then rubbed the bill Joe had given me. A slight difference, but *very* slight.

I told Campanelli that I believed the money was counterfeit and I may have known the man who was responsible. "We need to get Woz from Secret Service on the phone if we can, bring him in," I said.

The first of the patrol cars rolled up to the scene. Officers Watson and Houghton came in with guns drawn. As they entered the room you could see the look of surprise on their face. They were veteran officers who had been on the force for fifteen years. I knew them both. We exchanged hellos and they asked Campanelli what in the hell happened.

Joe filled them in as the rest of the patrols, Homicide, and the evidence team arrived. IAD, the Internal Affairs Division, also made an appearance since it was an officer-involved shooting. Joe turned over his gun, as was procedure. I volunteered mine and the shotgun George used. I had plenty more, so I grabbed another out of my safe. Felt better to have that familiar weight with me.

They placed crime-scene tape around the offices and closed off the building. The coroner was outside waiting for the teams to finish. I looked out my window and saw several news trucks out there. Channels Two, Four, and Seven and YNN News were all waiting for Harry DeSoto, the Police spokesman, to come out and make a comment. They were pissed it was taking so long—no one was going to make the six o'clock and would have to wait until the late broadcast.

I placed a call to my contractor, Jim Pauly, to have emergency repairs done and to start the restoration of my office. It looks like I'm paying for his daughter's wedding by the time all the work is done.

Thank God my building has more than one way out. George snuck Ingrid through the parking garage, thus bypassing all the news trucks and various other media. Joe and I decided to walk out with the Homicide boys and get deluged with questions as we walked by. We knew most of the media, and as usual gave them a "no comment." As we brushed by them a courageous brunette was waiting for us around the corner. She was Ashley Whittaker, the crime reporter for the *Buffalo News*. Ashley stood about five foot nine, had an hourglass figure. She was divorced with a daughter and quite intelligent. She was like a dog on a bone and wouldn't quit until she had the complete story. This was bad for us because she and Joe had an on-again-off-again relationship. So sooner or later Joe was going to be dropping a few hints to her.

"Lieutenant Campanelli, can you tell me what happened here tonight?" she asked. I don't know if she was formal for my benefit or not. Half the force and the news world knew all about the two.

"Ashley, you know I can't."

"Come on, what happened?"

"No comment, Ashley!"

She turned to me. "How about you, Romoso, any comment?"

"No comment." I said.

This continued as we walked toward the parking garage. The other reporters saw what was going on and rushed down the street to see if they could get in on the action. Campanelli stuck to his guns and said nothing. I slid my swipe card into the door. Ashley held her thumb and pinky fingers apart put them to her head and whispered to Joe to call her. How romantic. He pushed me into the garage and I began to laugh.

His car was down the street. I'd drop him off to get his car later.

I decided to take my Bentley. None of the media knew that car so there was less chance to be followed by them. Also, more River Rats may be lurking out there and chances were they didn't know this car, either. We got in and I started to reach for a cigar but remembered I don't smoke in any of my cars but the Lincoln. Damn! I looked at Tom and he just shook his head laughing knowing how bad I wanted a cigar. So he decided to throw me a shot, as good friends often will.

"Sucks, doesn't it?"

"Go fuck yourself, lover boy! Why don't you just marry her and get it over with."

He went somber real fast. "You know why."

Lieutenant Joe Campanelli was divorced with one son. His wife Marie divorced him after I got shot. She was a stunning woman and loved him very deeply, but she couldn't take not knowing if he would ever come home after work. It worried her sick. They were still great friends and still go out and Joe gets to see his son whenever he wants. Basically they still love each other. Joe wasn't going to quit, and she wasn't going to stop worrying, so they split. She didn't want his pension or child support because she knew Tom would always take care of their son and her pension was just as good as his. They split their assets fifty-fifty and are happier now than they were married. For some reason she accepts his job more now than before. Women. Go figure. It was too bad, they had everything going for them. Maybe one day they'll get back together.

"If you're so good at romance, numb nuts, why didn't you marry Lynn?" He shot back. "You remember, the one who worked at the private college and wanted to get married and you had more excuses than Carter had liver pills and put it off, until she got tired of it. She was perfect for you! Remember?"

He had me there. I screwed that one up big time. So I sat

there and took my medicine. We looked at each other and laughed. We were both losers when it came to matters of the heart. But life goes on.

As we drove around to where Joe's car was parked we saw the black Mercedes that followed George and Ingrid. I slowed down and Joe got the plate. He called it in to have them run the number. We didn't have to wait long.

"Thanks, Steve," Joe said into the phone. He hung up and filled me in. "It's registered to KYMF Enterprises, located on Michigan Avenue. Reported stolen last night."

"Perfect."

I dropped him back at his car. As much as Camp didn't want to, he had to return to the scene. He would have a lot of paperwork and interviews to do with IAD. Joe seemed relaxed despite having no control over things. He would let the chips fall where they might. Joe was good at that.

Not me. I hate not being in control. And that's where I was, mostly helpless to what was happening around me.

CHAPTER 22

OLD MAN FINNEGAN

I needed a drink. I wasn't ready to go home. Not yet, anyways. It was only 8:30 p.m. My nerves needed to calm down before I could even think about sleep. Since my office was blown to bits and crawling with cops and reporters, the only other option close by was Finnegan's.

After the short drive I pulled in and went inside. Brady was there, and immediately asked how I was holding up after the shooting. Damn, word certainly travels fast around here. The shooting just happened!

"How'd you hear about that so quick?" I snapped.

"Easy, big fella, your grumpy ass was just on the television, hustling away from cameras outside your building," Brady said.

I offered no more than a grunt, and ordered a cranberry and vodka. "And keep them coming," I said to Brady's back.

My phone buzzed. A text from Joe. The River Rats' clubhouse was deserted, and had been for at least a couple days, it appeared. They must have known this was going down and they sent everyone into hiding. If only things could have played out differently and we had announced ourselves before the shooting started . . . no, I can't play that game with myself. No good could come from it.

"Well if it isn't the gunslinger himself, in the flesh," I heard from behind me. The voice was aged, but there was still strength in it. I turned to see old man Finnegan. He was still a tall man, but the years had stooped his shoulders. He was also way thinner than I remembered.

"Where's the rest of you?" I asked.

"Doctor's orders," he said with a laugh. "They told me if I didn't get my act together, there wouldn't be any more acting."

Brian must be pushing ninety-five by now. Hell, he was already an old man when Brady was born. He was still solid and big and had a commanding presence, despite walking with a cane, the result of chronic pain from an old injury to his hip, something he would never talk about. He wore a black beret like his son, a long black western duster, and the same orange Converse sneakers as Brady.

He stepped forward and put a hand on my shoulder. It was a meaty paw, and still looked like it could do some damage if Brian had it in him to make a fist and take a swing at you. "Come on, Lou, come back to my office. There are things we need to talk about."

That was the last thing I wanted to do. But the old man said it in a tone that didn't leave any wiggle room for arguing. I had stood him up last time I was here. Might as well get this over with.

"Are you coming too?" I asked Brady as I got up from the bar. He kept wiping the bar down and shook his head no.

The old man led me into his, ahem, office. It was as big as a house. Floor-to-ceiling bookshelves on two walls, a real fireplace, bar, private bathroom complete with shower and spa. The office also had its own kitchen and dining room. Expensive stone work surrounded the fireplace. There was a giant mantle over the fireplace that had many pictures lined up on it. The furniture was all leather and large so big guys can actually sit in comfort. Can't believe they never invited me back here before.

As I slid into a chair he started right into it.

"Well, things around here are getting weird."

I took a sip of my vodka and cranberry rubbed my chin with my hand. "You can say that again," I said.

"Tell me about the case you are working on," Brian said.

I took another sip of my drink and dove in. It's hard to believe all that had happened in the past few days. I started with Ingrid showing up at my office, then backing up to the last case I worked with BPD, and how the money was likely from the same counterfeiter. I'm sure he knew about my run-in with the thug on Ganson, but not from my point of view.

I wrapped up with the details of the shooting at my office. Brian sat quiet for quite some time. His eyes were closed. Great, the old man fell asleep during my story. I wasn't going to tell him everything again.

Then he stirred, and opened his eyes, right on me. "What do you know about Kevin Young?"

I shrugged. "A whole bunch of nothing, other than he was a fifties gangster who ran a casino here in the First Ward, and disappeared without a trace."

"Yeah, he was always good at that," Brian said, then gave a short, sad chuckle.

"Wait . . . what? You know—knew him?" I stammered.

"How's your head?" Brian asked, changing the subject.

"Huh? Fine, other than a few headaches," I lied. "Now don't go avoiding the question, not now, not when I'm close to solving this thing."

"It all ties together, Lou. And it's quite complicated." He paused again, as if collecting himself to face some monumental task. "Ingrid, not the one who hired you, but her grandmother. Her and I were close friends."

"Is that why her note told me to speak with you?" I asked. I still wanted to press him on Kevin Young, but Brian was nothing if not stubborn. He would tell me in his own way.

He nodded. "She came to me with some of the counterfeit bills, and was worried it was all happening again."

"What, a counterfeiting ring led by some old geezer?"

Brian let out the same sad chuckle as before. "Yes and no. To get back to your original question, I do know him—Kevin— and knew him back in the day as well. That's because we are related. He's my brother."

"Bullshit." But as I thought about it, I looked harder at Brian, and thought of Brady. The blond hair—though Brian was now all white—goatee, large build. The mug shot I had of Kevin Young, even though it was black and white, showed an uncanny resemblance.

I got up and started to move about the room. Brian remained quiet. On the mantel above the fireplace were a number of pictures. I saw Mr. Finnegan in his younger days. One showed him and another who could have been his twin— and was also the same person in Kevin Young's mugshot.

Seriously? I turned to Brian, who motioned me to turn around. "Keep looking," he said.

I did. I went down the line, and saw something that defied all logic. One picture of Brian was with, of all people, me—a younger, thinner me, the person in the History Channel special. My drink fell to the floor as I examined one picture after another. My head was pounding once more, much worse than any of the other episodes. I couldn't believe my eyes, but there we were as plain as day.

Brian and this impossible look-alike were dressed in UB college football gear smiling and laughing. I moved over to the next group of photos. Brian was dressed in a formal Navy outfit and fake-me was in an Air Corps uniform. The next photo was of a beautiful blonde holding hands with my body double. I—he—was wearing a black tux and she was in a white wedding dress. Standing next to the couple in his tux was Brian, apparently the best man.

I staggered backwards and fell into a nice big and soft leather chair. I was in shock. How could this be? Then everything went dark.

***

A voice and a splash of cold water brought me back. "Lou, Lou, are you okay?" It was Brian.

Where was I? That's right, in the old man's office. I had passed out again. This shit was getting *really* old. I couldn't keep blacking out like this.

"Yeah, yeah, I'm fine," I lied. "What the hell is going on here, Brian? Why am I in—I mean, why is there some person who looks *identical* to *me* in all those pictures?"

The old man walked over to the bar and made himself a Scotch and soda. He also made me a new Vodka-cranberry. I took a stiff gulp of my drink and pounded it down my throat. The burning of the alcohol temporarily made me ignore the throbbing in my head.

The old man said nothing, just kept circling the office. He walked by me and took the empty glass from my hand and refilled it. He walked by me again and gave me my drink, never saying a word. I was getting impatient, and in case you hadn't noticed it's another one of my finer attributes.

Finally, I had had enough. "Will you please stop pacing and tell me what the hell is going on!"

I got up off the chair, a little uneasy on my feet. Staggering over to the fireplace, I needed to look at those pictures again. It also served to avoid grabbing the old man and shaking him, which I was close to doing. The picture of the gorgeous blonde was staring me in the face. I just stood and stared back, and then Brian's voice broke the silence.

"Beautiful, isn't she?"

I said nothing. My head was pulsating again, but I steeled myself and refused to go down again. There was such a familiarity about her, but as much as I searched my memory banks, nothing came to me.

"Lou, I know this is a shock to you, as it was for me, but believe me when I tell you this, you were a good man and husband to Ellen."

I remained silent. Ellen? There was a deep pain within me, a staggering sense of loss. I wasn't sure I could keep it together if I opened my mouth, and still didn't know the reason.

"Silence, shutting out the world, it's always been your method of operation," Brian said from behind me. "Women would get close and you'd do something to push them away. Ellen found a way in. You have to finally let that go if you are going to make it through this time."

I eyed my drink and played with the glass in my hand. A few minutes passed before I turned to Brian. "What the hell is going on? What do you mean she was my *wife*? I have no recollection of who she is."

Brian looked confused now. "Strange . . . I thought the connection had already been made."

"Connection? What the hell are you talking about?"

"I wish I had a reason why this is happening to you, but I don't," Brian said. "The questions you ask might create more questions."

"Try me. There is so much going on right now, whatever you say can't make it more confusing. My head is all jumbled up. I need to know all that you can possibly tell me. You've got to help me. Otherwise, I'm going to get myself fitted for a straitjacket and a padded room."

The brown eyes of the old man I knew began to flicker to life like a huge weight was going to be lifted off his shoulder. He smiled and began to spin his yarn.

"You are a time traveler. No, stop. Don't protest, and don't ask me how I know. Just know it's true. All the pieces you need to solve the case are there. In fact, the you in the past is working the same exact case, involving the same—"

But—"

"Lou, what the hell did I just say?" He paused and shook his head. "I guess the best place to begin is with Kevin Young. He's my brother and I loved him. I hate what he's become and what he's done.

"After what happened so long ago I thought he was gone from my life. He disappeared without a trace, and was thought dead. I was finally done with the shame and embarrassment he brought to our family. He reappeared a few years ago. However, rather than being an old man like me, he was still young. Something was off about him, though, like a piece of him was missing. His eyes were cold and empty."

"Wait a second, Brian," I said. "What are you saying? That Kevin can travel in time too? That makes zero fucking sense!"

Brian pointed to the mantle above the hearth. "And yet you are here, and you saw for yourself the evidence in the photos."

Nothing came to mind on how to respond. "Okay, fine. If he's figured it out, how the hell am I doing it?"

"No answer for you there, only that you are different

somehow," Brian answered. "Kevin doesn't have memories like you do."

"Huh?"

"He is still Kevin Young, nineteen-fifties gangster when he time travels. You, for some reason, had lives both now and in the fifties. That I cannot explain. A connection has been made . . . or will be made between you and the version of you in the past."

What the hell? If I had any sense about me I would make good on my threat and go straight to the looney bin and commit myself to that padded room. But I sat there and listened as Brian continued.

"When Kevin first showed up I about had a heart attack. Every day I had thought about him and what I may have done different to prevent all the bad things he'd done. Now he was here before me again. I half-thought I was going senile and this was all happening in my head, so I grabbed him by the throat. I felt my hands squeezing his throat tighter and tighter. He was turning blue and I didn't care. He refused to fight back. I almost killed him that day. Then out of nowhere his gang, the three bags of assholes you know well, pull me off of him. You had a personal encounter with Leary.

"Kevin apologized for everything that happened in the past. He was starting up again, and wanted to know if I wanted in. It took everything I had not to go after him again, even as an old man."

"You obviously said no, right?" I couldn't imagine Brian as a criminal. But then again, my imagination was never that great.

"I hemmed and hawed, but decided to take him up on it. I wanted all in, no holding back. So long as it didn't touch Finnegan's. I brought in Brady as well."

My anger was creeping up. "What the hell, Brian? What

are you trying to tell me, that I need to take you both down?"

"Nothing of the sort." He stood up with a bit of difficulty, leaning heavily on his cane. His desk was only a few short paces away, but it seemed to take forever. He took a key from his pocket and unlocked the bottom drawer. Within he pulled out a flash drive and tossed it to me.

"Everything you need to know about Kevin's latest dealings. From what I've heard, sounds like you know of the connection to the River Rats already. I'm old, Lou, and know I don't have that much longer. That's why I wanted Brady involved. If I died without gathering enough evidence against Kevin, he would've been able to continue on with no one to stop him."

My fury seceded, but only a little. They should have talked to me immediately. But would I have believed them? I would have thought both of them nuttier than I think of myself right now.

With my office shot to hell, I had no computer to look at the material he just gave me. "Brian, I'm so sorry. I wish I could do something."

"You'll figure it all out. As you know, the old casino is gone. I had it torn down. I didn't want any reminders of that God-awful place. I started Finnegan's Pub and it became a huge success—all legal, mind you.

"I changed my name soon after everything went down in the fifties. I had to. I certainly didn't want to be associated with my brother's reputation and knew I would not be able to get a liquor license being related to him. So I changed my name and stayed off the radar. I made enough money with all my business ventures and invested quite well. As a matter of fact, you gave me quite a few good tips at the track and on bowl games. So I did okay."

"Great, you got rich and I made a few lousy bucks. I could

always count on you for comfort, Brian."

We both laughed despite the situation. There were so many more questions I had to ask, though had no idea where to start. How did he know all of this? What wasn't he telling me?

Brian made us a couple more drinks. Brady came back into the office. I gave him a long look, but as hard as I tried I couldn't be mad at him. In the same situation I'd likely have done the same, and probably without the same cunning.

My phone started ringing: Campanelli.

"Hey, Joe, what do you got for me?"

"Nothing good. The rest of the Rats are in the wind, no trace of them. I'll let you know if anything else turns up. How are you doing?"

Should I tell him about the bombshell just dropped on me? Something I am having trouble grasping myself? No way, not until I can get everything straight. "I'm good, keep me posted."

I hung up and polished off my fourth drink. I'm not sure it was helping my mental capacity to grasp the situation, but it was doing its job in numbing the pain.

I told them about the Rats. Brady looked at me with that little smirk of his. "Trouble finding those little biker mice? You just need the right block of cheese."

CHAPTER 23
THE HIDDEN CLUBHOUSE

Brady, Brian, and I drove around the old First Ward. Looking for what, I don't know. They wouldn't tell me. Maybe it was just to calm me down, or just to build up more anger. If that was possible.

We cruised slowly down South Park, passing some old businesses that I used to go to as a kid. On the left was Reccio's Bowling Alley. My father and uncle bowled there for years, from the early fifties to the early nineties. They won a lot of money with their bowling skills. My uncle said he never gambled because he only bet on himself. I think Pete Rose used that defense.

Across the street was the Sorrento Cheese factory that previously was Mangano's Bakery. When we were kids my mother and grandmother took us there to buy bread. There was nothing like fresh, hot bread right out of the oven, especially when the butter melted into it. They also had the best peanut stick donuts and chocolate French crullers.

I pulled out a cigar from my pocket, lit it, and warmed my hands with the flame of the lighter. The night sky was cloudy and hinted at an impending snowstorm. There were no stars, no moon, nothing. Just darkness and the hazy glow of the old, worn-out streetlight.

There was an old dilapidated house just on the other side of Reccio's. This can't be it, can it? I looked over to Brady and he gave me a nod.

"It's either here or over at their warehouse," he said. "So best to start here."

We circled back and parked at Reccio's to hide the car, then walked back. As we approached the front door I looked in a window, which had bars welded over it and sheets acting as drapes hiding the interior of the room. Should we really do this? I was already teetering on the edge after what went down at my office. Here I was, five hours later, about to knock on the door of the rest of the crew that tried to take me out. Again. Then I thought, time to end this once and for all. I was sick and tired of getting shot at.

I shrugged my shoulders and pounded on the door for all it was worth.

The door opened a bit and out popped the head of one of the ugliest women I have ever set eyes on. Her streaky blond and gray hair was greasy. Teeth were either turning black or missing from years of meth addiction. She was probably a good-looking woman many years ago, but now she was ready for death.

She wore a black t-shirt with "I'm his bitch" printed on it, no bra—gravity had *not* been kind to her—and jeans that were sliding off her ass. She was starving and didn't care as she took a swig from a low-end bourbon bottle.

"Fuck do you want? No one's home! So get the fuck off my property!"

"Lou, Kathy here is not very neighborly, is she?" Brady said. How he knew this skank was anyone's guess. He must have known her from his dealings with the Rats.

"They ain't here, assholes! So hit the road before I call the boys to take care of you two."

"Who ain't?" I asked.

She looked from Brady, then back to me, but didn't say anything.

We knew she was four boys short. I took my hand and put it on her ugly meth-looking face and pushed her into the room. We walked in and she came charging at me. This was no lady. Just because she had boobs didn't make her one. She tried to kick us in the balls and scratch our eyes out. I finally had enough and clocked her in the face and down she went. She'd be out for quite a while. Probably be the best sleep she'd have in years.

We looked around at what was supposed to be a living room. The furniture was old and tattered and for all intents and purposes was useless. The only thing that looked sturdy was a random desk chair in the middle of the room. The paint was faded and the wallpaper was coming off the wall. The room was dark and stunk of stale beer.

The next room we checked was the kitchen. It was a mess, used for everything but cooking food. Looked like a mini meth lab, but you'd never be able to prove it in court. Even though the River Rats were evil, they were good at covering their tracks.

There was no one else in the house, so we decided to wait. Kathy was of no help lying out cold on the floor, and I was in no hurry to wake her up for questioning. Soon we heard a loud vehicle pull up to the house. I looked out the window and saw Dolan, the suspected top Rat in the organization, with a couple of other gang members and two biker chicks. They looked pretty good, and young, too. They hadn't had the pleasure of getting addicted to meth yet.

The two bikers with Dolan were Jim "Big Country" Regan, who stood six foot five and weighed 350 pounds with a long gray beard. The other biker was Mickey "The Chef" McDonald. He was a short man, about five foot eight and under two hundred pounds. Had a degree in Chemistry. We—the Buffalo Police and I, back when I was still hunting them with a badge— assumed he cooked the meth. He was a key member of the club and Dolan made sure he was protected around the clock.

I didn't want this to go the way of a shoot-out. Not again. Too much lead had polluted the Buffalo skies already this evening. We decided to wait on either side of the door to disarm them. Brian, old as he was, sat on the couch opposite of the door to draw Dolan's gaze to give us time.

It worked perfectly. Regan was puzzled as soon as he walked in and was greeted by a smiling Brian.

"Brian? What . . ." Regan said, but stopped when he felt two pistols at his temples. Brady grabbed him by his beard and dragged him into the room. I stepped out and greeted the others with a wave of my gun.

"Come on in, the party just started," I said.

In walked the two women, the Chef, and Dolan, who was none too happy. "What the fuck is this, Finnegan?"

"Your live-in walking-dead girlfriend let us in," I said, taking control. "We had to tie Kathy up because she couldn't control herself. Take a seat."

At the mention of her name Kathy started to stir again and out she went again. What a pain in the ass. Dolan took the hint, and took Brian's spot on the couch as the old man stood and moved to the side.

"Dolan, we want to ask you a few questions and we want straight answers," I said.

"Fuck you, Romoso! It's a shame those bullets didn't kill you a few years back."

I smashed him in the side of the head with my gun. "Wrong answer, asshole!"

Dolan was as defiant as I was stubborn, so one of two things was going to happen: I'd get tired of smashing his brains in—not likely—or he'd get tired of having his brains smashed in. Maybe. So let's see. He tried to stand so I pushed him back into the couch and proceeded.

"Who hired you to shoot me and my friends?"

"Fuck you!"

Another shot to the head for him. "Wrong answer again, Dolan!"

The women were in hysterics, jerking their bodies every time I hit Dolan in the head. Brady, very politely but with an icy demeanor, quieted them by saying he didn't want to tie them up like poor Kathy. The other two gang members lay there silently on the floor in the middle of the room. Brian had a gun on them, and they knew if they moved things wouldn't end well.

With everyone out of the way I could now focus all my attention on Dolan. I grabbed him off the couch and sat him in his desk chair and tied his hands to the armrests. In my front pocket I had placed a cigar, the one I had been smoking in the car. It's always good to have one lit when questioning an asshole. It has a tendency to make him talk. So I pulled out my lighter and fired it back up.

"Dolan, who hired you?" I asked again.

"Fuck You, Cannon!"

The old television show *Cannon* starring William Conrad? What a dick!

"Cannon? Really, Dolan, do all fat guys look like Cannon?" I saw Brady smirk at Dolan's last remark, so I flipped him the finger. "We already know the answer, so just say it." He remained silent. "Okay, hardball it is."

I'm usually not that sadistic but I wanted answers. So I took my lit cigar and grabbed Dolan's beard. The cigar made his beard smolder and start smoking. The room stunk of burning hair. Then painful screams erupted from his mouth. I kept the cigar there for a bit. He screamed louder and finally he said he'd talk. I put the fire out by slapping him in the face nice and hard so he'd get the message.

"Okay, douche bag, who hired you?"

Dolan was gasping for air and clearly in some pain. "Romoso . . . you're going to die . . . a painful death . . . when I get out of here."

Dolan was right. If he ever got free it was going to be painful for somebody, but I assure you it wasn't going to be me. "Yeah, yeah, yeah, I've heard it all before. Now talk."

"It was—"

Dolan was cut off by a loud commotion from the kitchen.

"You, my dear, old friend, are a hard man to kill!" A voice called out.

I turned, taking my eyes off of Dolan. What I saw was unexplainable. The hammering in my head started once more. The man looking back at me was the same one from the photos in Brian's office. His brother, Kevin Young. Damn! What in the hell is going on! The fingerprints found at Ingrid's home confirmed he was involved, as did Brian's story and outlandish claim of time travel.

But seeing him in person was a whole different story. I blinked a few times to make sure he was really there in front of me. He was. I could finally put to rest that theory that Dolan and company were using old identities to cover their movements. Not that I fully believed it before, but the proof was in the pudding.

He still looked like a young man. How is that possible? He should be over ninety years old! However, there was something off about him, like Brian had said. He looked almost gray. His eyes were sunken in as well, and there was a dull sheen covering them.

Two goons I'd never seen before, but still looked familiar, stood in the doorway to the kitchen with him. They had that same pallid look to them. Kevin's arm was in a sling. So it really was him in the window at Ingrid's. He had his second Colt .45 pointed at me while his two henchmen covered the room.

They had the drop on us. "Shit," I muttered, then put my weapon on the floor. Brady and Brian did the same.

"I guess good help is hard to find, Detective, isn't that right?" Young said.

Dolan started to scream. "He is going to kill us all, do something! He hired me and paid—"

Those were the last words anyone heard Dolan say. Young aimed his Colt and put a bullet into Dolan's head. The momentum of the shot forced Dolan to fall sideways to the floor, chair and all, as he was still tethered to it. There was grey matter and blood everywhere. On me, Brady, and all of the bikers in the room.

Kevin laughed and turned his gun on me. "You know, if you want something done right, do yourself."

"What did I ever do to you?" I said.

Kevin had a baffled look on his face. "What do you mean?"

"I've never met you before. Brian here said we have, but I have no recollection of it. So I ask again, what did I ever do to you?"

Kevin turned to his brother, still confused, and now with a bit of hurt in his look. "Is he serious, Brother? And was this your plan all along, to betray me?"

Brian didn't say anything. Nobody did for a while. The

pain in my head was debilitating. I couldn't think straight. But I know I didn't want this to turn into another shootout. Kevin had lowered his gun.

"Listen, pal," I said after what felt like hours, "I don't know you. What I do know, though, is you are wanted for attempted murder, money laundering, counterfeiting, and, oh yeah, how about *actual* murder, for killing my friend Dolan here. That little scratch you got there on your arm is nothing compared to what will happen."

Kevin looked me in the eye, and this time there was anger. "No, you don't get to lie to me. Your time is up, old friend."

He raised his arm. Everything was in slow motion. This was the end, my lights were finally going out. I guess the *fourth* time is the charm when it comes to trying to kill me.

Before he could get a shot off, though, Brady jumped from the couch and knocked me out of the way. He had reached down and gotten his throwaway .38 special from his ankle and fired. The shot missed, but the effect was achieved. One of Kevin's henchmen grabbed him as he was firing, and it pulled his arm in a wild arc across the room. He got off one shot, but nowhere near us. I scrambled to my feet, ran out after them, but the getaway car was waiting and the driver sped away down South Park and out of sight.

"Son of a bitch, he did it to us again!" I yelled.

The others were in hysterics as their messed-up brains couldn't comprehend what was going on. It was safe to say the River Rats were almost extinct. Without Dolan, and the crew taken out earlier in the night, hardly anyone was left.

Through all the commotion I didn't notice Brian laying on the ground. He had taken a bullet to the hip. Brady already was on the line with 911. I called Joe to fill him in. He was pissed. Not that I could blame him.

I cut the remaining bikers loose. They weren't much use to

me anymore, not with Dolan out of the way. They ran out the door like rats leaving a sinking ship. Hey, that was pretty good. Rats, ship—never mind.

Brian was losing a lot of blood, and fading. We did what we could for him, but that wasn't much. It didn't look good. The ambulance took forever to get there, but in reality it was probably under three minutes. They loaded him up quick, and Brady jumped in with him. The paramedics tried to stop him, which almost made me laugh despite the situation.

CHAPTER 24

AFTERSHOCK

E ventually BPD showed up. Joe got there first and wanted to go after the scattered Rats. I told him to let them go. They didn't know anything that could help us at this point. Besides, with five core members now down for the count, they wouldn't be a threat to anyone anymore.

I filled him in on what happened before the next squad car came. I left out some of the details, namely how Brian and Brady had dealings with the Rats. That I would hold onto until the right time. The flash drive with all Brian's evidence was still in my coat pocket. Officers Watson and Houghton climbed out of their car again. We met them at the front door.

Officer Watson was the first to speak. "Are you shitting me, you two again? Camp, what's going on tonight?"

"Wish I had an answer for you," Joe said. "At least this one wasn't my fuck-up." Then he proceeded to fill them in on what I had told him. Watson listened while Houghton took notes.

Another patrol car arrived and the officers secured the scene while waiting for Homicide to show.

"Camp that's your story? It's crazy!" Watson said.

"Crazy but true, Watts," Joe said. "Crazy but true."

"Lou, that really what happened?" He asked me.

"Yes, except when Young and his gang arrived I dropped my cigar and when they shot Dolan he fell on it and it lit his beard on fire. I slapped his face to put it out, or the house might've went up in smoke."

"Shit!" Watts said, drawing it out. "Camp?"

Joe said nothing, just shrugged.

Homicide arrived and asked the same questions and got the same answers. Detective Albert Martinez, a Homicide cop for ten years and a twenty-year member of the force, was the lead investigator and was not going to let us off the hook that easy.

He asked and re-asked the same questions and we gave him the same answers; this went on for two hours. Then he asked one question I couldn't answer or I'd be locked in the nut house.

"How can a man in his nineties get in here and overtake you, Lou?"

He had me. Apparently he has been doing some research and digging and came up with this on his own. I very well couldn't tell him he'd traveled in time. We were screwed. We had nothing! In my infinite wisdom I came up with this gem.

"Al, I frigging haven't a clue! He didn't move like he was an old fart. No one's seen him for fifty years! He could just have stolen the guy's identity. Or I don't know . . . maybe he traveled through time!"

He looked at me with a mean glare, like I was holding something back. "Being a wiseass isn't going to help you here."

"I'm sorry," I said. I held my hands up and shrugged. "It's

just that I'm as frustrated as you and I have no answer. We were too busy with Dolan."

"We will have to talk about that, too. You're really fucking up my case here."

He had a point. He was lead investigator on the shooting at my office, working with IAD since Joe was involved. The only leads he had on who hired the dead Rats were now in the wind or dead, mostly thanks to me. All I could do was shrug.

Martinez said he was going to put an APB out on the remaining members of the River Rats Motorcycle Club and figure out what was going on. I'm sure when he hears the bikers' story he'll be pulling his hair out as well. I also gave him descriptions of the two guys with Young, but it all happened so fast I couldn't give him much.

"One of them wasn't the one who put the boots to you a few days back?" Martinez asked.

"Don't you think I'd recognize that guy?" I said, a little angry at the tone Martinez was using. "If he was there, he'd be lying next to Dolan on a metal slab, that I can *guarantee* you."

"Okay, okay, Lou," Joe jumped in. "I believe you. Martinez does too." He shot Al a look. "Listen, we'll talk to Brady, see if he knew the guys."

Even though it was established I wasn't the shooter, I turned over yet another firearm to him for ballistic comparisons.

∗∗∗

They finally let me go after another hour or so. Midnight had come and gone, but I was still riled up. I called Brady, and he updated me. His father was still out, but pulled through surgery fine. The bullet was a ricochet, but had nicked a main artery. My brother, Mike, had sewed him up and put him in a medically induced coma to help with the recovery because he was too old to make it otherwise. Remind me to tell Mike to thank me for giving him so much work these past few days.

"Lou, before you go, my dad didn't get to tell you everything," Brady said.

"What do you mean?"

"About your role in all this as a time traveler."

"This shit again? Come on Brady, give it to me straight." I was fighting against it, even though in my heart it felt right.

"Listen. That iPod thing you pulled off of Leary, that has something to do with how Uncle Kevin and them do it. My guess is after tonight, they went back in time. There's too much heat on them now."

"Okay, let's assume that's the case," I said, pausing for a moment. "What the hell am I supposed to do?"

"Go home and listen to some old-time detective shows, get your mind off of everything so you can think."

"Great advice."

Brady sighed. "Lou, I've given you everything I know. You're the detective, just put it all together . . . listen, I gotta go, your brother is coming in here right now to check on Dad."

"Tell Mike he's still—" he had hung up on me.

Gave me all the answers he can? Brady may not have been lying, depending on how much Brian and/or Kevin had told him. It was still frustrating beyond belief to not know exactly what was happening. However, I was worried for my friend. Brian was the only one who had any idea what was actually going on. I couldn't lose him yet.

I called Ingrid from my cell phone and filled her in on the events of the evening after we parted. She didn't say much, which was not a good sign. I could tell she was pissed at being woken up so late at night.

The snow began to fall as large snowflakes danced across

my windshield. Despite everything going on I was enjoying my ride home for a change. A hot shower would feel good.

It was really late—or early, depending on your perspective—when I got home. All the adrenaline from two separate shootouts had started to wear off, which hit me like a ton of bricks. I became tired and felt every aching bone in my body. I was going to take a quick shower but changed my mind and instead turned on the steam and body sprays. I stood in the shower thinking and rethinking what to do. Young had to be stopped.

The hot water and steam soothed my aching bones and sleep was knocking at my door. I dried off, hit the sack, and slept like a baby until 8 a.m. when my phone woke me up. Brady let me know his father was still in a medically induced coma. That hit me like a body blow and took all the wind from my sails. I told him to hang in there, and I would stop by soon. I needed to pick his brain some more on Young's operation.

I soon pulled up to my building and my buddy's construction trucks were all around it. Luckily for me I had another office next to mine. I used it when I worked late and decided to crash and not drive home. The office was decorated with a nice big, blue leather couch and chairs. A sixty-inch TV adorned the wall opposite the couch. I had a few mementos decorating the place. My old high school and college football jerseys, and various NFL, CFL, and Arena League football helmets on bookshelves. As you can tell, I do love football. The office also had a complete bath and kitchen. Basically a tricked-out bachelor pad. I really didn't need a house but the idea of staying at the office twenty-four seven was not too appealing.

I peeked in and saw the Pauly boys working their asses off. Jim Pauly himself was there. We made small talk and I gave him fifty bucks to buy his gang lunch. My office was torn apart and Jim thanked me for paying for his daughter's wedding. I wonder, does this count as an expense? If it did Ingrid's bill was about seventy-five grand, and that's just in expenses. I know what you're thinking, how could I charge her? Don't worry, I probably won't.

A big payday and I can't even collect.

At five minutes to eleven in walked Campanelli.

"Shit! You are the last person I wanted to see right now," I said.

"Well good fucking morning to you too, asshole. I just wanted you to know that Martinez rounded up what was left of the River Rats hierarchy, that being Regan and McDonald."

I sat there expressionless as my mind played out several scenarios of how much shit I was in. Home invasion, holding someone against his or her will, even though she was a strung-out crack whore, and a murder rap. Campanelli stood there in silence waiting for me to respond. I said nothing for a while.

Finally I spoke up. "What did Martinez find out, and how much shit am I in?"

"Not sure what he got, but I couldn't sleep last night. So I decided to pull some old files out of the archives and do some ballistics comparisons. Some interesting stuff, Lou, and as much as I hate to say this you are on the right track."

"I know it's killing you. I told you I know what the hell I'm doing!" Juvenile yes, but it's not often I get to gloat.

We talked for a bit more before Joe had to go in and make a formal statement on his involvement in the shooting. I'd have to do the same at some point, but since I was no longer on the force I figured I'd wait until they made me. That gave me more time to think.

After Joe left I turned on the radio, tuned it to the old-time detective shows Sirius still played. I decided to take Brady up on his advice. It relaxed me, and I dosed. A few hours must have passed, then *The Mysterious Traveler* came on, one of my favorite programs.

I sat staring at the radio wondering where to go from here, how to get to Kevin Young. Absently I picked up Leary's device from my temporary desk. The screen on was blank. I fiddled with it. Nothing. The damn thing must be broken.

I tossed it back on my desk, and as I did the gadget kicked on and the room started to shake. The radio got louder, and my headaches returned. I stumbled and went to my knees. Were Pauly's boys next door using a jack-hammer or something? That was my last thought before my face hit the floor.

INTERLUDE

The Doc was beaming, and now he was the impatient one. "Tell me everything! When did they get this to work? How? Who traveled in time?"

"Easy, Doc," the tall man said. "A friend of mine, he traveled in time. As did a few others I know personally."

"Your friend, did he know Major Kruger?"

"You could say that . . . listen, would there be any side effects that you know of if someone travels in time?"

The Doc, who had still been standing at the chalkboard, made his way back to his desk. "Side effects, yes, we did theorize this. If time travel were natural, it would be something easily attainable. Our belief was that constant jumping would cause, shall we say, undesired results."

"Undesired how?" The tall man asked.

"Well, the body is made up of an uncountable number of atoms and electrons and protons. To successfully move through time, these atoms would need to undergo a serious charge of energy each time. That will take its toll, which will result in sickness, or possible mutations. Without testing, we would never surely know."

The tall man leaned back in his chair. He rubbed his chin in thought. After a few moments he broke the silence. "Okay, I can confirm the sickness angle, sort of. The people I know that traveled, they just looked pale, and out of it, like they were recovering from the flu or something. What about other things? Could something else happen?"

"What do you mean?"

"Well," The tall man said, "Would it be possible for someone to travel in time, but have a life in both eras? Like he has a family in both the past and the future?"

If the Doc was beaming before, he was practically jumping out of his shoes now. "Fascinating! Do you have more information?"

"Well, all I know is my friend, me and him both served in World War Two. But I also know that he had knowledge of things that happened in the future, a few years from now. He claimed he even had a life then, that he had memories from his childhood in the seventies."

"Amazing!" The Doc stood back up and paced, forgoing the use of the cane leaning against his desk. "Hmm . . . do you want my educated guess? I think what may have happened is somehow your friend unintentionally time-jumped. As he did, something bad happened—or something amazing, depending on how you wish to view it—and he became 'connected' to the future. Think of it like the movie The Matrix, where he can 'plug in' to the past or present."

"I don't know of his intentions. Problem is, he disappeared before I had a chance to really talk to him about it."

"Interesting . . . maybe once they became connected, they both could not exist anymore, or one of them died as a result. Did something happen to him before he disappeared?"

"Well, he was in rough shape before he left. And the version of him now, he seems to have no knowledge at all of this happening."

"Which would make sense," the Doc said. "For if it hasn't been sixty years since the incident you witnessed, then the future version of your friend would not have time jumped yet."

Both men sat quiet for some time. The Doc, who had finally sat back down, broke the silence. "Brian, what is it that you wish of me?"

Brian Young—or Finnegan, as he was now known— wasn't quite sure what he wanted. His long quest for answers had finally paid off, somehow. Lou had never been open with the time travel talk, and besides, the authorities who finally came in to clean up the mess left in Buffalo covered it all up. They in no way wanted this type of technology out there as public knowledge. They thought it best to keep it secret, in hopes the Soviets wouldn't get their hands on it. And Ingrid wouldn't talk about it, either, still holding a grudge since Lou abandoned them.

"Well, Doc, maybe you should meet my friend," Brian said.

"I think that would be a very good idea, but not until after the incident that links him to the past. If we talk at this point, he will call us both insane, and we will lose the opportunity to find out what happened."

1955

CHAPTER 25

LOU ROMOSO, TIME TRAVELER, AT YOUR SERVICE

I t was over in less than a minute. I found myself on the floor. The shaking stopped, my headache receded. I laid there with a blank mind. The ceiling was familiar and all wrong at the same time. Blinking my eyes a few times, I rose to a seated position. The office I found myself in was mine, but it also wasn't. What the hell is up?

Along one wall was a bar. *That* looked right. Woozily I made it to my feet and fixed myself a stiff drink. Vodka, straight. There was an old Philco radio playing the end of *Johnny Dollar* in the corner. The program was right, but I thought it was playing through my Sirius. I hadn't seen one of those old Philco's since I was a kid . . . in this same office?

That thought brought a return of the headache. I stumbled, then somehow made it to the chair behind a flimsy-looking table. The vodka helped dull the pain. As my head cleared again I started with the basics.

Who am I? Lou. Lou Romoso, private detective.

What was I doing? A case, it involved . . . money, counterfeit money, and Irish gangsters . . . Kevin Young! That's right! I just saw him, he shot my friend, Brian, and his son was there . . . Kevin was Finnegan's brother, somehow.

Brian was an old man, though . . . isn't he my age? He was telling me . . . I was something . . . it connected me to the past, and I didn't quite believe him.

Then it all rushed through my head at once like the Niagara over the falls. I hit the ground again and was out cold.

***

My eyes blinked open and I checked the clock. No time had passed. Time must just stop when I'm on ice. Maybe I *am* the center of the universe. That caused a chuckle to escape my lips despite the situation.

I must have created a ruckus because someone was running up the stairs to my office. I pulled myself up off the floor and back into the chair before the door burst open. It was Duffy. Both my uncle and a distant cousin. Pasquale was right behind him. My . . . father.

While gasping for every breath Duffy looked up and yelled, "What the hell is going on up here? I thought my bar was falling down! You faint again?"

I had, twice. But I didn't need him fawning over me again. Not while I was still working through everything.

"No, Duffy, Pasquale, really," I said, holding my hands out to keep him from getting too close. "Maybe it was the radiator, it has a tendency to shake and bang when it's working too hard."

I hoped that would satisfy their curiosity, because if not, I had nothing.

"Okay . . . maybe it was," Duffy managed. By the look on his face he wasn't convinced. "I'll check it out tomorrow." He gave me one last hard look before walking towards the door. Pasquale lingered a bit longer, but nodded and left as well.

Damn, that was surreal, standing face to face with my father. I was a few years older than him now! And my mother, Josephine, they weren't even married yet, And I wouldn't be born for years. What the hell?

At least my headache was long gone. That felt strange, but also right, like my brain was fighting against something, and had just triumphed. Or possibly relinquished and embraced whatever was coming. It didn't matter; everything fell into place. I don't know how to explain it; it was just right. Brian, my friend, was correct. I had traveled in time. My memories were filled with everything from my life here in the fifties and the future. The pain of losing my wife Ellen and unborn son was strong but was counteracted by the love felt from my family and friends.

Brian . . . would he know anything about this here in the fifties? I needed to talk to him. That's the only way to find out. Or can I go back, and talk to him in the future as an old guy? His son, Brady, he knew about the time travel too. And Ingrid, what did she know? Her granddaughter must have been oblivious to it, or she would have said something. As clear as everything was, there were still so many questions to ask.

Regardless, that all had to wait. People were after me. They were after both Ingrids, grandma and granddaughter, as well. They'd stop at nothing until we were in the ground. I'd made a promise to keep both of them safe. All the other stuff had to be tucked in my back pocket for the time being.

I could see the whole case laid out in front of me. All the clues were connected now. The River Rats, the counterfeiting,

Mickey Finn's, Ellen, the attempts on my life, all of it. The investigation in the present and the past were one in the same, and had the same asshole targets: Kevin Young and Heinrich Mueller, better known as Bernhard Kruger.

I sat back and soaked in the feeling of a simpler time: the fifties. I felt at home here, maybe because my parents were still alive, as well as all of my relatives. A tear formed in my eye as the thought that my parents and most of the relatives I get to interact with here are gone in my real world. Or was this my "real" world? Again, there were too many questions still unanswered that I'll eventually have to figure out.

I wiped the tear away; it was time to put the game plan together and take down the assholes.

"By the way," Duffy said, turning around in the door frame. I jumped a bit, totally forgetting he was there. "You have a couple visitors."

He turned and Ingrid, Russell, and Mary filtered in around him. Great, so much for that quiet time to think.

They weren't there for two seconds when there was a knock at my office door. Then it opened. I was surprised to see who it was. They walked in one at a time, all looking like they were ready for business.

First to enter was Fritz Kolbe. You remember him, the CIA agent. Agent Murphy from Immigration and Tom DeRosa, Buffalo PD Homicide, shuffled in after him. I watched as they filled my now cramped office.

Before anyone could start in on me I asked Tom about Alice.

"She made it through surgery. That nurse who told us she'd be lucky to survive was misinformed."

I sighed in relief. One less death to burden my conscious. "Any luck on the vehicle that struck her?"

Tom shook his head. "Still looking."

"I might have your answer on that." That turned some heads.

"Lou, I'm not quite sure what you have going on," Tom said, "but Alice told me she's been doing make-up at Shea's for five years. She loves her job because she gets to meet quite a few stars and the job doesn't pay too bad."

"Okay, Tom, let's get to the point," I said.

"That's the trouble with you, no patience."

He didn't know the half of it. "Thanks, it's nice to have friends."

Tom smiled back and continued. "Anyway, Alice said she was working a play about a year ago and a beautiful brunette came up to her during a rehearsal, introduced herself as Heidi, and asked her if she'd like to make some extra money. Alice asked her what she had to do. Heidi told her she had to make her look like a certain woman, and showed her a photograph of Mrs. Jessica Reitman. Alice recognized her immediately because she is a big supporter of the arts, especially Shea's. Mueller went on to explain that she was part of a group paying tribute to all the contributions Mrs. Reitman has made to the City of Buffalo and local businesses by creating a new play in her honor, with Mueller playing the lead.

"Alice said she took the job not only for the money but she wanted to play a small part in honoring Mrs. Reitman because she was always kind and generous to the behind-the-scenes workers. That's how Alice got involved. Heidi has been in every week without fail for over a year."

I took it all in and knew we were close to slamming the door on Mueller/Kruger and his counterfeiting. Now it was my turn to fill some holes. "Murph, I gave you the wrong name to research. Mueller is an alias. That's why you couldn't find anything on him. The names we are looking for are Bernhard Kruger, Erik Kruger, and Heidi Kruger."

Kolbe was taken aback by my revelation. Everyone else looked slightly confused, so Kolbe filled them in, retelling the story he had told me a few days ago, about Kruger and Operation Berhnard.

After he was finished, he asked me, "How can you be so sure?"

I couldn't really tell them the truth. That I time-traveled sixty years and watched a History Channel special. So I lied.

"I can't reveal my sources, Fritz. But it's a hundred percent a fact. Trust me."

I sat there looking at the faces in the room. There was no way I was going to tell Ingrid one of these vile human beings was personally responsible for the death of her husband. They were war criminals and had to pay the piper now.

Murphy was stunned and I could see his mind working already. "Let's not jump the gun, Murph," I said. "We need to nail them on all counts. Trust me, we will get them."

"I know, but I want these assholes today!" He yelled.

I couldn't let that happen and I wasn't going to. "I told you I'd let you in on this and I did. You have to trust me when I tell you we will all get our pound of flesh."

"Okay, Lou, I'm with you."

I could see the tears forming in Ingrid's and Mary's eyes, but now wasn't the time for me to be consoling.

Finally I was ready to lay my cards out on the table. We needed to bust them in the act. First, we had to catch them at the bank posing as Jessica and passing the fake bills. That would tie up one end. Second, we had to bust Mickey Finn's, where a big portion of the counterfeit bills were being passed. That would require more help, and would hopefully lead us to Bernhard's hideout where he was printing the fake money.

Kolbe was chomping at the bit to plead his case. Why, I don't know. Feds could do pretty much whatever they wanted to do. Maybe it was some strange professional courtesy he afforded me because I was a former cop and had paid my dues in the worst way one could. And I had proved my worth so far, getting closer than anyone to the former Nazis.

"Lou, lets nail this Heidi after she leaves the bank. We got her right where we want," Murph said.

"If we do, we lose the other two," Kolbe said, shaking his head. "And I want them bad. Especially Erik."

Murph was not happy but he acquiesced to my wishes. Kolbe was also in agreement with me, but he had his own agenda. Bernhard and Erik were wanted war criminals. Kolbe wanted the stolen art treasures and gold returned to their rightful owners if they were still alive, or to their kin.

"Phase one starts tomorrow at the bank," I said. "It'll be Monday morning, meaning Heidi is likely going to go in there to make a withdrawal. DeRosa, we need extra men to surround the area."

DeRosa nodded.

"Good. Be here tomorrow morning by seven thirty with your agents. Fritz and Murph, I'd like you both to be there too in case things change."

They responded both at the same time. "We'll be there."

DeRosa, cleared his throat and said, "Let's not forget that we have three unsolved murders; Sullivan, Leary and forgive me, Lou . . . Ellen. I know you have a pretty good idea who is responsible, so bring me and everyone else up to speed."

"Alright. Here is what I figured out so far, but I'll need more facts to bust them all. Kevin Young and Mueller are tied up together in counterfeiting. They run the bogus bills through the casino. They pay off the check cashers and suppliers in that crap too."

Some looks of doubt were spread across the room, but no one said anything. I continued.

"Young and his gang are responsible for the deaths of Sully, Leary, and Ellen, but I can't prove it until we track that black Ford. I have a line on where it is, but that's why we have to sting Mikey Finn's. Hopefully we can tie it in when we bust him for the counterfeiting. Young is also responsible for Alice the make-up artist getting run down."

Everyone was paying real close attention. Thankfully they weren't questioning how I knew all this. I'm not sure I could bullshit my way through an explanation.

"So, Tom, this is what we have. As of now we are all in the game, so let's all play nice, work together, and you can all share the headlines. I'll see you here tomorrow morning."

Everyone was excited to get rolling on this case and put an end to the killings, cheating of the hard-working, counterfeiting, and perhaps try to right the egregious acts of two of the most evil men remaining from the Nazi Party.

* * *

It was getting late, and we had a big day tomorrow. Everyone had left already as I stayed behind to have a drink and finalize my plans. When I went down to the bar there was a commotion across the room. The man was Vinnie "the Knot" Ardonato. He saw me and a wry smile came to his lips.

The Knot, who hailed from Syracuse, was built like a cement truck. He stood six feet tall and tipped the scales at 275 pounds with black hair, brown piercing eyes, and a temper like a hurricane. And let's just say he has a way with rope that no other man possesses. Vinnie isn't a killer, but he leaves his prey in pretty bad shape. His knots are so complicated that when his victims—usually another mobster who didn't follow the rules and needed an attitude adjustment—are found, they don't always survive. The knots tightened when the person fights against the restraints. Sometimes the doctor in the ER had to cut flesh away to remove the rope.

I always had a rapport with Vinnie. I should; I arrested him six times for various things. I went up to Vinnie and offered to buy him a drink.

"Vinnie, How are you? What are you drinking?"

"Detective Romoso, so nice to see you, too. You here to bust my balls or do you want me to teach you how to tie your shoes?"

"Vinnie, Vinnie, Vinnie, why so angry? Did someone you had locked up in a closet escape?"

Vinnie chuckled. "You are a funny man. What do you want?"

Vinnie was good for information on the street, and since I was no longer a cop, he made a few extra bucks on side helping find out things.

"Come on up to my office, I need your help," I said. It was more of a demand than a request, and Vinnie caught on.

We walked up the flight of stairs to my office. He made himself at home, grabbing a bottle of Canadian Club whiskey, some ice, and poured himself a triple.

"Easy, Vinnie, that stuff will kill you," I said.

"Don't be such a candy ass!" Vinnie shot back. "You want one?"

"No thanks. By the way, help yourself to a drink."

"Your hospitality reminds me of my time in prison. Did I ever thank you for that lovely stay?" He laughed and took a large drink of my whiskey.

"Look, what had you throwing a hissy fit downstairs?"

"Don't know what you mean."

"Bullshit. You know something. Now talk."

"Thanks for the drink, see you later." He got up to leave.

Unfortunately, I was not in the mood for his shit. As he got up, he turned his back to me to walk out. I grabbed him by the shirt collar and yanked him back to his chair.

Vinnie flew back so hard the chair almost fell backwards to the ground. He wasn't expecting that and began to stare at me. I've seen that look before so it didn't bother me and I pounded him in the face, just because. His head rocked back and he and the chair hit the deck. This time Vinnie got up and came after me. I was quicker than him, so when he charged me, I side-stepped him and hit him on the nape of his neck and down he went. He hit the floor like a load of dirt. He lay there for what seemed like an eternity and didn't move. Maybe I killed the asshole. That would be just my luck.

I didn't wait for him to move. I grabbed a pitcher of water from the bar and tossed it on him. He started squirming and slowly got up off the floor muttering to me. "You didn't have to get rough." He started to rub his neck.

"I don't have time for your bullshit tonight. I need answers."

"Okay, okay, Lou."

He held up his hands in the standard I-give-up motion, picked up his chair, grabbed his drink and sat down. He was shaking his head, clearing the cobwebs that I loosened and finally spoke.

"What do you want to know?"

"Why does it always have to be so difficult with you?"

"You know me," he said. He paused to finish off the whiskey. "I was in a bad mood because of that Irish fuck, Young. I'm going to kill that asshole."

"Then why give me the hard time?"

"A ton of people saw me come up here with you. If I come down without a scratch and they talk, certain people start asking questions. I don't need that kind of trouble. Capisce?"

"Yeah, Vin, I get it. What did Young do to you?"

"Cheated me out of five large."

"How so?"

Before he started he got up and refilled his glass. He downed it, and filled it up again. "I put a hundred on a long shot at Gulfstream and it hit. I went to collect and his lackey O'Connell told me that they didn't get it in on time because there was a problem with their phones. I knew that was bullshit and I tell him so. O'Connell tells me to go fuck myself and leave before he throws me out. I've never been thrown out of any place by anyone, and especially by no fucking mick.

"When I'm about to put his lights out I feel something cold on the back of my head. I know it's a gun and I figure well it's been a good run but I'm not going to take it laying down. Before I spin around, I hear 'don't try it, Vinnie! I'll blow your brains out right here!' It was Young. I told him to pay me and I'd be on my way. Now I'm expecting to hear 'fuck off, you dago prick, and get out of here before I grease your wop ass,' or something more colorful. Instead, he hands me the money and tells me to get lost. I left, but something didn't feel right so I came to see if Duffy knew anything."

"What do you mean something didn't feel right, Vin?"

"Young is an asshole, right?"

I just gave a short chuckle.

"Have you ever heard of him giving up a dollar, much less five grand, without causing a problem? I'll save you the trouble. No!"

"Then you came here to talk to Duffy about what?" I asked.

"I wanted him to take a look at the money Young gave me. Like I said, it doesn't feel right."

"Do you mind if I take a look at your cash?"

"Knock yourself out."

Vinnie threw me a bundled stack of hundred-dollar bills. I smelled them and the noticed that familiar scent. The printer's ink. Then I rubbed the bills between thumb and index finger and felt that all too familiar roughness to the paper, as fine as it was. Out of the stack only one was good.

"I got good news and bad news for you."

"The money is bullshit!" He pounded his fist on the table.

"Good news is Young gave you your hundred-dollar bet back. The rest is counterfeit."

"I'll get that mick fuck!"

"No you won't," I said. "I'm planning on taking him out myself and I don't need you fucking up my plans. Take your hundred back and be happy. I'm keeping the rest."

He looked like he'd put up a fight again, but finally relented. "For you, fine. I hope you know what you're doing."

"Don't worry, Vin. When have I ever been wrong?"

CHAPTER 26

SO IT BEGINS, AND NOT IN A GOOD WAY!

I left Marco's and got in Ingrid's Hudson. It was a cold night, even for January in Buffalo, so I let the Hudson warm up while I froze. I thought about the game plan for tomorrow and whether or not Murphy was right about nailing Heidi as soon as she left the bank. Figured I'd toss and turn all night over it because I wasn't going to get much sleep. The Hudson finally warmed up and I pulled away from the curb and headed to Ingrid's home. Took about fifteen minutes and as I pulled in I saw the front door open.

Russell. With his usual smile.

"Russell, how in the hell do you know it's me coming up that drive way?" I said as I got out of the car.

"It's a gift."

"Yeah, I'm sure it is."

Russell let out a laugh and said, "She is in the kitchen."

Ingrid had a late dinner waiting. It was a favorite of mine:

steak, salad, and potatoes. What can I say, I'm pretty basic when it comes to food. We ate, made small talk, and headed for bed. I hopped into the shower with the hot water turned way up and began to think.

As I stood under the pulsating shower stream a horrible thought popped into my head. "Fuck!"

I dried quickly, got dressed and woke up Ingrid.

Ingrid tossed and turned and swatted at my hand, yelling, "Leave me alone, I'm trying to sleep."

"Ingrid, we have a problem. Wake the hell up, your mother is in trouble!"

Ingrid shot straight up at that statement. "What did you say?"

"Your mother is in big trouble. Call her now!"

"It's one in the morning, she is sleeping."

"Ingrid, get on the phone and call your mother now!"

Ingrid picked up the phone and dialed it. It rang and rang and rang, no answer. I was now officially worried.

"Get Russell, he and I are going to your mother's house, now," I said.

Ingrid got him, and they came to the kitchen where I was pacing up a storm.

"Detective, what is going on?" Russell asked.

"Let's go, I'll explain on the road," I said. Ingrid made to follow us, but I stopped her. "Not you, I need you to stay here."

"If my mother is in trouble, I'm going. There's nothing you can do about it." The look in her eye left no room for arguing.

We all ran outside and Russell started up the Cadillac and headed down the driveway. I knew we were too late, but we had to try in the off chance we could make it to Jessica's in time.

"Okay, Lou, what is it," Ingrid said from the back seat.

I sighed and started talking. "For Mueller's plan to work

he needs Heidi in costume to pull it off, but there is one problem. Mueller had Young run down Alice, the make-up artist. I think those Nazi bastards are going to use Jessica to get her money, then God knows what they'll do."

The car went quiet. The only noise was the wiper blades rubbing across the windshield clearing the snow and slush away. Russell and I both knew Ingrid's mother was in trouble, as was the rest of her staff. We said nothing because we didn't want to make a bad situation worse.

When we got to Jessica's Ingrid jumped out of the car and rushed to the front door. Russell and I hustled after her, guns drawn. Ingrid tried the door. Locked. She went to get the key to her mother's house but in her rush to get here she left her purse on the kitchen counter in her home. Damn!

I knew we couldn't break these monstrous doors down and shooting the lock was no use. I yelled to Russell, "Get the carjack and crowbar."

Russell popped open the trunk and rushed back with them. "Take the jack and put the base by the hinge that sticks out a little sideways and the bumper holder lip between the two doors."

Russell did as I told him. I had the crowbar, so when Russell had that set up I stuck in the crowbar and cranked the jack for all it was worth. The door split just enough apart to separate the locks and dead bolt, which allowed us to open the door without much damage.

The house was eerily quiet and dark except for a reading lamplight and glow from the fireplace in the library. Russell and I walked slowly down the dark hallway. We told Ingrid to wait in the lobby and not to make a sound. We arrived at the French doors that decorated the entrance to the library. I signaled Russell to cover me as my hand reached for the doorknob. I turned it slowly and opened the door. Nothing.

I poked my head out from the protection of the hallway and looked in. Two shoes were pointing upwards. We were too late. Russell covered me as I walked in. A soft moaning sound carried through the still, silent air.

I signaled Russell to come in as I checked on the motionless body. Livingston. As I got close his chest was moving ever so slowly up and down. His face was a mess. His eyes were swollen shut and his nose broken, as well as his jaw. I checked his ribs and he cried out in pain; they were broken. The fingers on his right hand pointed east and west.

Livingston was tough. I've seen photos of this kind of beating once before, and that was one Michael Sullivan. How Livingston was still alive, I don't know.

"Russell, call for an ambulance!" I yelled.

Russell picked up the phone and called. As he was dialing Ingrid walked in and screamed at the sight of Livingston.

I yelled to Russell, "Get her out of here and check the rest of the house. I'll stay with Livingston." I leaned over to tell Livingston help was on the way when I noticed his left hand. His palm was facing the ceiling with a knife jammed into it along with a note. I had no choice.

I pulled the knife from the gravely beaten Livingston's hand. He moaned. I don't know if it was from relief or the pain. I found a towel to wrap around his hand to stem the bleeding. Other than that I was helpless until the ambulance arrived. The note was written in German. The only person I knew who could read it was lying there next to me.

I tried to make Livingston as comfortable as possible as we waited for the ambulance. It seemed like forever before it finally arrived. They gently put Livingston on the gurney as we all watched. He moaned softly and finally and mercifully passed out. The ambulance took him to Meyer Memorial Hospital.

DeRosa and his squad arrived and asked questions. We didn't have any answers for him, other than the rest of the place was empty. DeRosa sent his men to recheck. I was pissed and all I could do was stare at this stupid note written in German.

"Tom, those bastards stuck a knife in Livingston's palm with this." I handed DeRosa the blood-stained note. "It's written in German. I can't translate it."

He took the note and looked at it and shook his head. "I have a man who speaks and reads German fluently. You know him, Tommy Schultz."

"How long will it take to get him here?"

"He's home asleep."

"Get him here now. It's important!"

"Okay, Lou." He stepped away to make the call.

We waited for what seemed like an eternity. In the interim Russell went to pick up Mary so she wasn't alone. Forty-five minutes later Schultz arrived. Tommy Schultz was the Nazi Party's dream—five foot eleven, 170 pounds, blonde hair, blue eyes—except for one thing: he hated the bastards. Tommy was in Army Intelligence during the war and translated intercepted messages.

I greeted Tommy at the door with a handshake and a hug and thanked him for coming.

DeRosa handed Tommy the note. Tommy read the note a few times then asked if he could speak to Tom and I in private. He told us that he didn't want to talk in front of Ingrid because of the contents of the note.

"Lou, the note basically says that you interfered in this guy Heinrich's plans long enough. He has Jessica and if you don't stay away she will die. He also said you should have looked for microphones in the house and that Livingston should have known since he was British Intelligence. The note said

Livingston meddled in their affairs and got his face rearranged. Some guy named Erik gives his regards to Ingrid, and that he met her husband in Germany. The note also states they will raise the Nazi Party and third Reich from the ashes." He paused and handed the note back to me. "Lou, that's it in a nutshell. You want my opinion, this guy is crazy."

"Thanks for coming, Tommy, I owe you."

I stood there and looked at the wall regretting the day I asked Livingston to help me out. I remembered a quote I heard long ago, "Regret is an indulgence that you should not waste time with because by then it's already too late." How true. There was nothing I could do or take back. Only revenge.

Then a thought hit me. "Wait, the note doesn't mention Mary's mother, Maggie. We didn't find her here either."

Mary, in between sobs, managed to speak up from the access room. "She took a vacation. Mostly at Mrs. Wright's insistence that she get away to stay safe."

That was good. One less person we had to worry about protecting. My mind was working on what this would mean for my plans.

DeRosa must have had the same thoughts. He put his hand on my shoulder and said, "Lou, it's time for you to get off this case. It's personal now more than ever, and you know the two don't mix."

"You're right, but I want this sadistic asshole and his flunkies, and when I get my hands on them they're dead."

"It's beginning already. You'll get hurt, or someone else will get hurt. We'll get them, don't you worry."

If the shoe was on the other foot I'd be telling him the same thing. But there was no chance in hell I was backing away now. "Sorry, Tom, I'm in until the end. See you at my office. Seven-thirty sharp." I leaned in close so no one else could hear. "Also, I think we should put a car on Ingrid's house. Just in case they try to take her, too. I can't be with her twenty-four seven and still bring down Mueller."

DeRosa shook his head and said he'd get on it. I thanked everyone for their effort and headed back to the library. Everyone was quiet as they sat processing their emotions. Russell worried me the most as he sat wringing his hands. His jovial nature was gone. It would take everything I had to control him. Mary and Ingrid sat on the couch, both with red eyes. I think they were both cried out and were looking to me for answers. I didn't have many.

The truth about the letter found in Livingston's hand was the best and only approach.

"Ingrid, I'm going to tell you something . . . it's going to be hard to accept." I took a breath and grabbed Ingrid's hand. "Erik was in the SS during the war. He is the Nazi bastard who murdered your husband and his crew in Germany after they bailed out of the plane."

Ingrid burst out in tears and ran out of the library. I heard her running up the stairs and a door slam. I felt horrible but she needed the truth.

It's always wonderful to be the bearer of good news, right? I went upstairs to find Ingrid. I checked the multitude of rooms upstairs and finally found her in her mother's bedroom, laying on the bed, crying and staring at her wedding picture on the wall.

"Ingrid, I'm sorry you had to find out that way. I just wanted to see if you were alright."

She looked up at me through the tears. She didn't speak for a while, just sat there and cried. I sat next to her and wrapped her in my arms. "It's been ten years," she said finally, "and I'm still crying the same as the day I found out my Tom died. It sickens me that his murderer was this close the whole time. I want them all to suffer, like I did. My poor mother, Lou, what have they done with her?"

"She is still alive. They won't hurt her, they need her."

I sat with her a while more in silence before heading back to the library. Mary was staring into the fire, alone with her thoughts. Russell and I went up to the rooms that Heidi and Heinrich lived in. We rechecked dresser drawers, closets, and even looked for secret rooms and all we found were clothes that they left behind. I'm sure whatever money they had has been transferred to some bank in Switzerland. In other words, we got nothing.

Where the hell could they be? I couldn't let them get away this easily after all the damaged lives they left behind. I had to wait until tomorrow morning to begin getting even.

***

January 7, 1955. Needless to say sleep evaded me as my mind raced about the events that took place the previous night. I was up and pacing the floor at 5 a.m. I spent the night at Ingrid's house, most of which was spent in the library so I would not wake her.

Russell did not sleep much either. He brought me breakfast in the library. Eggs, bacon, and toast. I had coffee too, which is out of the norm for me, but I was cold since the fire burned itself out in the fireplace. I spent most of the night checking on Livingston and found nothing had changed. He was still unconscious and in grave condition. I said a quick prayer for him. Erik would never see another day if I could help it.

Russell stayed and chatted with me over breakfast.

"Russell, I have to change tactics now that Jessica has been kidnapped," I said. "The plan for the casino is off. It's too dangerous to put everyone in a bad spot, especially with what happened to Livingston. As for the bank sting, that will change, too. To what, I'm not sure. I guess we'll play it by ear. You are out, too. I pulled Livingston into this and I can't have anyone else going down on my account."

He thought over what I had said before responding. "That's a problem. I'm in and we are now a team. No, don't try to talk me out of it. There is no argument."

He was right. Even if he wasn't, he said it with an authority he hadn't displayed yet. There was no room for argument with him. I could see it in his eyes. Besides, I needed help, and if too many cops and Feds got involved people were going to die quick. I couldn't think of a better person to have my back.

"Okay, Russell, you're in. Let's get out of here and—"

Before I could finish Russell was already on his way to the car. I put on my hat, coat, and gloves while looking up the stairs at Ingrid's closed bedroom door. Hopefully she'd forgive me for leaving without saying anything.

Chapter 27

The Bank

Nine a.m. Showtime.

Thankfully the bank was not busy. The after-Christmas-I-have-no-money syndrome usually kicks in, so why go to the bank? I was in a room behind Mr. Simon's office, drinking coffee with Kolbe and Murphy. DeRosa, with Ruff and others, were strategically waiting in the surrounding areas in order to pursue the Germans as they left. Russell was a block away as well, ready in Pasquale's Plymouth just in case I needed him.

That was a surreal conversation, knowing what I know now. I was speaking to my father, who was over ten years younger than me! He was all for helping out, which was to be expected. He wanted all the way in, though, and I couldn't let that happen. I already had enough people involved. Trying to keep them all safe was too much. He understood, but was at the ready in case he was needed.

The plan was to move forward as originally intended, with

a twist. With Jessica kidnapped, we needed to track them back to their location to recover her and the counterfeit money. That meant no arrests at the bank unless absolutely necessary. There was some argument over that, but eventually DeRosa and I were able to convince the Feds.

As often with a stakeout, there was a lot of down time. Hurry up and wait, if you will. That's what we did. We were ready, or at least we thought we were, but you never knew. You had to be prepared for everything and anything.

We didn't have to wait long. About 9:30 a.m. the bank doors opened and let winter in. The cold wind could be felt through the entire lobby and sent chills down everyone inside. I peeked out and could see the ball was in play. In walked Jessica. She was wearing sunglasses, her winter coat, and a scarf. Her face looked swollen and she walked with a slow, unsteady gait. Her head was on a swivel, looking for something, anything reassuring. I would have loved to let her see me but couldn't, or it would ruin the sting. Jessica, not seeing any hope, continued her walk to Miss Jacobs' window.

Alongside Jessica was the black-haired beauty, Heidi. She was dressed in tight-fitting black dress, black heels, and a mink stole. I must admit, she was stunning, almost to the point it could make you forget she was dangerous.

Sandra's line was close to the office we were hiding in, so we could just make out what was being said.

Jessica asked, as I thought she would, to close out her account.

"Mrs. Wright, is it something we did?" Sandra asked.

"No, it's nothing the bank did," Jessica said. "I'm leaving Buffalo for a warmer climate."

"You'll have to speak to the bank manager, Mr. Simon. I'll go get him. Please have a seat in the waiting area. Can I get you some coffee?"

"No, thank you."

Jessica and Heidi went to the waiting area of the bank. It was a cornered-off area for the bigger clients. It had nice leather chairs, coffee and tea, and three newspapers: The *Buffalo Evening News*, my old friend the *Courier Express*, which I came home many a nights with—as the old expression once said, "I'm going home with the *Courier*!"—and the *New York Times*. I could see Heidi leaning over, talking to Jessica, but since I don't read lips I had no idea what the hell she was saying to her. The waiting area was too far away now for us to hear anything.

Sandra entered Simon's office. I needed to get in there and talk to them. With Heidi focused on Jessica and not paying attention to her surroundings, I took full advantage and snuck into Simon's office.

"Mrs. Wright wants all her accounts closed today and wants cash," Miss Jacobs said.

"Stick to the plan," I said.

"I know," she said. She turned to Mr. Simon. "That's why they are waiting to talk to you."

"Who is with Mrs. Wright?" Simon asked.

Before Sandra could answer, I jumped in. "It's a long story, but the gorgeous woman with Jessica Wright is her husband's wife, Heidi Mueller."

"What?" Came the response from Jacobs and Simon.

"You both know her better as Jessica herself," I answered. "She's just out of costume today."

Jacobs looked dumbfounded, but an eventual understanding as to what was going on hit her. Simon also looked confused, but like he was forcing it. "Now we have a lot of work to do," I continued. "Simon, you have to stall her here as long as possible. Try to give me twenty minutes."

"It will take at least that long to fill out the paperwork

required by our bank to close an account that large," Mr. Simon said.

"Look, just stall her and tell her she'll need to come back in an hour for the check so you can verify the accounts. Okay?"

"No sweat, Detective."

Heidi was just sitting next to Jessica now scanning the bank with her jade-green eyes. I had Simon personally get Jessica and Heidi, thus blocking Heidi's view of Simon's office. As Simon reached the two ladies I ran back to the spare office that we were using and filled everyone in.

"Alright, looks like—"

Both Kolbe and Murph looked troubled.

"What?"

Before they could say anything, the phone in the conference room rang. Murph picked it up immediately. He didn't say anything, just handed me the receiver.

I grabbed it, trying to figure out what was wrong. "Hello?"

"Lou, it's Tom. We have a situation."

"What is happening?"

"I can't get radio contact from White, he was posted up at Ingrid's. He was supposed to check in every half hour. He missed the 9:30 check. I called the house, and no answer. Then we got a call into the department that a black sedan was seen creeping through the neighborhood."

That wasn't good. There was no chance that car wasn't the black Ford we were after. I quickly thought through our options: Abandon the sting here at the bank, or send recon to the house.

"Okay, Tom, Here's what we'll do. I'm going to go check it out, you can handle the—"

"No, Lou," He cut me off. "If my guys are in trouble, I'll see to it that Ingrid is found and kept safe. If you rush out of there, it may tip off Heinrich. I'm hidden, my squad and I out here will take care of it."

I didn't say anything. If there was someone I could trust other than myself in this group, it was DeRosa. However, he wasn't the one who promised to keep both Jessica and Ingrid safe. I'd already failed on one of those. I didn't want to make it two for two.

But he was right. I relented. "Fine."

"Don't worry, Lou, I'll make sure she is alright."

I hung up the phone without responding. My mind was reeling. I looked to my companions.

"We need to take them now!" Murph said.

"I agree," Kolbe said. "Let's take Heidi now and rescue Jessica. We'll get the other two later."

I understood their position, but we had to give it more time. "If we do that we'll lose Heinrich and Erik, and possibly Ingrid. They won't stick around and wait for us to find them. Let's see how this goes."

There was silence for a couple moments.

"I disagree, but it's your show," Murphy eventually said, clearly agitated.

Fritz said nothing.

I took his silence as agreement and turned on the intercom. I had to isolate myself from everything else other than the task at hand.

With the volume low I hoped to God I could hear it, because my hearing isn't always the best. Some days, deaf guys would tell me what people were saying.

Now that they were all in Simon's office I moved Murphy outside to keep watch on things in DeRosa's stead. Fritz manned the radio and I listened intently as the transaction took place. The voices were fuzzy and distant on the ancient intercom speaker—at least considering the technology at my disposal sixty years from now.

"Mrs. Wright, I'll need you to fill out this tax form and a withdrawal slip," Simon said.

"Why does Jessica have to fill out this?" It was Heidi. There was impatience in her voice.

"Well, Heidi. It is Heidi, isn't it?"

"Miss Mueller."

"Very well, Miss Mueller. The form is for the IRS. Whenever a large amount of money is withdrawn the government wants to know to whom it is going. I'm sure you understand."

"Very well. Continue." She said it commandingly. I hope Simon didn't buckle. He didn't seem to have the spine for this type of thing.

Kolbe's face, normally impossible to read, was an open book. He wanted to grab Heidi, and now. I began to have second thoughts and wondered if we should just grab Heidi and hope for the best with Heinrich and Erik. But what did we have for proof? I couldn't get them for stealing Jessica's money because everyone in the bank would swear Jessica herself came to withdraw and deposit. I did have some of the counterfeit bills. But the source—Vinnie the Knot—wasn't exactly what you'd call reliable.

Alice could testify that she did make-up, but she was still laid up in a hospital bed. I'm sure Heidi could produce a dozen witnesses that would say she was putting on a play. We could get them on kidnapping, but I'm pretty damn sure Young couldn't be connected to any of this yet. So I had to wait and let it play out.

Simon's voice on the intercom interrupted my thoughts.

"Mrs. Wright, your address on the IRS form is different from the withdrawal slips. The address on the IRS form says Delaware Avenue, and on the deposit slip you wrote Ganson Street."

"Oh, I'm sorry, I was thinking about my Florida address."

"Not a problem, I'll just have you redo them."

Mr. Simon and Sandra stepped out of the office to get new withdrawal slips. After they left Heidi said, "If you ever try a stunt like that again that bitch daughter of yours dies a slow, agonizing death. Do you understand?"

What does she mean by "daughter?" Kolbe, who had come over to listen, picked up on it as well, because he immediately got on the phone. I radioed out to the net around the bank, but got nothing. Did DeRosa pull everyone to Ingrid's?

Jessica didn't answer. They sat in silence until Mr. Simon came back with the new withdrawal slips.

"Mrs. Wright, I have to inform you that at this time I'm only authorized to give you ten thousand in cash," Mr. Simon said. "You will have to return in an hour to pick up a cashier's check for the remaining sum."

Heidi guffawed through the speaker. "No, you will wire the money to the new account."

I could hear Mr. Simon start to babble. "B-but, we can't d-do that, there are regulations and—"

"You can if you wish to continue to do business with us."

"O-okay, I will get the necessary forms," Mr. Simon managed.

God dammit! Mr. Simon had the spine of a worm. I couldn't do anything about it, though, without blowing our cover. A few minutes later. Fritz and I watched through the cracked office door as Heidi abruptly left the bank with Jessica in tow.

Just then a blue Cadillac pulled up, with Erik behind the wheel. The door opened and the two women got in. What they didn't notice was the old Plymouth following their every move.

Russell pulled to the curb and Kolbe and I jumped in after rushing out of the bank. Murphy stayed at the bank to coordinate the rest of the operation and hopefully find out what was happening at Ingrid's.

Apparently Erik's time in the SS served him well, as he zigged and zagged his way through the city trying to make sure he wasn't followed. However, Russell was just as good and managed to stay far enough back to avoid suspicion.

I sat in the front seat of the Plymouth thinking about what went down in the bank and it struck me. Jessica's faux pas with her address in the bank. She was leaving a clue. Why didn't I catch that? Maybe she wrote the address of where they were being held. Ganson Street, but where? It was a long road with at least a hundred different places they could be.

I needed Murph to check the trash can in Simon's office, maybe Jessica wrote the full address on the withdrawal slip. No one was answering on the radio. I reached in my pocket to grab my cell phone and call the bank, however there was one tiny problem. Frigging cell phones still were not invented yet. Son of a bitch!

Russell was doing his best to keep the blue Caddy in sight but luck wasn't on our side. A slow-moving truck blocked traffic on a one-way street in the city, but not before Erik managed to get around it. The truck driver tried to turn left, now angled across two lanes. There was no way Russell could get around; we lost the Caddy.

I looked at Russell then to the Kolbe in the back seat. They both looked defeated, so I could only imagine how I appeared.

No one said a word for a few minutes before Kolbe spoke up. "Lou, it was a good try."

I nodded my head yes and told Russell to head back to the bank to get the others.

Murph saw us pull in the lot and was waiting for us in the lobby. "What happened?" He said.

"We lost them, that's what happened!" I pushed my way

past them and went right to Simon's office. They all followed me in. I picked up the trash can looking for the bad deposit slips. Nothing was there. Damn, Heidi must have taken them with her. I threw the garbage can at the wall and pounded the desk. They all looked at me like I lost my mind.

Murphy dropped some more bad news on me. "Um . . . Lou, DeRosa checked in. There was . . . no sign of Ingrid, or Mary. Officer White was incapacitated at the scene."

I slouched into Simon's chair. My head fell into my hands. How could I have fucked this up so bad? "So was this all just a setup? To get us away from Ingrid?" I asked.

Everyone thought about that for a while. Finally Kolbe spoke. "Probably, and they still get Jessica's money too . . . Lou, it's time for you to take a back seat. We tried it your way, but it failed. It's time for those of us who are still in law enforcement to take over. Russell, if you don't mind, please drive Detective Romoso back to his office to wait for us to call him."

Russell just nodded at him. He looked as angry as I felt.

I said nothing. Russell led me like a wounded puppy out of Simon's office. I heard the Feds talking about preparing for the search. I knew they'd find nothing. Zero. Nada. Zilch. Heinrich was too good for them to just stumble upon his hideout.

I was pissed. Not at them, but at myself. I had to find them. And quick.

***

At the curb in front of Marco's I noticed an unmarked police car. As I walked in Tom DeRosa was chatting with Duffy. They turned to face me as I came through the door. I was in no mood to talk with DeRosa so decided to walk past him. I saw Duffy shaking his head. Was I acting like a child? Probably, but I was still pissed.

As I neared DeRosa, he grabbed my arm and stopped me dead in my tracks. Tom was a strong man. I shook free and kept going. Then I heard Duffy's booming voice.

"Stop being an asshole and sit your ass down and listen to the man!" I stopped and slowly turned towards Tom.

"What do you want?"

"Lou, I'm sorry about what happened at the bank, and with Ingrid. Believe me, I wanted to keep you involved, but Fritz took over."

"Really! Since when do you take orders from the Feds!"

"I had no choice. I have to follow orders as well. Your buddy Kolbe made some calls. Believe me."

I stood there contemplating what Tom said. I'm sure he was telling the truth, he's had my back for a long time. I extended my hand to him and shook his hand and gave him a hug.

"No hard feelings. I was just upset, I have a bit of a temper."

He raised his eyebrows. "Really? I hadn't noticed."

Had the situation not been so serious, I may have laughed. Instead I bought a round of drinks for the bar. Thankfully it was early; there were only two other guys there.

"Fill me in on the scene on Delaware."

DeRosa jumped into it, sparing no detail. When they got there the front door was slightly ajar. A pool of red liquid coagulating on the floor greeted them. Smeared blood made a trail to the kitchen. Tom had two officers, Walters and Hoffman, follow him.

The kitchen was a mess. There were pots and pans and dishes thrown about. Shards of broken dishes and glasses were all over the floor. More blood, too. No puddle, but droplets leading towards the back door and into the garage. They tried the door but it wouldn't budge. All three worked on the door until it budged open enough to slip through. The body of a man was causing the blockage, Officer Thomas White.

Hoffman ran into the kitchen and called an ambulance. White was bleeding from a gunshot wound in his chest and barely clinging to life. Walters found a towel and gave it to Tom to stem the bleeding. The ambulance got there and loaded him up within five minutes.

"Obviously, the condition of the home indicated signs of a serious struggle," DeRosa said. "You don't have to put rockets in the air to figure that out. No sign of either Mary or Ingrid, either. The question, is where were they taken?"

That was a good question. The only answer I could think of was to upset me to the point where I would make a mistake. Not likely—well, I was furious, but I wasn't going to screw up again.

Tom had his evidence boys gather as much as they could. They dusted the entire house for prints and when they got done it looked like that game where you moved the graphite around with a magnet to make the guy's hair and mustache. Neighbors saw nothing. Most were working. Those homes had their views blocked of Ingrid's due to all the landscaping and snow banks.

None of that mattered. I knew who had them and why. I looked at DeRosa and he knew I knew. This night would not end well for someone or somebody.

"It's time to get nasty with Young and his boys," I said. "This is their work!"

"You think Young took them to the casino?"

"No, I think they're all on Ganson in one of those warehouses, with Jessica and Heinrich."

Tom had an exasperated look on his face. "You say that, but our evidence points elsewhere. Kolbe has everyone scouring the South Towns as we speak."

"Really? That can't be right. I've had nothing come up to point to Hamburg, Orchard Park, nowhere down there."

"Well, he swears by his source. What do you want me to do?"

I paused for a moment to gather my thoughts and figure out a plan. We obviously couldn't find what warehouse they were in, so we had to try and catch them on their way to or from it. To do that, I needed Tom's help. "I want you to get as many men as you can and watch the roads that access Ganson Street. Also keep an eye on the silos, the river, and the railroad tracks. Any car that comes down that road, especially the black Ford, stop them."

"We can't do that, don't have the man power."

"Fine, just post someone around Ganson, and have them be on the look out."

DeRosa agreed to that, and if he could get anyone else pulled off the search he'd let me know.

Tom left, and I sat alone at the bar to finish my drink. How did this all happen so fast? I lost Jessica, then Ingrid and Mary, the people I had sworn to protect.

Duffy looked at me and shook his head. "I hope you know what you're doing, kid."

Not twenty-four hours ago Vinnie the Knot had made the same comment. I didn't have the same confidence as before.

"Me too, Duff. Me too."

CHAPTER 28
MICKEY FINN'S - ISHED

I went up to my office to get some liquid courage. Home didn't sound right. I didn't need the drink, but my Italian guilt was getting the better of me. I could hear my mother in my head. *If you'd only listen you wouldn't be in this mess.* I was hearing this along with a few other guilt-ridden phrases. *She was such a nice girl, why did you screw it up!* Ah! Italian mothers, you got to love them.

Then I thought more about my mother, Josephine, alive and well, newly engaged to my father, Pasquale. It was great to see them young and full of life.

I poured myself a gin and tonic and lit a cigar. My thoughts turned to Officer Thomas White. I hoped he would survive. I thought of Ellen and how I missed her and now how much I wanted to save Ingrid. I thought of Livingston answering the door just as I got there and how I messed up his life. Could I ever apologize enough if they lived? How many other people's lives did I put in danger? I'm sure the list was long and distinguished. A tear formed and rolled down my cheek as I took a sip of my drink and relit my cigar.

A knock at the door pulled me back. Who the hell could that be? I shouted for them to go away, but the door opened anyways. It was Brian Young. And he looked both scared and angry, not a combination you'd often associate with him.

"Brian, how the hell are you? Long time no see."

"Lou, I need to talk to you."

Should I ask him if it had to do with time travel? I paused a moment to contemplate this, but decided to let him say what he came to get off his chest first.

"Sure, what's going on?"

He walked in, and Mike McMann followed him through the door. Seeing his face at that time was not good; he was one of the goons with Kevin back in 2015 at the Rats' hideouts. Now he has the audacity to come here? Did Brian turn on me? Thinking my end was imminent, I immediately jumped to my feet and drew my weapon. Before I could pull the trigger Brian moved in my line of fire.

"Dammit, Lou, wait! Just wait! He's here with me. He's got some things he needs to say."

I was fuming. What side was Brian on? Was he in on this scam the whole time? How could my best friend in the world do this? No . . . that couldn't be. He was helping me before, wasn't he?

"Don't tell me you've been in on this the whole time, Brian. Please don't say it. You already told me you weren't involved, now and in the future. Don't say you lied."

When I said future, McMann's head snapped from Brian to me. He looked guilty. Had he told Brian about the time travel? It appeared not.

"What? What are you talking about? No!" Brian said. "Mike here just came to me, explaining what was happening.

He couldn't take it anymore, but he knew if he came to you alone he'd never get a word out. You'd just shoot him."

Brian was right on that account. I wasn't so sure I could keep myself from doing it regardless. Never taking my eyes off McMann, I sat back down in my chair. The gun still pointed at him. I needed answers. Despite every fiber in my body disagreeing, I had to hear him out.

"Okay, Mike. You got one minute to sing before I blow your brains out."

He cleared his throat and started in on his tale, going all the way back to before the night my wife was shot. Kevin was worried I was getting too close to busting him and couldn't risk it, especially with his newfound partnership with the Germans. Sully's case would be solved in a matter of time. I had to be taken out. McMann, O'Connell, and Leary were tasked with the job.

"Honestly, Lou, I was sick about it. Killing in the war, that was no big deal. That was kill or get killed, right? But to murder you in cold blood? I wanted no part of it."

"Whatever, McMann, you mick piece of shit. Your time's running—"

Brian cut me off. "Enough, Lou! Let the man finish his story."

Normally no one could get away with talking to me like that. Brian was one exception. I bit my tongue and let him finish.

"I said I'd drive," McMann continued. "Didn't want no part of firing the gun. O'Connell jumped at the opportunity. He's sick in the head, Lou. We tracked you to Marco's, thinking you would be alone, only your wife was with you. As soon as I saw that I slammed on the gas. O'Connell yelled at me and started firing wildly. Believe me, Ellen was never supposed to be part of this. I'm so sorry."

284

At the mention of Ellen's name I became more sad than angry. I'd been waiting to know for sure who pulled the trigger, but actually knowing is a whole different thing. It was like a punch to the gut.

McMann continued, telling me he was in too deep, and couldn't figure a way out without himself going down for it, especially after Sully. He was driving the car after all. Leary was also the work of O'Connell. After the failed attempt to get me at Jessica Wright's home, Young was furious and had Leary taken out. DeRosa would be pleased. That's three open murders McMann just closed for him. A promotion might be in the works for my favorite Captain.

I looked at Brian, and he was almost as pissed as me. "How could you not know this was going on, Brian?" I asked him.

He shook his head, wouldn't meet my eyes. "I don't know. My love for Kevin must have blinded me to the truth. I couldn't . . . I wouldn't believe he was capable of such things. The past few days with everything happening my doubts were finally breaking down. I started to do some research, and eventually found some things that didn't look right with the finance deal through HK Arts and Maritime Central. Mr. Simon at the bank is either careless, or he was in on it. But I couldn't be sure. It's all right here." He put a file on my desk.

"Then Mike came to me earlier tonight, and I wanted to barge right in there and kill Kevin myself. But he talked me out of it, saying the only way we could do this is to come find you."

"Why?"

"Because," McCann said, "Kevin is the only one who knows where Ingrid and the rest of them are being held. Heinrich would only deal with him. The rest of us were kept from the inner circle. Security reasons, I guess."

"Well, he wasn't wrong, I'll give him that. You are sitting here singing like a bird to me right now," I said.

Each of us chuckled a little bit. The tension filling the room started to break. I had to formulate a plan to get to Kevin. Hopefully Brian could help me turn him. For all Kevin's flaws, his love for his only brother wasn't one of them. That unbroken bond could be my saving grace.

We sat in silence for a bit. I thought about my situation. It was a suicide mission, no doubt about it. All my allies—other than Russell—were either preoccupied or out of the picture. Right now it was just us staring up at an enemy that held the high ground.

I turned to Mike, mostly calmed down at this point. I still wanted to shoot him, but maybe just in the kneecap now. He and Brian were my only chance to make this work. Time to swallow my pride and finish this thing once and for all.

"Mike, I don't think I'll ever forgive you. I'm not sure the law will, either. But if you help me out, I'll do my best to make sure DeRosa and company take it as easy as possible on you."

To his credit, Mike never wavered, and looked me in the eye. Had to respect him for that. "I'm not looking for a break. This has got to stop."

"The letter to Ingrid was a nice touch," I said. He looked at me and smirked. Brian looked confused, but I told him I'd explain it later.

Brian then got up and paced the room. I could tell this was eating him up inside. He only paced like that when a major decision was looming in front of him. "Are you guys sure about this? The counterfeiting and all?"

Mike answered first. "Yeah, Brian. You were isolated, though. Kevin made sure of that. He didn't want to drag you in. Bills got passed through the gambling and check cashing."

"I agree with him," I said. I dug out the money I took from Vinnie the Knot, tossed it on the table. "This is from the bookmaking operation, paid to someone who thought he hit it big."

Brian grabbed the bills and felt them. "They feel fine to me."

"Trust me, Brian, they're fake. Damn good, but fake," I said.

He sat back down and let out a big sigh. "Okay, you win. Kevin isn't to be harmed. That's not negotiable."

I looked at Mike, but he showed no emotion either way. I know Brian loved his brother, but I wanted my pound of flesh.

"He won't be harmed if we can help it," I lied. "We need to get the place emptied, so nobody gets caught up in this that isn't involved."

"How are we going to do that?" McMann asked.

I smiled. "Exposure," I said, and laid out the plan.

Time to get back at it and finish this once and for all.

***

It was 8 p.m. by the time we worked it out and headed to Mickey Finn's. Russell had joined us. With McMann's loyalty still in question, having a man of Russell's caliber with us a must.

We took Brian's car to not arouse any suspicion. The night air was crisp and the snow on the sidewalk crunched beneath our feet as we walked towards the car. Lucky for us it didn't take long for the car to warm up. We made a right on Franklin to North Division Street to Michigan Ave, and straight to Mickey Finn's. The ride seemed longer than usual for some reason. I'm sure the silence had plenty to do with it.

We pulled up to the front of the casino and Brian stopped in front of the building. A new valet came over to the car. He was a nice kid, unlike that asshole Henderson. Thank God for that. If it was Sean, the plan may have been foiled before it started. The kid didn't recognize me or McMann. His name was Dave Leroy. He was eighteen years old, bright red hair, freckles, and built like a string bean. Brian said he was trying to earn money for college. I didn't have the heart to tell him tonight would be his last night.

Russell was to stay outside, in case anyone tried to make a run for it. I had him work his way around back to the secret driveway. If Young or his gang were going to take off, that would be the likely spot.

Brian, McMann, and I continued through the door and into the lobby. No matter how many times I come into this building the lobby was so impressive that you just had to stop and take it all in. The crystal chandelier had to be worth ten large, easy. The indoor waterfall was spectacular. The water crashing onto the rocks was soothing and calming, but the calm wouldn't last too much longer.

Before we could take another step, three bouncers met us in the lobby. They were built like Sherman tanks. I never had seen these three men before tonight. They were all over six feet tall and the smallest one weighed at least 225. They were solid from head to toe; obviously they spent their free time making out with iron. The first of the "hear no evil, see no evil, speak no evil" monkeys spoke.

"You're not welcome here, gumshoe. I think it would be wise of you to leave the premises now before I call the cops."

"Guys, he's with me," McMann said. "We're taking him to talk to Kevin. His orders."

The three goons looked at each other and shrugged. "Okay, Mr. McMann," the first one said.

We walked through. McMann made his way to the back to check in. He'd been gone for a while, and we didn't need Kevin getting suspicious. I went to the casino, while Brian headed to warn those who were clean to vacate the premises.

The place was booming with customers. I reached into my pocket and pulled out a few one-hundred-dollar bills. Of course they were the counterfeit ones from Vinnie the Knot. I'm not going to waste my own hard-earned cash. It was time to gamble everything on the roll of the dice. I squeezed in next to a beautiful curvy brunette in a tight-fitting sweater and skirt. She smiled at me and said, "You can get closer if you like, honey."

My mind wandered as usual when you get the opportunity to be that close to a beautiful woman. Come on now, what guy's mind hasn't wandered? After all, we are guys. Then I realized I had something better waiting for me and it wasn't worth it.

I threw my money on the craps table and the box man— that's the guy who is seated at the table and handles the cash— grabbed my money to exchange it for chips. He got an odd look on his face immediately after grabbing my money. He didn't reach for any chips. Instead he signaled over to the pit boss and whispered in his ear. The pit boss, Ronny Smith, walked over to me and signaled for me to come over to him. A sharp Irishman from the First Ward, Ronny hung out with Kevin Young back when they were kids. Smith was about five foot six and 115 pounds soaking wet with black hair and blue eyes, wearing a three-hundred-dollar suit. He probably could have gotten it for a lot less at the boys department at Robert Halls. He went to college, studied business, and became a foreman at the GM plant on Delevan Avenue in the city. Kevin gave him a chance to triple his earnings so he jumped at it.

I have to admit, I would have too. Behind him were two bouncers, the Gondola brothers, Vincent and Giovanni. They weren't particularly tall, about five foot ten, weighing 220. They both had barrel chests and huge arms. They worked for their father's concrete business during the day and moonlighted as bouncers at Mickey Finn's.

They both nodded their heads at me. I guess that was their way of saying hello. It was typical for these two. They didn't talk much. Didn't have too.

I nodded back and said to Ronny, "What's the problem?"

He looked right and left to make sure no one heard him but me. "Your money is no good here, Lou."

"Why is that?" I said a little louder, drawing a few eyes around us.

"You know why. Look, you either take this money and leave or go back into your pockets."

"If I don't?" I said, louder still. We were starting to attract some more attention.

"Then I have the Gondolas here throw you out on your ass."

I refused to move. Everyone around us stopped. They were all looking at Ronny and me.

"Lou, we don't need your business." Ronny had ditched the whisper and was making his voice heard now. "I asked you to leave nicely and you wouldn't so now we do it the hard way. Throw him out, boys!"

The Gondola brothers moved towards me. I was not about to fight these guys man to man, much less two on one. So I called on my trusted friend: my gun. They stopped dead in their tracks. Ronnie looked at my gun. I could see the sweat pouring from his forehead. He knew things were heading south fast and he needed a way out.

"Okay, you win. Your money is good here."

This was my chance. I had everyone's attention in the casino. I stood up on a chair and jumped up on the craps table.

"You see, ladies and gentlemen, these guys don't want me to gamble. That's because I know something they don't want you all to know. This casino pays off in counterfeit money." Any color that was left in Smith's face was gone. There were some murmurs from the crowd. "That's right. You've been paid off in fake money. It's no fucking good." I snatched my money from Smith's hand and threw it on the craps table.

"Go ahead and touch it. The paper is no good, it feels different than the real deal. Here, try it out for yourself."

I threw a good bill on the table and they all took turns comparing the bills. I could see the stunned look on their faces. Ronnie and the Gondola brothers started to backpedal towards the exit. The other employees who weren't in on the scam were just as shocked as they realized that they may have been paid in bad money. Everyone was looking for a pit boss. They wanted an explanation. I smiled and left the gaming room. My next stop was the bar. It was crowded as well. There were plenty of scoopers left spending their hard-earned checks.

I walked in and one of them asked, "What the hell is going on in there?"

I smiled. "If you must know, the players just found out that they've been getting paid in counterfeit money. And if I'm a betting man, which I am, I'd say you all have been getting paid in bullshit money too."

I could see their faces getting redder by the second. They all turned to get an explanation from the bartender, but he headed for the hills. The scoopers were pissed and they were looking for someone in charge, but they had deserted the place at the first sign of trouble. With those Brian had cleared out, the place was almost void of employees. The angry mob forming started to tear apart Mickey Finn's. Some of them went to the second floor. Four bookies were taking bets. They knew payouts were made in counterfeit cash and Young's casino was a house of cards. Unfortunately for them, the only way out was the fire escape. The scoopers were on them before they could reach it. There is nothing worse than an angry gang of hard-working, drunken men who have been cheated and are out for revenge.

I could see the place coming unglued as windows broke, tables were busted, and anything that wasn't nailed down was destroyed. A loud crash sounded from the lobby; the chandelier had been knocked down into the fountain. I could hear the screams of the unfortunate bosses who didn't make it out. It wasn't my problem.

Most of the angry patrons started to make their way out after a bit. That was good, just like I wanted. The less people around for what was going to happen the better. I met Brian by the bar. We waited for McMann for a few moments, but decided he may already be with Young to put up a good front. I wish I had a way to contact Russell. Hopefully he was staying alert now that the wheels had been put in motion.

We made our way through the remnants of Mickey Finn's to Kevin's office. Now things were really about to begin.

Chapter 29

Silencing the Opposition

There it was, my quest was reaching its conclusion. I reached the door to Young's office. I thought about the best way to enter and figured why not do what I always do. Be a bull in a china shop. No sense changing now. Ellen always said I was about as subtle as an atom bomb. I thought about kicking the door down. However, this was no ordinary door. It was steel.

"I can see you want to kick it down," Brian said. "Just try the knob, it's probably open."

Sometimes I can be thick. I grabbed the handle and it opened fine. Brian led the way.

But he stopped dead in his tracks. I walked right into him. I leaned to the side to see what made Brian stop.

Kevin Young was sitting tied up in his desk chair looking like he went ten rounds with Rocky Marciano. Punching bags didn't get that much abuse. His arm was in a sling, probably from when I shot him in the future. He slowly looked up and struggled to get out a sentence.

"Looks like we all lost, Lou," Kevin managed to spit out.

Brian ran to untie him. Before he got there, Heinrich stepped out of the shadows with a Luger in his hand.

Where was McMann? He was my ace in the hole. I made a move to my gun, but felt some cold steel on the back of my neck. O'Connell. Damn!

"Welcome, Detective Romoso, we've been waiting for you," Heinrich said. "It's time, as you Americans say, to tie up loose ends. You were the last remaining piece. Mr. Young here has worn out his usefulness. Mr. O'Connell, though, he has potential."

"Fuck you, Heinrich, I'm not alone here," I said.

He laughed. That couldn't be good. "McMann? How stupid do you think I am? Erik, if you would."

The back door opened and in walked McMann with a gun to his head. He smiled, even though his face had taken a beating. Erik looked cold as ice, but somehow had an air of satisfaction about him. He was one sick bastard. No Russell, though, so maybe we still had a chance.

Before I could say anything O'Connell clocked me in the head with his gun and down I went. Erik, not to be outdone, came over and kicked me in the ribs. I scrambled to my knees and thought it was over. I failed everyone. But I wouldn't go down without a fight.

"Come on, Bernhard, your fight is with me, not them." I motioned to Brian and McMann. "Let's you and me figure this out. Man to man."

He looked at me with surprise. "Bernhard, no one has called me that for years. Maybe you are better than I gave you credit for, Romoso." He walked around the desk and sat on its edge, just a few feet from me. "But you are too late. My plan is already in motion. Jessica's money was wired to my account this afternoon. All the remaining art has been loaded up and is on its way back to Switzerland."

"How far will that ten million get you?" I said. I needed to keep him talking. Maybe the chaos out in the bar would soon attract some cops and we could still wiggle out of this. "Yeah, it's a lot of money, but hardly enough to restart the Nazi Party. I don't think you and this idiot brother of yours could pull that off."

That earned me another kick to the ribs. Damn, Erik was quick. I never even saw it coming. I forced myself back up to my knees, wincing in pain.

"Do you think Buffalo is the first city I've hit? Hardly," Bernhard said. He stood up and started pacing around the spacious office, like he was some big-shot college professor. "No, Buffalo is merely my base of operations. I've been all over the country spreading the counterfeit bills, fulfilling Hitler's original dream of crashing the U.S. economy. Jessica's ten million is merely an added bonus. We've been able to amass billions through the US, Canada, and Argentina with our efforts."

"How, it's only you three!" He had to be lying. No way could he have organized something like that, not with the likes of Kolbe after him. And then I thought about Kevin, and him travelling to the future, and working with the River Rats.

"You poor American fool," he said, laughing. Erik joined him. Even O'Connell chuckled. "Your friend Mr. O'Connell has been in my pocket this whole time. Kevin was just a means to an end. And where do you think the rest of the Nazi Party survivors are, Mr. Romoso? Why, they are helping me in this grand plan to restore the Third Reich into power. You stupid Americans are too busy squabbling with the Soviets to even notice. If not for Agent Kolbe, that traitor, and the Israeli death squads, no one would even care about us."

He had a point there. Only a decade later and people were already forgetting what the war was all about. That damn McCarthy had totally shut everyone off to any other issues. It was all about communism now. No one cared about fascists.

"So now what, you just kill me, then time travel your ass out of here?" I said.

"Time travel?" Brian said. "What the hell are you talking about, Lou?"

I forgot Brian was in the room. Everyone else already knew about it.

"I was wondering when you'd get to that," Bernhard answered for me. "One of Hitler's great gifts to the world. It's a pity we can't share it any longer." Bernhard started in on a tale I would have never believed if I hadn't already traveled through time myself.

Bernhard, in charge of the counterfeit operation to bring down the Western economies, also oversaw what he called "Betrieb Wurmloch." Hitler recruited the brightest minds in Europe, some by choice, others by force. Together they poured over Einstein's old theories and put them to the test.

"The scientists were getting close to a breakthrough," Bernhard continued. "However, the Soviets were closing in on our location. SS units, Erik's included, were brought to the front to slow their advance. I wanted no part of being caught by them, so I had Erik execute the scientists and we put their machine to the test. If it failed, we would die. Better that than to be in the hands of Communists."

"Let me guess, the machine worked," I said sarcastically.

"Ja, but not as you would expect."

They ended up in the German countryside, Erik, Berhnard, and Heidi. The year was 2005, sixty years in the future.

"We had no way to know where or when the time was set

to send us. We had hidden much of the wealth confiscated from the Jews. The time machine was damaged, but we took with us all of the scientists' work. With that and the Jewish gold we hired new scientists. They were amazed by the research we had, and quickly duplicated it and created much smaller devices we could use."

He pulled one from his pocket. I happened to have one of those, but it was broken. Or I just didn't know how to use it.

"So did you have a life in the future as well?" I asked.

Bernhard looked perplexed. "What do you mean, Romoso?"

"I mean, I have a life here and in the future. Family and the like. Do you too?"

"Nien. I do not know what you speak of."

Huh, that's strange. What made me so lucky?

"What are we waiting for?" O'Connell said. He looked like he was starting to get nervous. "Let's get out of here. If you hadn't heard the commotion out here, Mickey Finn's is done. The cops should be here any minute."

He was right. Cops would have been here by now, if they were coming at all. This stalling wasn't working. Kolbe must have pulled all available resources to deal with hunting down the Germans and finding all the kidnapped. If he got his head out of his ass and headed here, we could end this. Sometimes the Feds' thought process was too one dimensional.

"I don't think so," Bernhard said. "If Agent Kolbe stays true to form, the entirety of the police force is out searching for us in the South Towns. We have all the time in the world. Besides, they won't find anything."

He was too confident. I didn't like it. They must have sent in an anonymous tip to the police.

"Those new scientists wanted to publish the work. I had other ideas. We were presumed dead, and no record of any of us three existed in the future. That was too easy to continue our work. Erik put the scientists in the ground, and then we began to rebuild Hitler's empire.

"Our only setback was the sixty-year restriction. The scientists tried to explain it, but I did not understand their talk of wormholes and time paradoxes. We could set the location, however, and traveled back in time to Argentina, where we knew many of our Nazi brethren were hiding."

Sean Henderson came bursting through the back door. "Hey, boss, we are ready to go."

"Did you make the call?" Bernhard asked him.

Henderson laughed. "Yeah, that smug asshole Kolbe believed every word."

What a prick. I knew he was no good. Looks like Kolbe's source had been selling him a bill of goods.

I needed to get more out of Bernhard about time traveling. And I wanted to know exactly how I had a life in both eras. That didn't make sense at all.

"You asshole, Henderson, how could you do this!" Brian yelled before I could say anything.

I looked over at Kevin. He was still conscious, but hadn't moved in a while. He sat in silence, knowing it was all over. If I hadn't wanted to kill him myself, I would have felt bad for the guy. His entire empire had been ripped out from under him, undone by two of his closest confidants. And the third had flipped on him to the good guys. Poor asshole.

"Erik, Mr. O'Connell, let's escort our friends down to the garage," Bernhard said.

If Russell was still in play, I needed to keep Bernhard and Erik's attention. I started to ask more questions, but Erik cuffed me over the head good. I kept my mouth shut as we were shuffled to the basement of the casino. There was the Ford, just where I thought it would be, and Bernhard's blue Cadillac.

Kevin had installed a basement garage when he rebuilt Mickey Finn's. That was the driveway to nowhere I saw back in present times, the one Teddy pointed out to me.

Alongside them were two 1950 blue and white Ford delivery vans. The vans were used for, believe it or not, a legitimate business Brian owned. Brian had started a delivery service as a part-time venture during the off season in his days playing football. It was called Bringing You Service Delivery.

The cops weren't going to suspect them in these vans, even if some of them were still in the area. They were on the lookout for the other two cars parked next to them. It was the perfect vehicle to use for what was going to transpire. No one would think twice about a delivery van making its way towards the warehouses on Ganson. Hopefully someone could put two and two together and think it couldn't be a coincidence that Brian Young's company was making the deliveries. I wasn't keeping my hopes up.

Even better, there were two goons I'd never seen before in the driver's seat of each car. Again, guys the cops wouldn't be looking for. These Nazi assholes knew what they were doing, that's for sure. One of those goons opened the back door, and there lay an unconscious Russell. Shit. So much for a rescue.

They still hadn't cuffed us, though, which I thought was strange. McMann and Brian were close in the garage, and Brian caught my eye. I knew what he was going to try. McMann picked up on it as well. This wasn't a good idea, but maybe it was our only shot. Erik was busy loading Kevin into one van. It wasn't an easy task, since he was mostly dead weight. Henderson had a gun on us, but Bernhard had turned his back to speak to O'Connell and the drivers.

Brian made his move. Even as a hulk of a man he was quick on his feet. Henderson didn't have a chance. Brian head-butted him with everything he had, and Sean was out like a light. He hit the cement basement floor with a sickening thud. Blood started to trickle out from behind his head, and was already flowing from his busted nose. His body spasmed a couple times then went still. He wasn't going to make it.

McMann had picked up the gun and got one shot off before anyone knew what happened. Erik and O'Connell were fast, though, and took out McMann before he could get another shot off.

I stood there stunned in silence. Everything had happened in a second or two, and I never reacted. It was all over almost before it started. McMann was down, and I rushed to his side.

"Hang in there, Mike," I said.

He coughed, and blood spurted out of his mouth. "I'm sorry, Lou, I'm s-sorry." And he was gone.

I looked up and tried to assess what was going on. Erik and O'Connell had guns on Brian, and Bernhard and the drivers had me covered. Brian was wincing in pain. He must have taken a bullet, too. His hip was bleeding bad.

"You've got to help him, he'll bleed out if we don't!" I yelled.

Erik, cold as ever, looked to Bernhard, who nodded at him. Erik understood, raised his gun and fired into Brian's chest.

"No!" I screamed. This couldn't be happening. I scrambled away from Mike and over to him. Brian gripped my hand tightly. His eyes were wide and he looked at me. I put pressure on the wound with my other hand. His grip started to fade quickly, and he passed out.

Kevin had managed to sit up in the van. He still couldn't speak, but he was crying. I knew it was from the pain. Not of the beating he took, but from possibly losing the one person in this world he truly loved.

"You assholes!" I yelled. Tears were also falling down my face.

Bernhard grabbed me and dragged me to my feet. "This is your responsibility, Romoso," he said angrily. "It wasn't supposed to happen this way. Had you just listened, no one would have died."

I doubted what he said, but I was too broken at the time to respond. Erik still showed no emotion.

O'Connell had a smirk on his face. He bent down and grabbed Henderson's weapon and tucked it into his belt. "He won't be needing that anymore," he said, and then he laughed. If Erik was cold, O'Connell was insane.

Defeated, but not done. Erik came over and tied my hands behind my back. Bernhard wound up and backhanded me across the face. "No more, or I'll start killing everyone else at the warehouse."

I hate getting hit in the face. It gets me wild. Though my hands were tied, my feet weren't. I pretended to buckle over from the slap but that just put me into position to throw my shoulder into Bernhard. I drove him into the wall with a thud. He wilted like a seven-day-old rose. Erik was on me like lightning, though. Before I could sidestep him he took my legs out. My face hit the brick wall. He and O'Connell picked me up and threw me in the van without any fight from me.

That was the last thing I remembered before my mind shut down.

CHAPTER 30
PUNCHING-BAG TACTICS

I t had to be about an hour before I woke up. I was sitting in a wooden chair with my hands tied to the armrests and my ankles tied to the legs. As I opened my eyes they were all there. I was like a teacher at the head of the class. They were tied up to wooden chairs as well. The room was painted an off-white with a concrete floor. Nothing special. The floor was wall-to-wall plastic. I guess they didn't want to make a mess in case they had other guests to entertain. There were no windows and the room was cool.

Ingrid was in front of me. She had a bruise on her face. I figured it was from that bitch Heidi. On her left was Jessica and her right Russell. Mary was next to Jessica. Kevin was behind them all. He still didn't look good, but was conscious. It was like old home days. I guess Bernhard wasn't kidding when he said he was tying up loose ends.

In walked Heidi dressed in a tight-fitting skirt and top. She did look great. Amazing what passes through a guy's mind, especially when he is about to die.

Heidi walked up to me and ran her fingers over my shoulder and put her lips next to my ear. "You should have declined to take this case. You'd be alive to see tomorrow."

"You're wasting your time," I said. "If I were you I'd leave now, because when I get out of here you're going to be a widow, sitting alone in a cell waiting for the chair."

"I highly doubt that." Her lips moved to mine and she kissed me. I shook my head to get her away.

Ingrid was pissed. I guess that was the whole idea. "Heidi, when I get out of here you won't have to worry about the chair, because I'm going to kill you myself!"

Heidi just laughed, walking around the room. She stared at each of us in turn. I had no idea what she was thinking. She grabbed her purse from the desk that was in the corner of the room and pulled out a .38 and walked over to Mary. She put the barrel to Mary's forehead and held it there, finger on the trigger.

"You were Sully's girl, yes?"

Mary didn't flinch, which surprised Heidi. I could tell by the perplexed look on her face, the first real emotion she'd shown since I met her a few days back.

"You know how he got shot, Sully's girl?" Heidi said. "I tell you. The swine tried to pick me up, and when I laughed at him, he got mad. So he forced me to shoot him and I did, right in the knee. Your Mr. Sully had a wandering eye. He really didn't love you." She pulled the gun away and moved back towards her purse. "No matter. Soon you can take the matter up with him. I have to admit, I enjoyed shooting him. I never liked him."

Mary said nothing.

"Nothing? No response from you, my pretty little redhead?"

Heidi seemed to be enjoying her mental torture of Mary, but she was not done.

"Do you know how the swine Sully really died?" Mary looked up, and showed the first sign of irritation. Heidi smiled pure evil, and nodded to Erik. "Erik here is to blame. He tied him up in a chair like you are now."

Heidi went into detail I had long suspected but never wanted to hear. Somehow Heinrich had caught wind Sully was talking to the police, and wanted to know what was revealed. Sully, being the stubborn piece of shit he was, gave them nothing. That didn't stop Erik from trying, though. He pistol-whipped him multiple times in the head and face. When that didn't work, he used his fists, raining down body-blows. Sully responded by spitting blood at him. Erik then broke each one of his fingers, one at a time. Not once did Sully scream, Heidi told us. Say what you will about the man Sully was, but you couldn't deny he was one tough son of a bitch.

Mary had tears running down her face by the end of the story. I couldn't blame her. Heidi seemed to get more excited with each gory detail of the demise of Michael Sullivan.

Jessica was next on her hit parade. "Jessica, how can such a smart businesswoman be so blind? Did you really think my Bernhard was in love with you? He was in love with the opportunity to *use* you. Do you think he actually liked sleeping with you, knowing I was in the next room? It took you long enough. You too will be joining your pathetic husband."

Jessica, unlike Mary, spoke. "Don't be too proud of yourself, your dear sweet Bernhard couldn't perform!"

That infuriated Heidi, especially since I started laughing out loud. That wasn't such a good idea on my part. It put Heidi over the edge. These Nazis were so easy to piss off. She started ranting in German and I had no clue what she was bitching about so I kept laughing. The more I laughed the worse she got. I have that effect on women.

Bernhard walked in the room while I was having my laughing fit. Erik came over and gave me a shot to the ribs. The air left my lungs like a balloon popped by a pin. That hurt, but I smiled through the pain. I also noticed something else that happened once he hit me. Well, two things. One, if I smiled every time he hit me I could drive him crazy and he'd make a mistake. Two, the chair they tied me to was very old, so old that every time I moved from getting hit the armrest would crack a little.

Bernhard must have grown tired of the banter. "We have wasted enough time with these sub-humans. Erik, take care of Detective Romoso and the rest of this, this scourge of mixed races."

That bastard lied. "Bernhard, you fuck, you told me no one else would get hurt! Let the women go, for God's sake."

He smirked. "Goodbye, Detective. Come, Heidi, meine liebste." He and Heidi made for the door. He turned to get one last shot in. "Oh, before I forget. Jessica, thank you for the hospitality." He and Heidi both laughed as they walked out.

Jessica's head dropped, as did Ingrid's and Mary's. Russell and Kevin were still hurting. Erik decided to start with Kevin. He put on a pair of black gloves and began reigning body shots right to his ribs. Normally I'd be cheering in the front row with a box of popcorn watching Kevin take a beating, but I felt sorry for him. It's one thing to get hit in a fair fight. But to be tied up and beaten? No one deserved that. Blood began to trickle from his swollen lips. The damage was becoming severe. Kevin moaned with every punch. The women were sobbing hysterically.

After Kevin mercifully passed out I needed to focus Erik on me. He slowly walked up and down the front of the room eyeing his next victim. He stopped in front of Ingrid. My heart began to race as I struggled to get free. There was no way she could take a beating from Erik. She'd be dead in seconds.

The armrests were loose, but not loose enough. Erik grabbed Ingrid by the throat and squeezed. As he tightened his grip he spoke in an eerie tone. "I get to see you die as I did your frightened husband."

I began to rock the chair for all it was worth and managed to tip myself over. The commotion caused Erik to let go of Ingrid's throat. I could hear her coughing and gasping for air. It worked.

Erik came over to me as I lay on the floor still tied to the chair. He was pissed. I made it worse by laughing. "Erik, you coward. You killed unarmed men, and now you torture a helpless female? You're a candy ass!"

Well, that did the trick. He kicked me with his steel-toed shoes. I didn't see that coming. He stomped on my exposed rib cage and drove his boots into my sides. I wouldn't make a sound, as hard as that was. I was hurting bad but each blow was further loosening the armrests.

Erik got tired of my zero response and lifted me back to a seated position, then headed to Russell. One thing I'll say about Erik, he was an equal opportunity torturer. He'd hammer one of us for a bit then start another project.

Russell was bandaged up. Erik ripped off the bandages, then he grabbed some rock salt. Where the hell he got salt I didn't know. Obviously this guy carried his own tools of the trade. He took a handful and ground it into the wounds on Russell's arm. He was tough and held his own until the pain became unbearable. Erik then hit him in the face and Russell's nose exploded in blood, spraying the plastic-covered walls. Some of it made it above the edge of the plastic, though, and splattered and started to drip underneath the covering.

I had to get him back to me. My arms were almost free.

"Erik, your painter is going to be frosted that you got blood on his wall. I think your big brother will take it out of your allowance. Bad boy!'

Erik hated me by now, but that was inevitable. Everyone I meet eventually does. "I kill you, Romoso!"

"Fuck you, Nazi!"

He sprinted over and caught me with a left in the jaw. Damn, that hurt.

"Is that all you got? Did Hitler teach you to hit like a girl? Storm Troopers, ha! More like seamstresses!"

Bam! Another blow to the face, he drew blood with that one. "I bet you got hit by your grandmother harder than I just did, you goose-stepping pussy!"

Erik was irate and out of control, which was good. He was screaming in German, bouncing off the walls. The thought of someone openly defying him drove him nuts. Especially me. Erik caught himself and was breathing heavily. He was getting tired. He punched me again in the back of the head. I saw stars with that one. My head was spinning. It couldn't have been his fist. It wasn't. It was a sap.

I didn't remember passing out, but I do remember waking up to a cold bucket of water. I shook my head and caught my breath. And there was Erik and Bernhard right in front of me. Bernhard grabbed my hair and slapped my face. As I told you before I hate that. When he slapped me, though, the armrest loosened more. Almost free.

He wasn't happy. The smile was wiped from his face. "Welcome back, Detective," Bernhard said. "I see you managed to work my brother into a frenzy. I had to come in here and calm him down."

Erik took off his gloves and wiped his sweat-soaked brow, quite pleased with himself; he was beating up another defenseless man. The room was quiet except for the moans of the injured, which was just about all of us.

Bernhard was getting edgy. They were wasting too much time. They needed to get rid of all of us. We were all witnesses. Especially me!

"Erik, finish with my friend Detective Romoso and then make quick work of the others."

Erik walked over to my chair and circled like a shark stalking his prey. I started to smile at him; he took exception and punched me in the side of the head. That stung. I saw spots in front of my eyes. It was like looking at floating dice.

"No smiling, dead man," Erik snarled.

I couldn't resist, so I did. Bam! A shot to the ribs. It sounded like a loud slap. The air shot out of my lungs and I was gasping for breath.

"You're going to have . . . to hit me harder than that . . . asshole! I've been hit . . . harder by mosquitos."

As usual I don't know when to shut my mouth and he began to use my rib cage as a punching bag. He seemed to be enjoying his work. The more he punched me the harder he laughed. He was fucking crazy. I could hear the battering of my ribs as they were turning to mush. It was getting harder to breathe. Erik was surprised that I was still conscious and not begging him to stop. I would never give this Nazi bastard the pleasure. I'd die first. I'm stubborn that way.

As Erik rested I could hear Ingrid sobbing. "Erik, stop! You're killing him. Lou, Lou, are you all right? Please wake up!"

I shook my head to clear the cobwebs. I heard Ingrid crying as well as everyone else screaming for Erik to stop.

"Ingrid I'm fine, don't cry. You hit harder than he does, the piece of shit!"

I wasn't fine. I was dying.

"Detective, beg for your life now and he will end it quickly and painlessly," Bernhard said.

"Eat shit and die you Nazi piece of shit!" It's tough to get creative with insults when you're almost down for the count.

Erik put his face close to mine, grabbed my face with his hands so I was looking him straight in the eyes and he began to laugh, then he punched me as hard as he could. I went tumbling backwards in the chair. The only good thing was the armrests broke and my arms were free.

The bad part was the last punch finally did me in.

CHAPTER 31

LAZARUS

I was looking down on myself. I could see my head fall to my chest as it heaved, trying to catch every lifesaving breath. My eyes rolled back into my head as I lost consciousness, but I really didn't care. I could hear Ingrid crying, as well as the other women. Russell was screaming for me to hang in there and keep fighting. But I didn't want to fight anymore. I was done. Time for something better and more peaceful.

I found myself floating towards a bright white light. At the end of the light was a man with long hair dressed in the brightest, whitest robe I have ever seen. It was almost blinding. He was smiling, and the smile warmed my heart. He was standing in front of a beautiful white mansion. The landscaping was spectacular. The grass, trees, and shrubs were the greenest green; the blue in the sky made you feel so at ease. Where was I? I recognized the longhaired man from paintings I've seen in churches. It couldn't be, was I dead? I must be, because it looked like heaven. I made it. Don't ask me how, but I made it.

If I made it to heaven the man must be God. Holy crap, I met the Big Guy. He never said a word. He just smiled and pointed toward the white light.

I looked toward the white, warming light and there they were waiting for me. They were all smiles and all looking healthy as ever. There was my father and my mother, who passed away a year apart from each other, my grandparents, seemingly alive and well.

I saw my grandmother Elvira holding a roll of quarters, which she gave each of us every year on Christmas. I saw my other grandmother and the grandfather I never met smiling and waving me to come to them. My father was laughing and my mother was right by his side, waving me to come. They were all smiles.

Then I saw an angel as the group split to let her through. It was Ellen and my son, Lou. She was more beautiful than ever. Her blond hair was golden, her eyes were the deepest blue I've ever seen, and her smile was intoxicating. My son looked great in his little football jersey. I ran as fast as I could towards Ellen and the rest of my family, all my injuries forgotten and gone. I couldn't wait to hug them all. There wasn't any pain. Tears flooded my face. I put my arms around Ellen and Lou Jr. and hugged them for all it was worth.

Ellen didn't say a word. She hugged me back then stepped back and pointed to the rest of my family. The white light grew brighter and more comforting as I hugged each of them.

Ellen pointed to another place and said, "Lou, watch and listen."

I did as I was told. You know when they say your life flashes before your eyes? Well guess what, it's true. I watched. I saw myself as a boy in both times, past and present. Every good thing, every mistake. No one said a word. My time as a fighter pilot, my time as cop, my time with Ellen, everything, every moment. Guess time has no value in heaven. I didn't care, I was with my family.

Then Ellen spoke. "I have to show you something. You are not going to like it, but you have to see it."

Ellen looked and I followed her eyes, I was holding my son's hand as I watched.

Ellen was right; what I saw wasn't easy. My battered body, lifeless on the chair with the armrests broken free, laid in audience as Erik one by one turned to the rest of my ragtag group, and shot them.

"Ellen, why are you showing me this?" I asked. All the euphoria I was feeling was fading away.

"Because it is not your time to die. You have to go back."

"No! My place is here with you and my son. I let you down before and I'm not leaving you. Or them." I pointed to my family.

"Lou, listen to me!" It was a male voice. I looked up and saw my father, Pasquale. "You have to go back. This is not your time or place right now. We will all be here when it is your time. I promise."

I couldn't understand. "Why don't you want me here?"

Ellen squeezed my hand tighter and kissed my cheek. I'm sure she could taste the salt from my tears of joy and sorrow. I did not want to go back to the land of the living. Quite frankly it was a pain in the ass sometimes. Ellen gave me a love tap to my head.

Damn, she could read my thoughts. I must be the only guy to die, go to heaven, and get sent back. Must be because I'm such a calming influence. The Romoso luck continues.

"Lou, stop feeling sorry for yourself. It is time for you to return, those people need you." Ellen pointed to Ingrid. "She needs you. You now know we will be waiting for you. Go to them. We all love you very much and we will be here when it is your time."

Ellen kissed me on the lips and the man I first met tapped me on the shoulder. I looked at him. He smiled, and I felt reassured.

***

The white light got dimmer as I floated back towards Earth. It was being replaced by a flood of pain. I could taste blood flowing from my mouth and my ribs felt like a broken bag of bones. My head throbbed. Even my frigging teeth hurt. My eyes were almost swollen shut, but I could see, blurry as it was. Then I felt it. My arms were free. Erik had his gun pointed at Russell. Ingrid and the other women were crying. I had to think. I had to get Erik back to me.

"Hey, you Nazi pig, leave him alone. You can't even kill people right. You suck!"

I was now awake. Hurting, but awake. I scanned the room and everyone seemed to perk up. Ingrid and Mary yelled at the same time.

"Lou, you're alive!"

"Lazarus has nothing on me," I said as I tried to get up. But the legs of the chair were still attached and movement was a struggle.

Erik forgot about Russell and sprinted over to me. He grabbed my sweat- and blood-soaked hair and pulled my head back. His eyes were wide open and I could see the evil in them. His pupils were racing side to side. Who knows what he was seeing.

He put his gun away and pulled out a knife. Oh come on now, a frigging knife! Where did this guy keep all of these weapons? He stared at the blade as the light reflected in the polished steel. This ass was going to cut my throat. He started to move his hand, holding the knife, and tightened his grip on my hair to pull my head back to gain access my throat.

Ingrid screamed. "No!"

The scream distracted Erik for a split second. It was the opening I needed. As he closed in his head got closer to mine. He wanted the best seat in the house to watch me die, this time permanently. He didn't see me move. The armrest still tied to my arm provided a great weapon.

I blasted Erik in the head with the armrest. The jolt dazed him for a moment. As he moved back my other arm crushed his ear. Erik yelled out in pain like a wounded animal, letting go of my hair. The momentum of that last head slap knocked me sideways onto the floor. The legs on the chair broke and I was free.

I leg whipped Erik. He went down and hit the floor hard. It stunned him and gave me time to get up.

A shout came from behind me. Ingrid. "Lou, watch out, here he comes!"

Erik charged at me like a bull, knife out and running full steam ahead. His head was down so it was easy to sidestep him. As he ran by I stuck out my foot and tripped him. He hit the deck and slid head first into the wall. I loved it. He was out of it. It was my chance to make sure he was out for good. I kicked the knife out of the way.

I moved towards the lump of flesh lying on the floor when I heard, "That will be far enough, Detective Romoso. Put your hands up and turn around. Slowly!"

I'm usually the one saying that line, but this time it was Bernhard. He had the equalizer in his hand. His Luger. I raised my hands up over my head. However, he was too focused on me to notice Russell, who had finally managed to slip out of his bindings. I needed to keep Kruger talking.

"So, Bernhard, what's your plan after you take care of us? I'm sure the police and the feds have found this place, and are making plans to storm it as we speak."

He was clearly frustrated, and wanted this over with. O'Connell had stepped into the room and was helping Erik. Bernhard wasn't in the mood for talking, and raised his luger and pointed it at me.

"Time to die, Romoso," he said.

Russell sprung like a coiled spring. He grabbed Bernhard's arm, pulled it down, and knocked the gun out of his hand, but not before he got a shot off. The bullet grazed my shoulder. It wasn't enough to drop me, but it stung. Russell turned him around and connected with an uppercut. Bernhard was knocked woozy and fell to the floor.

I walked over and picked up the gun and turned it on Erik and O'Connell. O'Connell backed away, and Russell hit him over the head with a broken chair leg and he was out cold. Erik still was lying motionless. I didn't trust him and I was right not to.

I saw it just in time. The Nazi inbred had another knife. Where in God's name does he hide this shit? The knife sliced my shin and stopped me from getting any closer. It also made me drop the gun. I jumped back and Erik slowly rose from the floor. He had the knife in his right hand.

"You are a dead man!" He screamed.

He charged me again, only this time a little slower, slashing at the air with his knife. I went for his knife hand. I grabbed his arm with my left hand and his wrist with my right hand and drove him into the wall. When his back hit the wall I kept slamming his knife hand and arm until the knife dropped. It hit the floor and I kicked it away from Erik towards the chairs. Then it was just Erik and I, no weapons. Erik was strong and could fight. Not to mention he was fucking crazy. Once he lost the knife and I had stopped slamming his arm into the wall he was able to get his left arm around my neck. He began to choke me. I tried to pull his arm away but he had a good hold so I bent over and flipped him over my back. He rolled away and hopped right up to his feet.

He spied his knife on the floor and went to pick it up. I charged him and nailed him, if I do say so myself, with an impressive tackle. Hit him in the midsection and heard one of his ribs crack. This was my chance. He was gasping for air. It was time to give Erik a taste of his own medicine.

I picked him up and threw him against the wall and began to use *him* as a punching bag. I hit him hard with lefts and rights to the rib cage. No stopping until every rib cracked. He needed to know what it felt like. It was payback time for all the defenseless people he killed: the soldiers in Belgium, Tom Reitman, Sully, and me. I wasn't going to stop until he was dead.

Finally two big arms wrapped around me and pulled me away. It was Russell.

"Enough, Lou, he's finished. Let the Law take care of him now."

Erik slid to the floor in a mass of flesh and broken bones. He was barely breathing.

I kicked him once in the ribs and spit the blood that was still flowing from my mouth at him. I wanted to kill him, but the beating I received was taking its toll. Standing was becoming more difficult and I could barely see. My eyes were almost swollen shut. Erik did one hell of a number on my face, or what was left of it.

Everyone was now untied, including Kevin, but he wasn't moving very fast. Russell collected the guns and knives from the floor. Jessica and Mary were tying up their previous captors.

Ingrid came over to me to see how I was doing. I couldn't see her very well but I could feel the warmth of her tears as they dripped onto my face. She hugged me for all she was worth and I lurched in pain. I was too sore to move and it took everything I had to smile back.

"Lou, I'm so sorry I got you into this. I'm so sorry."

I grimaced in pain. "I've been worse."

When, I don't remember. Who the hell just takes the beating of his life, dies, and says he had worse? No one, that's who. Only an idiot. But I loved Ingrid and she felt bad enough. Figured I could milk this for quite a while. And I would.

I wish I could say it was over, but it wasn't. I called Russell to me. He had to complete the final act of this tragedy. On more person was missing.

"Russell, Heidi must still be in this warehouse somewhere. Find her and bring her here."

"Will do."

"Be careful, she is probably armed and knows how to use it. There may be some other henchmen around, too."

I asked Jessica to get outside and find the cops. They had to be close. I collapsed in a chair from pain and exhaustion.

CHAPTER 32
TYING UP LOOSE ENDS

A ll there was left to do was wait for the cavalry to get there and close the case. My job was done, but I needed to go to the hospital. I was in bad shape.

The Krugers would be taken to the hospital and interrogated once they recovered. Most likely Bernhard and Erik would face a trial and be hung. What a shame. Heidi was the lucky one, although she had to answer for the crimes she committed in the US, such as bank fraud, kidnapping, assault with a deadly weapon, counterfeiting, grand larceny, and a litany of other federal, state, and local charges, to name a few. If she were lucky she'd get life.

There was one problem with that. Where was she? She had to be still in the building. And if she was Russell would find her.

Kevin Young was still a problem, too. He ripped off his own friends, relatives, the rich, and the struggling, hard-working people of his community, South Buffalo. He didn't care, and quite frankly, I don't care either. He was going down.

Russell set out to find Heidi and got as far as the door. Russell ran right into the barrel of Heidi's .38.

"Get back inside and drop the gun!"

What choice did Russell have? He backed into the room with his hands in the air. Russell threw the gun towards Mary. Heidi wasn't paying much attention to where it landed. Her eyes scanned the room and saw Erik slumped in the corner. She laughed at the bloody mass. What is wrong with these people? They have zero compassion, even for their own. They're frigging animals.

"You!" Heidi pointed to Russell. "Yes, you, the one they call Russell. Bring Erik here."

Russell was in a bind and did what she said. He grabbed Erik by the collar and dragged him over to Heidi.

She looked down at him and smiled and shook her head. "I told you that temper would be the end of you. I can't have incompetent fools in my organization."

What the hell was going on here? Was Heidi running the show? Erik turned his head up to face Heidi. He was still gasping for air. The pain had to be intense. But for the first time there was a hint of fear in his eyes.

"Erik, you are swine. I never liked you. I kept you around because of your brother. For some reason he loved you. You have used up your last chance for redemption."

She put her gun to his head and blew his brains out. My eyes could not believe what they saw, as blurry as it was. I thought Erik was nuts. Heidi makes him look like a choir boy. This woman has ice flowing through her veins. Think I dated a girl like that once.

Heidi moved over and aimed her gun on me. Son of a bitch, doesn't Bernhard have another brother she could shoot?

"You, Russell, bring Bernhard to me."

Russell complied. He grabbed him, untied him, picked him up by his collar and dragged him over. As he did Bernhard was starting to come around. He looked at Heidi and smiled as he slowly rose from the floor. Bernhard was still shaky and rested on the wall. He looked over at the pile that was once Erik. He stared in silence for a while, tears forming in his eyes.

"Who killed my brother, Heidi?"

Heidi didn't miss a beat. "I did. He was hurt bad and he put us in a bad situation. We must scramble to leave this place."

I looked up at the two Germans. "You better listen to her, Bernie. You better leave in a hurry, the cops will be here in a few minutes."

Heidi walked up to me and put the barrel of the .38 into my forehead. I was too spent to resist. She bent down whispered in my ear.

"The police are going to be delayed."

My mind became scrambled as thoughts of Jessica lying dead somewhere in this building ignited my temper. I tried to swat her gun but was too slow. My injuries slowed me up a ton and Heidi was able to move the gun out of the way.

She laughed, but it was a cold laugh, completely emotionless. "Relax, she isn't dead. Not yet. She is lying in the hallway bleeding."

"You bitch! You're just as bad as Erik. I will kill you."

"No, you won't. I see the way you look at me. You wish your woman was half the woman I am. She doesn't have my looks or intelligence. You dream about me."

She grabbed my hair pulled my head back and kissed me again. She really was crazy. The picture was becoming clearer. Heidi was the mastermind behind this whole counterfeiting enterprise. But how was that possible? Was she the puppet master?

In the corner of my eye Mary was bending down real slow as not to attract attention to herself. I had to keep them talking.

"So, Bernie, tell us one thing before you kill us. I'm dying to know. Never mind the pun."

He didn't say anything, just looked at me with a mix of anger, sorrow, and curiosity painted across his face.

"Who's in charge of this little crime syndicate?" I asked.

Heidi didn't wait for him to answer. "If you must know this was all my idea. I met Bernhard in Berlin while I was working for the Führer. We, as you Americans say, hit it off. We knew the war was ending and had to escape. Our possessions and a large collection of art and Jewish wealth are hidden throughout the mountains and we came back for them a little at a time.

"Bernhard knew how to counterfeit American money, so I formulated the scheme to defraud wealthy widows and gain access to their bank accounts. Every widow that Bernhard met was almost the same size as me and it was easy to hire a make-up artist. None were suspicious and we were able to complete our task. That is, until you came into the picture, Detective.

"Bernhard dealt with Mr. Young. He gave Young the startup money for that poor excuse of a casino. Go to Monte Carlo to see a real casino."

"If I have the time, Heidi."

She laughed again, just as cold as before. "I don't think you will in this lifetime. Perhaps in another."

"Perhaps," I said. She was falling right into my plan; her vanity couldn't help itself and had to tell us just how much smarter she was than everyone else.

"I told Bernhard we should have killed that entire drunken Irish gang long ago. When that idiot Young bought off Mr. Sully, he got greedy and he had to die. Erik enjoyed killing him almost as much as I enjoyed shooting him in the knee." She paused and walked toward me. "I will enjoy killing you just as much. Then your bitch girlfriend, Sully's girl, whom he treated like the dog she is, and your girlfriend's classless mother."

Heidi lifted her arm and took aim. It looks like I was going to die for a second time this night, but there probably wouldn't be any coming back from this one. Ingrid began to scream. You could see the look of terror in her eyes. She was about to lose another person she cared deeply for in her life. She could look no longer and covered her eyes with both her hands.

Strangely I wasn't afraid. I was already at the pearly gates once, so I knew what to expect. It was okay with me. Behind all the commotion Mary had quietly bent over and picked up the Luger Russell had kicked towards her. The Krugers paid no attention to her because they were focused on me.

Heidi was now ready to put an end to the one man who ruined all their plans. Me! "Any last words?"

"Now that you mention it, I do. First, thank you for recognizing my talents enough to ruin your criminal enterprise. Second, I don't think you're going to be able to see your dream of killing me come true."

Heidi's face showed a hint of confusion, but was still cold. "Why do you say that?"

"Mary, if you please!"

Heidi turned around and saw Mary standing there with a gun. Before Heidi could swing her arm into range, Mary fired. Heidi screamed out in pain as she crumbled to the ground. Mary had shot her in the knee. How ironic! I didn't have time to admire Mary's shot because Bernhard was taking aim on Mary. Unfortunately I was useless. The beating I took kept me from reacting. But a blur rushed in from my left. Russell was running at him, putting his shoulder into his rib cage. Bernhard pulled the trigger but the errant shot hit the ceiling.

Heidi was on the ground screaming as Mary approached

her. "How does that feel, bitch?" She took her foot and stomped on her wounded knee. Heidi screamed out in pain. Memo to self: Women can be mighty nasty when provoked or looking for revenge.

Russell retied Bernhard's hands behind him. He squirmed to no avail. Russell threw Bernhard in the corner next to O'Connell, who was still unconscious, bound up at the feet and wrists. He would enjoy a lifetime stay at the bars motel. No doubt about that. He had three bodies to answer for.

After securing the bad guys, Russell went to look for Jessica. Ingrid comforted a hysterical Mary. For Mary, closure finally came, but at what cost? She endured the loss of her first love, though she paid a big mental price to get to that point. Mary had her revenge but I highly doubt it brought her any solace.

Russell walked back into the room with Jessica. Thank God she was fine—a little worse for wear, but alive. Ingrid followed shortly thereafter and said the cops were on their way in.

I could hear the sirens coming and a wave of relief hit me. The case was over. As with everything else, reports had to be filed, interviews conducted, criminals arrested and booked, and lives put back together.

Myself, all I cared about were the people who stood by me and put themselves in harm's way to help me solve this case. I put my back to the wall and slumped down to the floor. Couldn't tell you what hurt worse, so I went with everything.

What sounded like a herd of buffalo came tramping through the doors of the warehouse, led by Tom DeRosa. I looked up at him and shook my head and let out a little laugh. DeRosa looked pissed. I'm not sure why, but if I had to guess it was because Kruger and company put them on a wild goose chase.

Kolbe and Murph ran in a moment later to get their fair share of recognition.

"Well, look who finally showed up to the party," I said. Even this beat up I still had to stay true to my sarcastic self.

DeRosa bent down and took a closer look at my face. "You look like a tank ran you over."

"Nice to see you too, Tom."

Ingrid was by my side trying to ease the pain, but there was really nothing she could do. She was angry, upset, worried, and I'm assuming she felt like she was of no help to me whatsoever. It wasn't true, of course. She was a big help, or she was going to be once she paid her bill. Only kidding.

Well, half kidding.

I whispered to DeRosa, "Tom, you can charge O'Connell with the murder of Leary and my wife and kid, conspiracy to commit murder, counterfeiting, bookmaking, and anything else you can think of. You won't get him for the murder of Sully. That was the Nazis.

"McMann had flipped, that's why I'm here right now. Don't drag his name through mud." I shifted a bit to try and get more comfortable, not that it was likely. "But he's not with us anymore. You'll find him and Henderson dead back at Mickey Finn's." I paused again, tears forming in my eyes. "Brian Young, too. He got caught up in it and shot by that Nazi fuck Erik."

"We know," DeRosa said, putting a hand on my shoulder. "But we found Brian alive, and he's in surgery as we speak. Ambulance will be here in a minute, so hold in there."

That was good news on Brian. "Before we went to Finn's, Brian gave me a file on the finances behind the bar. Simon at the bank is probably dirty, but it may be hard to prove. It's all in that file."

I let out a loud sigh. It was finally over . . . but wait, was someone else missing? The pain was really getting to me now. Blood was dripping down the side of my mouth and I was coughing it up as well. It hurt just to breathe. If it kept up I'd be in trouble . . . who wasn't there? Kevin Young. Where did he go? I turned and looked frantically and he was nowhere to be seen. Dammit!

He must have slipped out when Mary was attacking Heidi. DeRosa had moved away and was talking with the Feds.

"DeRosa! Kevin's missing. He was here with us!" I yelled to him. He and all the others stopped what they were doing.

Agent Kolbe turned and yelled at me. "How could you let that happen, Romoso!"

What an asshole. If he couldn't tell, I was practically dying on the floor. Hell, I already *had* died once. No point in arguing with him, especially with the condition I was in. Instead, I pushed myself up off the floor with Ingrid's help and walked over to them.

"He was beat up pretty bad, so he couldn't have made it far," I said. DeRosa got a squad to scour the warehouse in search of him. "Tom, help me out, let's drag this piece of shit Nazi out of here."

Tom hauled Bernhard up off the ground, and each of us grabbed an arm. Ingrid walked by my side to keep me steady. Kolbe was right behind us. I don't know how I made it that far. I don't remember any of it. When we made it outside, my eyes suddenly saw stars and black dots. Our pictures were being taken. When I finally was able to see again I recognized the men taking the pictures. They were crime photographers from the *Buffalo Evening News* and the *Courier Express*. Also, there was a guy I didn't know taking film of us coming out of the building. It hit me. This was the scene I saw on the History Channel. The only difference was this was really happening.

We made it to the street and the waiting black and whites.

Bernhard and Heidi Kruger, Nazi war criminals and master counterfeiters, were put in the back of a car, defeated. I collapsed into an ambulance.

The last thing I remember is looking into the lovely eyes of Ingrid.

CHAPTER 33

AFTERMATH

January 10, 2 p.m. I awoke two days later with everyone waiting for me. Ingrid, Tom DeRosa, Kolbe, and Murph. Tom saw me stirring in bed.

"Ladies and Gentlemen, the king has arisen. All hail the king!" He said.

"Very funny, asshole."

"Good to see almost dying didn't affect your sense of humor," DeRosa said, laughing.

I looked over and saw Ingrid. She was no worse for wear. She had a couple of black eyes from her confrontation with Heidi, though, like a raccoon. A beautiful raccoon. I smiled and she smiled back.

"Hi, Ingrid. You know the black and blue of your top matches your shiners. I like a girl who is color coordinated."

Ingrid leaned over and kissed me on the lips. She didn't say a word. Didn't have to. I could see her eyes were red and spotted a tear forming in her eye. The tear began to fall; I raised my arm and wiped it away with my thumb.

"Don't cry. I promise I'll replace any of your cars that got damaged."

She finally laughed and called me an idiot.

"Ingrid, really, how are you?" I asked.

"I'm fine, really."

"How about everyone else?"

"Mother and Mary are all doing well. Russell too. It's been touch and go for Livingston, but he is going to make it. They beat him within an inch of his life, Lou. He doesn't remember much of that night right now but the doctors think his memory will slowly come back."

I was becoming exhausted and I had a few questions for Tom and the others. "Tom, how is Alice and Officer White doing?"

"Alice is doing well and on her road to recovery." He paused for a beat and looked somber." White . . . he didn't make it."

No one talked for a while. We lost some good people, and for what? So some insane assholes could try and resurrect the most awful government in the history of the world? What a shame.

After a while, I asked, "And Brian Young?"

DeRosa shook his head. "He's alive. The shot to his chest missed his heart by less than an inch but went through clean. The hip was worse, nicked a main artery and shattered some bone. No normal man could have survived. He's one tough son of a bitch."

It was good to know my friend might pull out of this yet. Hell, I know he's still around sixty years from now. I'd hate it if my stupidity changed history.

"Kevin?" I asked.

"No one has seen hide nor hair of him since that night,"

DeRosa said, baffled.

Damn, that wasn't good. But I had confidence in the BPD. They'd track him down. I was sure of it. Unless . . . did he still have access to the time travel devices? If so, he was gone forever.

Next on the hit parade was Kolbe. "You'll be glad to know that Heidi and Bernhard Kruger will be tried as war criminals and one or both will hang. I will escort them to Israel for their trials. It should be interesting."

Kolbe went on to say they got their hands on the counterfeit bills still at the warehouse. They would now be able to trace most of the bad cash in the area, but it would take time to recover it all and get it out of circulation. Tens of Millions alone had been spread through the Buffalo area. They were coordinating efforts in other cities to try and recover as much of the bad money as possible. In the raid they recovered Bernhard's books and could see all the cities and countries his counterfeiting was reaching.

Murph wasn't able to trace how the Krugers got into the U.S. They had Swiss passports in their fake names, but there wasn't any record of them ever entering the country. They were stamped for entry to Germany, Argentina, and others. I wasn't surprised by that, seeing as they had been time traveling. No need to worry Murph about that, though. Let him keep digging.

Soon everyone left but Jessica and Ingrid. Jessica decided she was going to pick up the entire tab for my work. Ingrid had argued with her mother about who was going to pay my fee and as we all know you never win that argument. Jessica bent over and kissed me on the cheek, handed me a check and whispered to me.

"Ingrid and I are eternally grateful for all you've done for us. You saved our lives and the lives of our friends. We can never fully repay you."

I smiled. "All in a day's work."

I almost cried when I saw the amount of the check she wrote to me. I've never seen that many zeros. Unless you counted my grades in math class.

"Jessica, I can't accept this. It's way too much money."

I was holding on to that check for dear life. Jessica just laughed.

"That check is the money Heinrich . . . Bernhard . . . or whatever his no-good name is, stole from me. I don't need it and you saved me from bankruptcy and much more embarrassment than I already have endured. It's yours to do whatever you want."

"Thank you, Jessica."

Ingrid was all smiles, most likely because she didn't have to pay my bill. Ingrid rubbed my arm, leaned over and said, "This is your lucky day, Detective Romoso."

"Right here in the hospital?"

Jessica started to laugh and Ingrid blushed and punched my arm. "No, smart-ass."

She handed me an envelope. Inside were a set of keys. They were attached to a car brochure for a new Lincoln Continental Capri in navy blue. There was no note attached. Ingrid just smiled and said keep looking. So I did.

She sighed and hit me in the shoulder playfully. "Not at me, Lou. Inside the envelope."

What can I say, I'm a guy. It doesn't make me a bad guy.

I put my hand inside and pulled out two first-class airline tickets to Italy with lodgings in first-class hotels.

"A car, plane tickets, hotel suites. I told you, there was no charge," I said.

"Lou, shut up."

"Can you find me a phone? I want to call Miss Jacobs to

see if she can get some time off."

Ingrid's face got flush and she started to get mad. "Louis Romoso, are you kidding me, Miss Jacobs! You're going to ask Miss Jacobs!"

I started laughing, and believe me, it hurts to laugh with broken ribs. "Calm down, of course I'm going to take your mother. God knows she deserves it."

Ingrid finally caught on and she smiled. "That's better." Ingrid bent over and kissed me and whispered, "I love you."

It was a good day. The doctor came in a little while later.

"You are healing well," the Doc said. "No reason to keep you here any longer. I'm going to discharge you in an hour."

"Thanks, Doc."

I wanted to do some things before heading to Ingrid's. She protested, but I told her not to worry. Everyone who wanted me dead was gone.

First stop, the bank to deposit my newfound wealth. I closed out my account at my now former bank and decided to pay Miss Jacobs a visit. She was glad to see me because, well just because. We made small talk and she flirted with me. I enjoyed it, but at the end of the day Ingrid was all I needed. Plus I feared for my life if Ingrid ever found out.

After the bank I wanted to stop by my office. I wasn't planning on doing any work or taking on new cases. No way was I ready for that. But I needed to sit in my chair. Something about the pictures on the walls, the bar, my cigars . . . it just felt right.

I took the back way up rather than walking through the bar. The parade of people through the hospital had worn me down. Walking through Marco's would start that up all over.

At the top of the stairs the hair on the back of my neck stood up. Something was wrong. I turned and my door was ajar and the radio was on. Who could be in there? Instinctively I reached for my holster. Damn, my guns were all locked up in the safe in the office. I haven't had one on me since the warehouse. Weapon or no, I was going in there. Too much had happened to me in the last few days to care.

My hand was on the door and I threw it open. What was sitting at my desk stopped me dead. Not what. Who. Kevin Young.

"Hey, Shamus," Young said with a smile on his face. He was holding his remaining Colt .45, with the barrel pointed straight at my head. "Come on in, have a seat."

I did. My body was in no condition for a struggle. Smarts had to get me out of this.

I'm in deep shit.

"Kevin, what are you doing? How'd you get in here?"

"Back stair, same as you," he answered.

He looked remarkably good, considering the beating Erik laid on him. "You were two steps away from death last I saw you," I said.

"Who do you think taught Brian everything he knew about fighting? He never would have won that Golden Gloves without me in his corner. I can take a punch. And can act with the best of 'em."

"If you kill me, you won't walk out of here alive."

He stood up angrily. That must have touched a nerve.

"You think I give a fuck about my life?" He said. "You took Mickey Finn's from me. That in itself isn't enough to kill you. That's just the business we're in. But you took the only person in my life I ever loved. The only family I had. The one part of my life that was good. Brian would still be here if you didn't get him involved."

He was in tears now. Again, if I didn't hate the son of a bitch, I might have felt bad.

"Kevin, Brian was there on his own," I said, trying to calm

him down. "McMann told him what you were into, and he was livid. He wanted to take you down, if only for your own good. There was nothing I could do to keep him out of it . . . besides, he's still hanging on at Buffalo General."

"You're a liar!" Kevin yelled. He raised his gun up and aimed right between my eyes. "Say a prayer, Romoso, because your time is done."

Right then, the volume on the old Phillips radio turned way up. A Johnny Dollar episode was blaring. The room began to shake and both Kevin and I hit the floor. My head was pounding and everything was spinning. . . .

2015

CHAPTER 34

THE BITTER END

I dragged myself up off the floor of my spare office. My head was still pounding, but I was alone. And . . . I was back to present times. That was sad. I was enjoying the 1950s—other than getting my ass shot at and nearly killed. Not to mention that's where Ingrid was. What did I have here? Nothing except a shot-up office, a possible police investigation into my handling of this case, and no prospects of love.

There was at least . . . what happened to Young? He disappeared on me again. I thought he could travel in time too? Was I out so long that he took off?

I got up and walked around my desk to the chair and sat down. Pulled a cigar out of my humidor and lit it. A feeling hit me that the case was closed in the past. I wouldn't be heading back there anytime soon.

The only thing left to do was to finish what I started, and find Kevin Young to stop this insanity. But where to start?

On my desk was a copy of the *Buffalo News*. It made me

think about how the newspaper business was dying. Gone was the *Courier Express* and countless other local papers. With them it seemed journalistic integrity had gone, too. Before reporters really worked a story. Now it feels like being first is better, not being right.

The paper, dated January 10, 2015, was open to the crime section. Had I really been out for three days? When I picked it up, the image of Brian Finnegan struck me. He was in his marine uniform. The article talked about his service to his country, his role in bringing down a counterfeit ring in the 1950s, and now his involvement with a biker gang that saw him get shot twice. What the hell? Then I remembered everything that had happened. He was still at the hospital in a coma, and doctors were unsure if he'd ever wake up, seeing as he was ninety-five years old.

Without thinking about it I was out in my car and on the way to the hospital. I'm not sure what I hoped to accomplish, but I had nowhere else to go. I checked my phone and my voicemail box was full. They alternated between family and Lieutenant Campanelli. My family would want to hear every detail of the showdown with the Rats. If I talked to Joe, he'd try to make me come in to make my formal statement about the shootings. I wasn't quite ready to do either—especially my family. Not until I had all the answers of what was actually happening, anyways.

I listened to Joe's last voicemail. "Lou, where the hell are you? It's been over two days, and no one has heard from you. This isn't funny anymore. Call me."

Damn, how would I cover my ass on this one? Who would believe me that I traveled in time? Brian was laid up at the hospital. Maybe Brady could help me sell it. Otherwise I was going to be giving measurements for my straight jacket.

Visiting hours were over at Buffalo General but I had

connections through my brother, Mike, and the attendant at the nurse's station looked the other way. I headed up to Brian's room.

As I got there I heard another person talking. Was Brian up? I slowed and waited by the door. Only one voice was speaking. It sounded like a younger man; someone else was in the room. I had my gun on me. Just to be safe I loosened it in my holster.

When I opened the door the person said, "I was wondering how long it'd take you to get here." It was Kevin. Turns out I am a pretty good detective after all.

Brian was hooked up to so many wires and machines it was tough to look at. I know he's old, but he never really looked it until now. His skin looked paper thin and ghoulish. It seemed as if he'd dropped forty pounds since I last saw him. And that was only a few days ago.

Kevin stood up from the chair next to the bed. He turned to face me, and he saw the barrel of my Glock pointing at his chest.

"There's no need for that, Shamus," Kevin said. "I'm unarmed, and I'm done fighting."

As much as I didn't want to, I believed him. He wasn't the same guy I saw the day before at the River Rat's clubhouse. Or sixty years ago while sitting in my office. He finally looked old and tired.

"So what happened?" I asked. I didn't elaborate, but Kevin seemed to know what I was talking about.

"I have no clue. After your office started shaking, I got a terrible headache and blacked out. I came to after a bit, and I was alone. You were nowhere to be seen."

Kevin paused and rubbed his forehead. He went on to explain to me how when he walked out of the building, he felt like he was in the twilight zone. He was still in the 1950s. He made it back to his hideout, where he had stored away some emergency funds. There was no more life for him in that era, not being tied to Nazi war criminals in such a public way. Seeing no alternative, he took what he could with him and used the time travel device he still had to return to the new millennium.

"So how did you get hooked up with the River Rats?" I asked. It was the first thing I had said for quite a while.

Kevin smiled. It was a sad, defeated smile. "That was my doing, at the behest of those German bastards. I wish I had never gotten involved with them. That ruined everything. It all escalated and there was nothing I could do about it.

"But the best part about moving to the future is no one knew who I was, since I was supposed to be a missing person from the fifties, presumed long dead. One of my sources said some Homicide detective named Lou Romoso was investigating the Rats. I nearly choked when I heard your name. So I decided to check you out. I was tickled pink when I saw you. Carrying a few extra pounds, but it was you. That's when the plan hatched. How did you figure out to time travel, Romoso? How did you blend in so easily?"

I said nothing. I was afraid if I did I'd get too angry and shoot him before he could finish telling me everything.

He continued. "I kept trying to figure it out. How could you have a family here and now, and in the past? It didn't make any sense. Not that it mattered. You needed to go."

It didn't make any sense to me either. What was so different about me? The only person who had any sort of answers was in a coma. The others were trapped in the 1950s, the Nazis. The rest of Kevin's crew was dead and buried.

Kevin kept going, but I knew most of the rest. He claimed the Germans were responsible for all the bad things that were happening to me. I had trouble believing it, but he looked genuinely remorseful. He had Dolan put the hit out on me at the behest of Kruger. Unfortunately for them, I proved to be a very difficult person to kill. I'm stubborn that way.

"So where does that leave us?" I said. "Am I supposed to let you walk off into the sunset? Are we supposed to forget all about this?"

"I don't know, Lou, but I'm done. All this hate I've held in these years has worn me down. I thought killing you would sate that anger, but now it's no use. We killed Ellen, Sully, even that prick Leary, and for what? A few extra bucks?"

He had a tear rolling down his cheek and didn't bother to wipe it away. I didn't know what to do. My gun was still in hand. Kevin didn't flinch. Instead I holstered it grabbed my cell phone. Man, it was nice to have that back. I dialed up Camp. He started shouting at me, but I shut him up and told him there'd be time for explaining things later. I told him where to go, that I got a tip on something. He asked why, but I didn't tell him. Didn't need the whole force coming down and creating a big scene.

I hung up and turned back to Kevin. "Listen, before a few days ago, I didn't even know you existed. When Ingrid—Ingrid's granddaughter—came to me it started this whole train of events and I was in a whirlwind. But now that it's all over, I'm tired, too. And I just want the pain of everyone I've lost to go away. Not that it's likely." I paused, and moved closer to Kevin. "I'll never forgive you for killing Ellen. I will live with that memory for the rest of my life."

Kevin stared at me, and after a bit gave me a slight nod. It was officially over now. Our battle through time was done.

I turned and started to walk away. Before I got too far, I looked back to him. "Lieutenant Campanelli of BPD should be here in about five minutes or so. I didn't tell him what he'd find. If you're here, great, if not, makes no difference to me."

I got back to my car and before getting in lit the last cigar I had in my coat pocket. Savored the taste. Both of my cases were done. I looked up at the bright moon and clear sky, blew a kiss to my mother and father, and to Ellen and Lou Jr., and got in my car.

About the Author

Lou Rossi was born and Raised in Western New York. He attended Maryvale High School, and was a member of the 1975 graduating class. For college he stayed in the Buffalo area, attending Buffalo State College. Lou graduated with a Bachelors of Arts in Economics in 1979.

His coaching career has spanned the high school, college, and professional levels. He has coached at Williamsville South, Nichols, and St. Francis High Schools, and Buffalo State. At the professional level he coached for four years in the Arena Football League, spending one year with the Rochester Brigade of AF2, and three with the Buffalo Destroyers.

Lou has also been a police officer. He recently retired after over three decades as an officer at the University at Buffalo in Buffalo, New York.

Cigar Boys: Stories from the Ashes, his first journey into the world of writing, is a collection of short stories written about the patrons of a fictional Western New York cigar shop. *The Counterfeit Matter* is his first novel.

More from Lou Rossi

You have to be a certain type of individual to be a regular at a cigar shop. At the Box that statement couldn't be any truer. Those who frequent the Box are one sorry collection of humanity, and we here at the Box Burns Gazette love them for it. The Gazette was created in order to document all of the crazy stories and events that have happened at the Box and to its customers. So follow along as we detail all the shenanigans our friends and lovable losers manage to get themselves into in *Cigar Boys: Stories from the Ashes*, a collection of short stories by Lou Rossi.

www.ingramcontent.com/pod-product-compliance
Lightning Source LLC
Chambersburg PA
CBHW060848250626
47159CB00015B/2529

* 9 781943 706198 *